Claws and Effect

*Also by Rita Mae Brown &
Sneaky Pie Brown in Large Print:*

Rest in Pieces
Murder at Monticello
Pay Dirt
Murder, She Meowed
Murder on the Prowl

*Also by Rita Mae Brown
in Large Print:*

High Hearts
Bingo

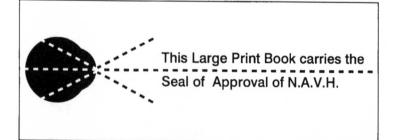

This Large Print Book carries the
Seal of Approval of N.A.V.H.

Claws and Effect

RITA MAE BROWN & SNEAKY PIE BROWN

Illustrations by Itoko Maeno

Thorndike Press • Waterville, Maine

02 0591

A Mrs. Murphy Mystery

Illustrations by Itoko Maeno

Published in 2001 by arrangement with Bantam Books,
an imprint of the Bantam Dell Publishing Group,
a division of Random House, Inc.

Thorndike Press Large Print Basic Series.

The tree indicium is a trademark of Thorndike Press.

The text of this Large Print edition is unabridged.
Other aspects of the book may vary from the original edition.

Set in 16 pt. Plantin.

Printed in the United States on permanent paper.

Library of Congress Cataloging-in-Publication Data

Brown, Rita Mae.
    Claws and effect / Rita Mae Brown & Sneaky Pie Brown ;
  illustrations by Itoko Maeno
        p.   cm.
    ISBN 0-7862-3484-9 (lg. print : hc : alk. paper)
    1. Haristeen, Harry (Fictitious character) — Fiction.
2. Murphy, Mrs. (Fictitious character) — Fiction.   3. Women
postal service employees — Fiction.   4. Women detectives
— Fiction.   5. Women cat owners — Fiction.   6. Virginia
— Fiction.   7. Cats — Fiction.   8. Large type books.
I. Maeno, Itoko,   II. Title.
PS3552.R698 C57 2001c
   813´.54—dc21   2001034754

Dedicated to the people who work in animal shelters. You're overworked and underpaid but you have given your life to a different kind of reward.
God bless you.

Cast of Characters

Mrs. Murphy Beautiful, brainy, saucy, she is the perfect cat. Just ask her.

Pewter A gray cat with strong opinions, she is often reluctantly pulled into Mrs. Murphy's schemes.

Tee Tucker A courageous corgi who loves Harry. She loves Mrs. Murphy and Pewter as well but she thinks the cats can be awful snobs.

Mary Minor "Harry" Haristeen Energetic, organized, very task-oriented, she provides her friends with laughter just by being herself. She's the postmistress of Crozet although a graduate of Smith College. Many people consider her an underachiever.

Mrs. Miranda Hogendobber She's older and a good friend to the thirtyish Harry. Her husband was the former postmaster of Crozet. She's widowed and rather religious.

Big Mim Sanburne The Queen of Crozet, a contemporary of Miranda's, is imperious and relentless in her efforts to "improve" Crozet and its inhabitants.

Little Mim Sanburne The Princess of Crozet is often resentful of languishing in her mother's shadow but she's beginning to emerge. It's about time; she's in her thirties.

Jim Sanburne The Mayor of Crozet is the affable husband of Big Mim. He married well above his station.

Aunt Tally Urquhart The Dowager Queen, in her nineties, she passed on control of the town to her niece years ago. This does not mean she doesn't want to get her own way.

The Reverend Herbert C. Jones He's the beloved pastor of the Lutheran Church. By his position and by his nature, he can often help others. His two cats, Cazenovia and Elocution, appear to have religious impulses.

Dr. Bruce Buxton Sought out by athletes because he is a celebrated knee specialist, he's also sought out by single women because he's single. Bruce has a big head.

Sam Mahanes The administrator for Crozet Hospital juggles the budget as well as the doctors' egos. With a few exceptions, he gets along with people.

Tussie Logan The head nurse in Pediatrics is dedicated to her job. She's attractive and available.

Hank Brevard The plant manager at Crozet Hospital lives to complain. People just tune him out.

Susan Tucker As Harry's best friend she has to be a good sport. She's a wife and mother, drawing comfort from her family. She bred Tee Tucker.

Ned Tucker Susan's lawyer husband, who works hard and loves his family.

Danny Tucker and Brooks Tucker Their teenaged son and daughter, respectively.

BoomBoom Craycroft She's a dazzler who upsets other women by simply walking into the room. Too many people assume that because she's beautiful, she's dumb. Boy, have they got a wrong number.

Dr. Larry Johnson He's an older, trusted general practitioner who tried to retire once with dismal results. He knows many secrets and keeps all of them.

Sheriff Rick Shaw Overworked, understaffed, and underpaid, he nonetheless loves his job and plays strictly by the book — well, most times.

Deputy Cynthia Cooper Bright, on the rise in her profession, she, too, loves law enforcement. She hangs out with Harry and the gang in her free time and she's beginning to wonder if there's a man out there ready for a wife who's a cop.

Fair Haristeen, DVM Harry's ex-husband is a sought-after equine practitioner, who still loves Harry. He's a big enough man to have learned from his mistakes. He's open-minded and thoughtful.

1

"People tell me things. Of course, I have a kind face and I'm a good listener, but the real reason they tell me things is they think I can't repeat their secrets. They couldn't be more wrong."

"People tell __me__ secrets." The corgi looked up at Mrs. Murphy, the tiger cat, reposing on the windowsill at the post office.

"You're delusional. Dogs blab." She nonchalantly flipped the end of her tail.

"You just said people think you can't repeat their secrets but they're wrong. So you blab, too."

"No, I don't. I can tell if I want to, that's all I'm saying."

Tucker sat up, shook her head, and walked closer to the windowsill. *"Well, got any secrets?"*

"No, it's been a dull stretch." She sighed. *"Even Pewter hasn't dug up any dirt."*

"I resent that." A little voice piped up from the bottom of a canvas mail cart.

"Wait until Miranda finds out what you've

11

done to her garden. She hasn't a tulip bulb left, Pewter, and all because you thought there was a mole in there last week."

"Her tulips were diseased. I've saved her a great deal of trouble." She paused a moment. *"And I was careful enough to pull mulch over the hole. She won't find out for another month or two. Who knows when spring will come?"*

"I don't know about spring but here comes Mim the Magnificent." Tucker, on her hind legs, peered out the front window.

Mim Sanburne, the town's leading and richest citizen, closed the door of her Bentley Turbo, stepping gingerly onto the cleared walkway to the post office because ice covered much of central Virginia.

Odd that Mim would own a Bentley for she was a true Virginian, born and bred, plus her family had been in the state since the early 1600s. Driving anything as flashy as a Bentley was beyond the pale. The only thing worse would be to drive a Rolls-Royce. And Mim didn't flaunt her wealth. Miranda, who had known Mim all of her life, figured this was a quiet rebellion on her friend's part. As they both cruised into their sixties, not that they were advertising, this was Mim's salvo to youth: Get Out Of My Way.

People did.

Mary Minor "Harry" Haristeen smiled when Mim pushed open the door. "Good morning."

"Good morning, Harry. Did you have trouble driving in today?"

"Once I rolled down the driveway I was fine. The roads are clear."

"You didn't ask me if I had trouble." Miranda walked up to the counter dividing the post office staff from the public. As she lived immediately behind the post office, with just an alleyway in between, she slipped and slid as she made her way to work on foot.

"You haven't broken anything so I know you're fine." Mim leaned on the counter. "Gray. Gray. Cold. Hateful."

"Four degrees Fahrenheit last night." Miranda, passionate gardener that she was, kept close watch on the weather. "It must have been colder at Dalmally." She mentioned the name of Mim's estate just outside of town. As some of Mim's ancestors fled to America from Scotland they named their farm Dalmally, a remembrance of heather and home.

"Below zero." Mim strolled over to her postbox, took out her key, the brass lock clicking as she turned the key.

Curious, Mrs. Murphy dropped off the

windowsill, jumped onto the wooden counter, then nimbly stepped off the counter onto the ledge that ran behind the postboxes, dividing the upper boxes from the larger, lower boxes. She enjoyed peering in the boxes. If a day dragged on she might reach in, shuffle some mail, or even bite the corners.

Today she noticed that Susan Tucker's mailbox had Cracker Jacks stuck on the bottom of it.

Mim's gloved hand, a luscious, soft turquoise suede, reached into her box. Murphy couldn't help herself; she peered down, then took both paws and grabbed Mim's hand, no claws.

"Mrs. Murphy. Let me have my mail." Mim bent down to see two beautiful green eyes staring back at her.

"Give me your glove. I love the smell of the suede."

"Harry, your cat won't let me go."

Harry walked over, slipped her fingers into the mailbox, and disengaged Murphy's paws. "Murphy, not everyone in Crozet thinks you're adorable."

"Thank you!" Pewter's voice rose up from the canvas mail cart.

Harry gently placed her tiger on the counter again. A pretty woman, young and fit, she stroked the cat.

Miranda checked the bookshelves for cartons. "Mim, got a package here for you. Looks like your coffee."

Mim belonged to a coffee club, receiving special beans from various world-famous cafés once a month. "Good." She stood at the counter sorting her mail. She removed one exquisite glove and slit open envelopes with her thumbnail, a habit Harry envied, since her own nails were worn down from farm work. The older, elegant woman opened a white envelope, read a few sentences, then tossed the letter and envelope in the trash. "Another chain letter. I just hate them and I wish there'd be a law against them. They're all pyramid schemes. This one wants you to send five dollars to Crozet Hospital's Indigent Patients Fund and then send out twenty copies of the letter. I just want to know who put my name on the list."

Harry flipped up the divider, walked over to the wastebasket, and fished out the offending letter.

"Sister Sophonisba will bring you good fortune." She scanned the rest of it. "There is no list of names. All it says is to pass this on to twenty other people. 'If you wish.' " Harry's voice filled the room. "Send five dollars to Crozet Hospital's Indigent Patients Fund or your microwave will die."

"It doesn't really say that, does it?" Miranda thought Harry was teasing her but then again . . .

"Nah." Harry flashed her crooked grin.

"Very funny." Mim reached for her letter again, which Harry handed to her. "Usually there's a list of names and the top one gets money. You know, your name works its way to the top of the list." She reread the letter, then guffawed, "Here's the part that always kills me about these things." She read aloud. "Mark Lintel sent five dollars and the Good Lord rewarded him with a promotion at work. Jerry Tinsley threw this letter in the trash and had a car wreck three days later." Mim peered over the letter. "I seem to recall Jerry's wreck. And I seem to recall he was liberally pickled in vodka. If he dies he'll come back as a rancid potato."

Harry laughed. "I guess he had to get rid of that old Camry somehow so he decided to wreck it."

"Harry," Miranda reprimanded her.

"Well, I liked your death threat to microwaves." Mim handed the letter over the worn counter to Harry, who tossed it back into the wastebasket, applauding herself for the "basket."

"Two points." Harry smiled.

"Seems to be local. The references are local. None of this 'Harold P. Beecher of Davenport, Iowa, won the lottery,' " Mim said. "Well, girls, you know things are slow around here if we've wasted this much time on a chain letter."

"The February blahs." Harry stuck her tongue out.

"Ever notice that humans' tongues aren't as pink as ours?" Tucker, the corgi, cocked her head, sticking her own tongue out.

"They are what they are," came the sepulchral voice from the mail bin.

"Oh, that's profound, Pewts." Mrs. Murphy giggled.

"The sage of Crozet has spoken," Pewter again rumbled, making her kitty voice deeper.

"Well, I don't know a thing. What about you two?"

"Mim, we thought you knew everything. You're the —" Harry stopped for a second because "the Queen of Crozet" dangled on the tip of her tongue, which was what they called Mim behind her back. "— uh, leader of the pack."

"At least you didn't say Laundromat." Mim referred to a popular song from the sixties, before Harry's time.

"How's Jim?" Miranda inquired after Mim's husband.

"Busy."

"Marilyn?" Miranda now asked about Mim's daughter, Harry's age, late thirties.

"The same, which is to say she has no purpose in this life, no beau, and she exists simply to contradict me. As for my son, since you're moving through the family, he and his wife are still in New York. No grandchildren in sight. What's the matter with your generation, Harry? We were settled down by the time we were thirty."

Harry shrugged. "We have more choices."

"Now what's that supposed to mean?" Mim put her hands on her slender hips. "All it means is you're more self-indulgent. I don't mind women getting an education. I received a splendid education but I knew my duty lay in marrying and producing children and raising them to be good people."

Miranda deftly deflected the conversation. "Don't look now, but Dr. Bruce Buxton is flat on his back coasting down Main Street."

"Ha!" Mim ran to the window, as did Mrs. Murphy and Tucker. "I hope he's black and blue from head to toe!"

Bruce spun around, finally grabbing onto a No Parking sign. Breathing heavily, he pulled himself up, but his feet insisted in traveling in opposite directions. Finally steadied, he half slid, half skated in the direction of the post office.

"Here he comes." Mim laughed. "Pompous as ever although he is handsome. I'll give him that."

Dr. Bruce Buxton stamped his feet on the post office steps, then pushed the door open.

Before he could speak, Mim dryly remarked, "I give you a 9.4," as she breezed past him, waving good-bye to Harry and Miranda.

"Supercilious snot!" he said only after the door closed because it wouldn't do to cross Mim publicly. Even Bruce Buxton, a star knee specialist at Crozet Hospital, knew better than to offend "The Diva," as he called her.

"Well, Dr. Buxton, I gave you points for distance. Mim gave you points for artistic expression." Harry laughed out loud.

Bruce, in his late thirties and single, couldn't resist a pretty woman so he laughed at himself as well. "I did cover ground. If it gets worse, I'm wearing my golf spikes."

"Good idea." Harry smiled as she opened his mailbox.

"Bills. More bills." He opened a white envelope, then chucked it. "Junk."

"Wouldn't be a letter from Sister Sophonisba, would it?" Harry asked.

"Sister Somebody. Chain letter."

"Mim got one, too. I didn't." Harry laughed at herself. "I miss all the good stuff. Say, how is Isabelle Otey?"

Harry was interested in the gifted forward for the University of Virginia's basketball team. She had shredded her anterior cruciate ligament during a tough game against Old Dominion. UVA won the game but lost Isabelle for the season.

"Fine. Arthroscopic surgery is done on an outpatient basis now. Six weeks she'll be as good as new, providing she follows instructions for six weeks. The human knee is a fascinating structure . . ." As he warmed to his subject — he was one of the leading knee surgeons in the country — Harry listened attentively. Miranda did, too.

"My knees are better." Mrs. Murphy turned her back on Bruce, whom she considered a conceited ass. *"Everything about me is better. If people walked on four feet instead of two most of their problems would vanish."*

"Won't improve their minds any," came the voice from the mail cart, which now echoed slightly.

"There's no help for that." Tucker sighed, for she loved Harry; but even that love couldn't obviate the slowness of human cogitation.

"Pewter, why don't you get your ass out of the mail cart? You've been in there since eight this morning and it's eleven-thirty. We could go outside and track mice."

"You don't want to go out in the cold any more than I do. You just want to make me look bad." There was a grain of truth in Pewter's accusation.

Bruce left, treading the ice with slow respect.

In ten minutes Hank Brevard, plant manager of Crozet Hospital, and Tussie Logan, head nurse in Pediatrics, arrived together in Tussie's little silver Tracker.

"Good morning." Tussie smiled. "It's almost noon. How are things in the P.O.?"

"The P.U.," Hank complained.

He was always complaining about something.

"I beg your pardon." Mrs. Miranda Hogendobber huffed up.

"Cat litter." He sniffed.

"Hank, there's no litter box. They go outside."

"Yeah, maybe it's you," Tussie teased him.

He grunted, ignoring them, opening his

mailbox. "Bills, bills. Junk."

Despite his crabbing over his mail, he did open the envelopes, carefully stacking them on the table. He was a meticulous man as well as a faultfinder.

Tussie, by contrast, shuffled her envelopes like cards, firing appeals, advertisements, and form letters into the wastebasket.

Miranda flipped up the dividing counter, walked out, picked up the wastebasket, and started to head back to the mailbag room, as she dubbed the working portion of the post office building.

"Wait." Tussie swiftly dumped two more letters into the trash. "If you don't open form letters you add three years onto your productive life."

"Is that a fact?" Miranda smiled.

"Solemn," Tussie teased her.

Miranda carried the metal wastebasket around the table to Hank. "Any more?"

"Uh, no." He thumbed through his neatly stacked pile.

"Can't you ever do anything on impulse?" Tussie pulled her mittens from her coat pocket.

"Haste makes waste. If you saw the damaged equipment that I see, all because some jerk can't take the time. Yesterday a gurney was brought down with two wheels jammed. Now that only happens if an orderly doesn't take the time to tap the little foot brake. He pushed, got no response, then pushed with all his might." Hank kept on, filled with the importance of his task. "And there I was in the middle of testing a circuit breaker that kept tripping in the canteen. Too many appliances on that circuit." He took a breath, ready to recount more problems.

Tussie interrupted him. "The hospital does need a few things."

He jumped in again. "Complete and total electrical overhaul. New furnace for the old section but hey, who listens to me? I just run the place. Let a doctor squeal for something and oh, the earth stops in its orbit."

"That's not true. Bruce Buxton has been yelling for a brand new MRI unit and —"

"What's that?" Harry inquired.

"Magnetic Resonance Imaging. Another way to look into the body without invading it," Tussie explained. "Technology is exploding in our field. The new MRI machines cut down the time by half. Well, don't let me go off on technology." She stopped for a moment. "We will all live to see a cure for cancer, for childhood diabetes, for so many of the ills that plague us."

"Don't know how you can work with sick children. I can't look them in the eye." Hank frowned.

"They need me."

"Hear, hear," Miranda said as Harry nodded in agreement.

"Guess we need a lot of things," Hank remarked. "Still, I think the folks in the scrubs will get what they want before I get what I want." He took a breath. "I hate doctors." Hank placed the envelopes in the large inside pocket of his heavy coveralls.

"That's why you spend your life in the basement." Tussie winked. "He's still looking for the Underground Railroad."

"Oh, balls." Hank shook his head. If they had been outside, he would have spat.

"I've heard that story since I was a kid." Miranda leaned over the counter divider. " 'Bout how the old stone section of the hospital used to be on the Underground Railroad for getting slaves to freedom."

"Every house and bush in Crozet has historical significance. Pass a street corner and some sign declares, 'Jefferson blew his nose here.' Come on, Tussie. I've got to get back to work."

"What are you doing here with doom and gloom?" Harry winked at Tussie.

Hank suppressed a little smile. He liked

being Mr. Negative. People paid attention. He thought so anyway.

"Chuckles' car is in the shop."

"Don't call me that," Hank corrected her. "What if my wife hears you? She'll call me that."

"Oh, here I thought you'd say 'people will talk.'" Tussie expressed much disappointment.

"They do that anyway. Ought to have their tongues cut out."

"Hank, you'd have fit right in during the ninth century A.D. Be in your element." Tussie followed him to the door.

"Yeah, Hank. Why stop with cutting people's tongues out? Go for the throat." Harry winked at Tussie, who joined her.

"Mom's getting bloodthirsty." Mrs. Murphy laughed.

"Let me get Chuckles back to his lair." Tussie waved good-bye.

"Don't call me Chuckles!" He fussed at her as they climbed into the Tracker.

"They're a pair." Miranda observed Hank gesticulating.

"Pair of what?" Harry laughed as she emptied the wastebasket into a large garbage bag.

The day wore on, crawled really. The only other noteworthy event was when Sam

Mahanes, director of the hospital, picked up his mail. Miranda, by way of chitchat, mentioned that Bruce Buxton had slid on his back down Main Street.

Sam's face darkened and he replied, "Too bad he didn't break his neck."

2

"Whee!" Harry slid along the iced-over farm road, arms flailing.

The horses watched from the pasture, convinced more than ever that humans were a brick shy of a load. Mrs. Murphy prowled the hayloft. Tucker raced along with Harry, and Pewter, no fool, reposed in the kitchen, snuggled tail over nose in front of the fireplace.

Susan Tucker, Harry's best friend since the cradle, slid along with her, the two friends laughing, tears in their eyes from the stinging cold.

Slowed to a stop, they grabbed hands, spinning each other around until Harry let go and Susan "skated" thirty yards before falling down.

"Good one."

"Your turn." Susan scrambled to her feet. Instead of spinning Harry, she got behind her and pushed her off.

After a half hour of this both women, tired, scooted up to the barn. They filled up water buckets, put out the hay, and called the three horses, Poptart, Tomahawk, and Gin Fizz, to come into their stalls. Then, chores completed, they hurried into the kitchen.

"I'll throw on another log if you make hot chocolate. You do a better job than I do."

"Only because you haven't the patience to warm the milk, Harry. You just pour hot water on the cocoa. Milk always makes it taste better even if you use one of those confections with powdered milk in it."

"I like chocolate." Pewter lifted her head.

"She heard the word 'milk.' " Harry stirred the fire, then placed a split dry log over the rekindled flames. Once that caught she laid another log parallel to that, then placed two on top in the opposite direction.

"I'd like some milk." Mrs. Murphy placed herself squarely on the kitchen table.

"Murph, off." Harry advanced on the beautiful cat, who hopped down onto a chair, her head peering over the top of the table.

"Here." Susan poured milk into a large bowl for the two cats, then reached into the stoneware cookie jar to give Tucker Milk-Bones. As Susan had bred Tee Tucker, she loved the dog. She'd kept one from the litter and thought someday she'd breed again.

"Did I tell you what Sam Mahanes said today? It was about the only interesting thing that happened."

"I threw out junk mail along with the Cracker Jacks in my postbox. That was the big interest in my day," Susan replied.

"I didn't do it."

"Then why didn't you clean it out? You're supposed to run a tight ship at the post office."

"Because whoever put the Cracker Jacks in there wanted you to have them." Harry smiled.

"That reduces the culprits to my esteemed husband, Ned. Not the Cracker Jacks type. Danny, m-m-m, more like his father. Must have been Brooks." She cited her teenaged daughter.

"I'll never tell."

"You won't have to because when I get home she'll wait for me to say something. When I don't she'll say, 'Mom, any mail today?' The longer I keep quiet, the crazier it will make her." Susan laughed. She loved her children and they were maddening as only adolescents can be but they were good people.

"The hard part was keeping Mrs. Murphy and Pewter from playing with the Cracker Jacks."

"What was your solution?"

Mrs. Murphy lifted her head from the milk bowl. *"Catnip in the Reverend Jones' box."*

Both women laughed as the cat spoke.

"She's got opinions," Susan remarked.

"I put catnip in Herb's mailbox." Harry giggled. "When he gets home and puts his mail on the table his two cats will shred it."

"Remember the time Cazenovia ate the communion wafers?" Susan howled recalling the time when Herb's sauciest cat got into the church closet, which was unwisely left open. "And I hear his younger kitty, Elocution, is learning from Cazenovia. Imagine kneeling at the communion rail being handed a wafer with fang marks in it."

Harry giggled. "The best church service I ever attended. But I hand it to Herb, he tore up bread crusts and communion continued."

"What happened with Sam Mahanes?" Susan asked. "Didn't mean to get off the track. I do it all the time and I'm not even old. Can you imagine me at eighty?"

"I can. You'll be the kind of old dear who walks in other people's kitchens to make herself a cup of tea."

"Well — at least I won't be boring. Eccentricity is worth something. You were going to tell me about Sam Mahanes in the post office today."

"Oh, that. Miranda told him that Bruce Buxton took a header on the ice. He turned a nifty shade of beet red and said, 'Too bad he didn't break his neck,' and then he slammed out of the P.O."

"Huh." Susan cupped her chin in her hand as she stirred her hot chocolate. "I thought those two were as thick as thieves."

"Yeah, although I don't know how anyone can stand Bruce on a long-term basis."

Susan shrugged. "I guess in order to be a good surgeon you need a big ego."

"Need one to be postmistress, too."

"You know, in order to be good at anything I suppose everyone needs a touch of ego. The trick is hiding it. Bruce might be wonderful at what he does but he's stupid about people. That's one of the things I've always admired about Fair. He's great at what he does but he never brags." She sipped a moment. "And how is your ex-husband?"

"Fine. It's breeding season so I won't see much of him until mares are bred for next year and this year's mares deliver." Fair was an expert on equine reproduction, a veterinarian much in demand.

"Oh, Harry." Exasperated, Susan cracked Harry's knuckles with a spoon.

"You asked how he was, not how we're doing."

"Don't get technical."

"All right. All right. We were keeping to our Wednesday-night dates until now. We're having fun." She shrugged. "I don't know if lightning can strike twice."

"Me either."

"I get so sick of people trying to get us back together. We've been divorced for four years. The first year was hell —"

Susan interrupted. "I remember."

"I don't know if time heals all wounds or if you just get smarter about yourself. Get more realistic about your expectations of other people and yourself."

"God, Harry, that sounds like the beginnings of maturity." Susan faked a gasp.

"Scary, isn't it?" She stood up. "Want more of your hot chocolate?"

"Yeah, let's finish off the lot." Susan stood up.

"Sit down."

"No, let me bring the cup to you. Easier to pour over the sink."

"Yeah, I guess you're right." Harry picked up the pan and carefully poured hot chocolate into Susan's cup and then refilled her own. "The weatherman says it's going to warm up to fifty degrees tomorrow."

"You wouldn't know it now. I don't mind snow but ice plucks my last nerve. Especially with the kids out driving in it. I know they have good reflexes but I also know they haven't experienced as much as we have and I wonder what they'll do in that first spin-out. What if another car is coming in the opposite lane?"

"Susan, they'll learn and you can't protect them anyway."

"Yeah. Still."

"Aren't you amazed that Miranda has kept to her diet in the dead of winter?"

"Still baking things for the store and her friends. I never realized she had such discipline."

"Shows what love will do."

Miranda had lost her husband over ten years ago. By all accounts it was a happy marriage and when George Hogendobber passed away, Miranda consoled herself with food. Ten years of consoling takes a long time to remove. The incentive was the return of her high-school boyfriend, now a widower, for their high-school reunion. Sparks flew, and as Miranda described it, they were "keeping company."

"The football team."

"What?" Harry, accustomed to abrupt shifts in subject from her old friend — in-

33

deed she was often guilty of them herself —
couldn't follow this one.

"I bet that's why Sam Mahanes is mad at
Bruce Buxton. Because Bruce operates on
all the football players, and didn't he just get
a big write-up in the paper for his work on
the safety? You know that kid that everyone
thinks will make All-American next year if
his knee comes back. And Isabelle Otey, the
girls' basketball star. He gets all the stars.
Jealousy?"

"Buxton's always gotten good press. De-
served, I guess. Being in Sam's position as
director of the hospital I'd think he'd want
Bruce to be celebrated, wouldn't you?"
Harry asked.

"You've got a point there. Funny, every
town, city, has closed little worlds where
ego, jealousy, illicit love collide. Even the
Crozet Preservation Society can be a tempes-
tuous hotbed. Good God, all those old ladies
and not one will forgive the other for some
dreaded misdeed from 1952 or whenever."

"Sex, drugs and rock and roll." Mrs.
Murphy climbed back up on the chair to
join the kitchen discussion.

"What, pussycat?" Harry reached over,
stroking the sleek head.

*"People get mad at other people over
juicy stuff."*

34

"Money. You forgot money." Tucker tidied up the floor, picking up her Milk-Bone debris.

"A little bit around here wouldn't hurt," Pewter, ever conscious of her need for luxury, suggested.

"Well?" Mrs. Murphy pulled forward one side of her whiskers.

"Well what?" The rotund gray kitty leapt onto the remaining free kitchen chair.

"You want money. Get your fat butt out there and earn some."

"Very funny."

"You could do shakedowns. People do it. Ask a small fee for not tearing up gardens, not leaving partially digested mice on the front steps, and not raiding the refrigerator."

Before unflattering words could be spoken, Harry leaned over, face-to-face with the cats. "I can't hear myself think."

"They certainly have many opinions," Susan said. "Not unlike their mother."

"M-m-m." Harry glanced out the window. "Damn."

Susan turned to observe.

"More snow," Tucker lamented. Being low to the ground, she had to plow through snow. It was the only time she admitted to admiring larger canines.

3

"Spike!" Isabelle Otey shouted from the sidelines as Harry, on the opposing team, rose up in the air, fist punching into the volleyball. Although Isabelle's main sport was basketball, she loved most team sports and she enjoyed knowing the "townies," as residents of the county were called by UVA students. Languishing on the sidelines, she supported her team vocally.

Isabelle's team, knowing of Harry's skill, crouched in preparation but not only was Harry strong, she was smart. She spiked the ball where they weren't.

"Game," the ref called as the score reached 21 to 18.

"Rocket arm." Cynthia Cooper slapped Harry on the back.

Isabelle, her crutches leaning against the bleachers, called out to Harry, "Too good, Mary Minor. You're too good."

Throwing a towel around her neck, Harry joined the coach of the opposing team. Coop, a deputy on the county's police force, joined them.

"Isabelle, they need you. Basketball team, too." Cynthia sat next to her.

"Four more weeks. You know it isn't really painful, the swelling went down fast but I don't want to go through this again so I'm doing what Dr. Buxton told me. What scares me more than anything is going out to the car, walking across the ice with crutches."

"Calling for rain tomorrow." Harry wiped her face with the white towel. "The good thing is it will melt some of the snow. Bad thing, won't melt all of it and at night everything will be more ice."

"Keeps me busy." Cynthia grinned. "I have to earn my salary somehow. You know, most people are pretty reasonable about fender benders. A few lose it."

"You must see a lot of stuff." Isabelle couldn't imagine being a law-enforcement officer. She envisioned a career as a pro basketball player.

"Mostly car wrecks, drunks, a few thefts and" — she smiled devilishly — "the occasional murder."

"I wonder if I could kill anyone."

"Isabelle, you'd be amazed at what you could do if your life depended on it," Cynthia said, running her fingers through her blonde hair.

"Sure. Self-defense, but I read about these serial killers in the paper or people who just go to a convenience store with a shotgun and blow everyone to bits."

"I have a few uncharitable thoughts in the post office from time to time," Harry giggled.

"Oh, Harry, you couldn't kill anyone — unless it was self-defense, of course," Isabelle said.

"It's not a subject I've thought much about. What about you, Coop? You're the professional."

"Most murders have a motive. Jealousy, inheritance money. The usual stuff. But every now and then one will come along that makes you believe some people are born evil. From my point of view our whole system allows them to get away with it."

"Are we going to have the discussion about suspending civil rights?" Harry asked Coop.

"No, we are not because I'm going to hit the showers. I've got a date tonight."

Both Harry and Isabelle perked right up. "With who?"

"Whom," Harry corrected Isabelle.

"With Harry's ex."

"For real?" Isabelle leaned forward.

"Take him. He's yours." Harry nonchalantly waved her right hand.

"Oh, don't be such a hardass. He loves you and you know it." Coop laughed at Harry; then her voice became animated. "That's it. Confess. You could have killed BoomBoom Craycroft when they had their affair."

"Ah, yes," Harry dryly replied. "The affair that ended my marriage. Actually, that's probably not true. Marriages end in a variety of ways. That was the straw that broke the camel's back. Could I have killed BoomBoom? No. She was no better than she should be. I could have killed him."

"So — why didn't you?" Isabelle, having not yet fallen in love, wanted to know.

"I don't know."

"Because you aren't a killer," Coop answered for Harry. "Everyone in this world has had times when they were provoked enough to kill but ninety-nine percent of us don't. I swear there are people who are genetically inclined to violence and murder, and I don't give a damn how unpopular that opinion is."

"Why are we sitting here discussing my former marriage?"

"Because I'm going on rounds with Fair tonight."

Fair Haristeen had invited Cynthia Cooper to accompany him when she expressed an interest in his work.

"I didn't know you were interested in horses." Isabelle stood up as Harry handed her her crutches.

"I like them but what I'm really interested in is seeing some of the farms from the back side. Meeting the barn workers. There might be a time when I need their help. And I'm curious about the technology."

"A lot of the stuff that's eventually used on humans is used in veterinary care first."

"Like the operation on my knee." Isabelle swung her leg over the bottom bleacher, stepping onto the wooden floor. "I wonder how many dogs, cats, and horses tore their anterior cruciate ligaments before I did." She paused a moment. "Har, I'm sorry if I put you on the spot about when your marriage broke up."

"Here, let me carry your purse." Harry picked up the alarmingly large satchel, throwing it over her shoulder. "Everyone in Crozet knows everything about everybody — or thinks they do. He fooled around and I got sick of it. And being married to a vet is like being married to a doctor. You can't plan on anything, really. Emergencies interrupt everything and sometimes days would go by and we'd hardly see one another. And I married too young."

They both watched with lurid fascination as BoomBoom Craycroft pushed open the gym doors. "Speak of the devil."

"Hi, girls." The buxom, quite good-looking woman waved to them.

"What are you doing here?" Harry asked, since BoomBoom had skipped gym in high school. Her only physical outlet, apart from the obvious, was golf.

"I saw everyone's cars parked outside and thought I might be missing something."

"You did. We beat the pants off them and then discussed whether we were capable of murder," Harry deadpanned.

"Ah. Well, the other reason I stopped by was that I saw Sheriff Shaw at Market Shiflett's store. Coop, he knows you have plans but will you work tonight? Bobby Yount came down with the flu and he thinks it's going to be one of those nights. He asked for you to call him in his car."

"Damn. Oh well. Thanks, Boom." Cynthia turned to Harry and Isabelle. "There goes my date with Fair." She knew this would tweak BoomBoom's raging curiosity.

Eyes widening, BoomBoom edged closer to Coop, hoping to unobtrusively pull her away from the other two women, to get the scoop on what sounded like a romance or at least a real date.

Harry took care of that by saying, "Gee, Boom, maybe you ought to fill in."

"You can be hateful. Really hateful." BoomBoom turned on her heel, the heel of an expensive snow boot bought in Aspen, and stormed off.

Isabelle's jaw dropped at the adults' antics.

"Spike." Coop clapped Harry on the back.

4

In one of those weather shifts so common in the mountains, the next few days witnessed temperatures in the middle fifties. The sounds of running water, dripping water, and sloshing water filled everyone's ears as rivulets ran across state roads; thin streams crossed the low spots of meadows spilling into creeks; streams and rivers rose halfway to their banks, and were still rising.

The north faces of ravines held snow in their crevasses, lakes of pristine snow trackless since animals avoided the deep drifts. Ice, turquoise blue, was frozen in cascades over rocks on the north face of outcroppings.

Fearing the onslaught of another sweep of Arctic air soon, farmers scrubbed and filled water troughs, suburban gardeners added another layer of mulch on spring bulbs, car dealers washed their inventory.

An early riser, Harry knocked out her farm chores, rode one horse and ponied the other two, climbed up on the ladder to sweep debris out of the barn gutters and the house gutters also.

Mrs. Murphy hunted mice in the hayloft, careful not to disturb Simon, the sleeping possum, the hibernating blacksnake, or the huge owl dozing in the cupola. Pickings were slim, since the owl snatched everything up, so Simon ate grain from the tack room. However, neither the owl nor Murphy could eradicate the mice living in the walls between the tack room and the stalls. The mice would sit in their cozy home and sing just to torment the cat.

Pewter, not one to get her paws wet, reposed in the house, flopped on her back on the sofa. Tucker followed Harry, whom she considered her human mother, which meant her stomach was filthy but she too felt a great sense of accomplishment. She picked up the small twigs and branches which had fallen, dragging them over to the toolshed. Small though the corgi was, she could pull four times her weight.

She'd grab the fat end of a branch, plant her hind legs, jerk the weight up a bit, then backpedal. Her yard work always made Harry laugh.

By eleven Harry was ready to go to town this Saturday. Fox-hunting was canceled since the rigs and vans would get stuck in the mud. Parking was always a problem on rainy or muddy days.

"Tucker, let's clean you up in the wash stall. You're not getting in the truck like that."

"I could sit in one spot. I won't move." Her ears drooped since she wasn't thrilled about a bath in any way, shape, or form. On the other hand she'd happily sit in a puddle, leap into the creek. But there was something about soap married to water that offended her canine sensibilities.

"Come on."

"Why don't you wash off Mrs. Murphy's paws, too?" A gleeful malicious note crept into Tucker's voice as she headed into the barn.

"I heard that, you twit." Murphy peeped over the side of the hayloft.

"Any luck?" Harry called to her beloved cat.

"No," came the growl.

"Slowing down, aren't you?" Tucker wanted to get a rise out of her friend. She was successful.

"I could smoke you any day, lardass. Tailless wonder. Dog breath."

"Ha. Ha." Tucker refused to glance upward, which further infuriated the sleek, slightly egotistical cat.

"All right. If you won't stand I'm going to put you in the crossties," Harry warned the little dog.

Turning on the warm water, she hosed off Tucker's stomach, which now returned to its lovely white color.

Mrs. Murphy, keen to enjoy her friend's discomfort, hopped down from the hayloft to sit on the tack trunk in the aisle. *"Cleanliness is next to godliness."*

"You think you're so smart."

"Cats are smarter than dogs."

"That's what you say but it's not true. Cats don't save shipwrecked humans. Newfoundlands do that. Cats don't rescue people in avalanches. St. Bernards do that. Cats don't even herd cows or pull their weight in the fields. Corgis do that. So there."

"Right. I told you cats were smarter than dogs. Further proof: You'll never get eight cats to pull a sled in the snow." She hurriedly washed her paws since she didn't want Harry to think she could wash her down.

"You two are chatty." Harry finished with Tucker, cut the hose, then wiped her off with an old towel.

A frugal soul, Harry saved everything. She had a pile of old towels in a hanging basket in the aisle outside the washroom. She also kept old towels in the tack room and she even picked up worn-out towels from the country club, purchasing them for a few dollars. For one thing, she needed them, but for another, Harry couldn't abide waste. It seemed like a sin to her.

"Beauty basket." Murphy smiled slyly at Tucker.

"Thank you. I thought you'd never notice. If she's cleaning me up it means we're going somewhere. Wonder where?"

"Well, Augusta Co-op for feed, always high on Mom's list. Wal-Mart. A and N for jeans if she needs any. Oh, don't forget AutoZone. She'll pick up a case of motor oil, windshield-wiper fluid, oil filters. Then again she might go to James River Equipment to get oil and oil filters for the tractor. You know her. It won't be the jewelry store. She's the only woman I know who would like a new set of wrenches for Valentine's Day as opposed to earrings or even flowers."

Tucker laughed. *"She loves flowers, though."*

"She'll send Fair flowers." Murphy laughed because in most ways Harry was quite predictable, but then cats always knew humans better than humans knew cats.

47

"Let me look at you." Harry walked over to Mrs. Murphy, who didn't bother to run away from her. After all, if she did and made Harry mad, she wouldn't get to ride in the truck, and Murphy adored riding in the truck, lording it over lowly cars.

"Clean as a whistle."

Harry inspected each dark paw, the color of Mrs. Murphy's tiger stripes. "Pretty good there, pussycat."

"Told you."

Harry picked up an animal under each arm, strode outside and put them inside the truck. No dirty paw marks on her seat covers. To haul her horse trailer, a year ago she'd bought a new dually, a one-ton truck with four wheels in the back for greater stability. She'd agonized for years over this decision, fretting over the financial drain, but it worked out okay because Fair helped a bit and she watched her pennies. But for everyday running about she used the tough old 1978 Ford, four-wheel drive, half ton. She'd bought cushy sheepskin covers for the bench seat as she'd worn out the original sheepskin covers.

When she closed the door, she thought about Pewter, then decided to let the cat sleep. True, Pewter would be grouchy on their return but she wanted to get rolling.

Once a job was completed, Harry wanted to move on to the next one.

Her grandmother once said that Harry was "impatient of leisure," an apt description.

Once on the road they headed toward Crozet instead of going toward Route 64, which would take them to Waynesboro where Harry shopped. She avoided Charlottesville for the most part since it was so expensive.

"Bag Augusta Co-op." Murphy observed the sodden landscape.

Both animals were surprised when Harry turned down the long, tree-lined drive to Dalmally Farm, passed the chaste yet still imposing main house, and continued on to a lovely cottage in the rear not far from the stables, so beautiful most people would be thrilled to live in them.

"Little Mim?" Tucker was incredulous.

Little Mim, Harry's age, was not an especially close friend of Harry's. Little Mim had attended an expensive private school whereas Harry, Susan Tucker, BoomBoom, Fair, and the gang all attended Crozet High School. Then, too, Little Mim had a chip on her shoulder, which Harry usually knocked off. One would not describe them as close friends under any circumstances. Over the years they had learned to tolerate one another, always civil in discourse as befit Virginians.

"Now don't get off the sidewalk or she won't allow you in the house. You hear?" Harry ordered.

"We hear."

Neither animal wanted to miss why Harry was calling on young Marilyn Sanburne.

Little Mim opened the door, greeted them all, seating Harry by the fireside. Her Brittany spaniel kissed Tucker, who didn't mind but felt the display of enthusiasm ought to be tempered. Murphy sat by the fireside.

"I'll get right to the point." Little Mim pushed over a bowl of candies toward Harry. "I'm going to run for mayor and I need your help."

"I didn't know your father was stepping down," Harry said innocently, for Jim Sanburne had been mayor of Crozet for almost thirty years. Jim was good at getting people together. Everyone said Mim had married beneath her when she selected Jim from her many beaus. She did, if money and class were the issues. But Jim was a real man, not some fop who had inherited a bundle of money but no brains nor balls. He worked hard, played hard, and was good for the town. His Achilles' heel proved to be women; but then men like Jim tend to attract more than their share. Mim used to hate him but over time they had worked things out. And she had to admit she'd married him on the rebound after a torrid affair with Dr. Larry Johnson back in the fifties. She'd had a breast cancer scare a few years back and that more than anything settled down Jim Sanburne.

"He's not," came Little Mim's blithe reply as she leaned back on her sofa.

"Uh, Marilyn, what's going on?"

"Crozet needs a change."

"I thought your dad was doing a great job."

"He has." She crossed one leg over the other. "But Dad wants to bring in more business and I think that's going to damage the town. We're doing fine. We don't need Diamond Mails."

"What's Diamond Mails?"

"Dad's trying to lure this big mail-order book club here from Hanover, Pennsylvania. You know those book clubs. There's all kinds of them: history, gardening, investing, best-seller clubs. He wants to build a huge warehouse out there just beyond the high school, where the abandoned apple-packing shed is, on the White Hall Road?

The groves are still behind it — on that nasty curve."

"Sure. Everyone knows where it is."

"Well, that's where he wants them to relocate. He says he'll take the curve out of the road. The state will do it. Fat chance, I say, but Dad has friends in Richmond. Think about it. This monstrous ugly warehouse. About fifty to sixty jobs, which means sixty houses somewhere and worse, think of the mail. I mean, aren't you already on overload?"

"But they'll have their own shipping and mailing."

"Of course they will but the workers will go through you. Private mail."

"Well — that's true." Harry had just shoveled piles of Valentine's Day cards. A future with more canvas bags bursting with mail loomed in her imagination.

"It's time for our generation to make our contribution. You know everybody. People like you. I'd like your support."

"That's flattering." Harry's mind was spinning. She didn't want to offend Little Mim and she certainly didn't want to offend Mim's father, whom she liked. "This is an awful lot to think over. I'll need a little time. And I'm not crawfishing. I do want to think about it. Does your father know you plan to oppose him in the fall election?"

"Yes. He laughed at me and said there's many a slip twixt the cup and the lip." Her face darkened. "And I said that's for sure and who knows what will happen between now and November."

"What's your mother say?"

"Oh." Marilyn's face brightened. "She said she was neutral. She wouldn't get in the middle of it. That was really good of her, and I didn't expect that."

"Yes." Harry thought Big Mim was taking the only sane course of action.

"The other thing is that Dad and Sam Mahanes plan to raise the money for a new wing on the hospital, which I don't oppose but I want to make sure nothing slips under the table, you know, no sneaky bond issue. If they want a new wing then they can raise the money privately. Larry Johnson agreed to head the drive. Dad talked him into it."

"You wouldn't by any chance know what's going down between Sam and Bruce Buxton, would you?"

"Budget." She clipped her words.

"You mean the hospital?"

"Bruce wants everything brand spanking new. Sam preaches fiscal responsibility. That's what Dad says."

"Well, I guess people will always fight over

resources." Harry had seen enough of that.

"It's turned into a feud too because other doctors support Bruce but the nurses support Sam. They say they know how to work the older equipment, old IVAC units and stuff, and they don't want stuff that's so technologically advanced that they have to go back to school to use it."

"Larry Johnson will calm them down." Harry knew that Larry and Mim had had an affair but as it was long before she was born she paid little attention to it. He'd come back from the war to establish a practice. He was handsome, but Mim's mother had felt he wasn't rich enough or classy enough for her daughter. She broke up the relationship and Mim had never forgiven herself for her cowardice. She should have defied her mother. Marrying Jim certainly was an act of defiance although too late for Larry, who had subsequently married a girl of his own class. As it turned out, Jim Sanburne had a gift for making money in construction, which over time had somewhat mollified Mrs. Urquhart, Mim's mother. And over time, Jim and Larry had become friends.

"He certainly will," Little Mim agreed.

"Thanks for asking me over. I've got to run some errands. The feed truck couldn't get into the farm last week and Thursday's delivery day. So I'd better get odds and ends just in case we get clobbered again. February is such a bitch."

"Doing anything for Valentine's Day?"

"No. You?"

"Blair's in Argentina on a photo shoot. So no." She paused. "Do you know if Bruce Buxton is dating anyone?"

Harry, wisely, did not comment on what Marilyn perceived of as a romance and what Blair Bainbridge thought of as a growing friendship. At least, that's what Harry thought was her peripatetic neighbor's position regarding Little Mim. "I don't know much about Bruce other than that he comes in for his mail. He's a little bit moody — but I never see him with a woman. Too busy, I guess."

Little Marilyn stood up, as did Harry. "You can talk to anyone you like about my candidacy. It's not a secret and I'll make a formal announcement March first."

"Okay." Harry reached the door, Mrs. Murphy and Tucker behind her, and then she turned and stopped. "Hey, did you get a chain letter last week?"

"I probably did but I throw them in the trash after reading the first line. Why?"

"Your mother got one and it upset her."

"Why?"

"Just junk mail, but you know how those things predict dire consequences if you don't send out the money and pass them along."

"A tidal wave will engulf your home in Tempe, Arizona." A gleam of humor illuminated Little Mim's attractive face.

"Right, that sort of thing. Oh well. I'll see you." Harry opened the door as her cat and dog scampered for the truck.

A tidal wave wasn't about to engulf Tempe, Arizona, but the creeks were rising fast in Crozet.

As Harry headed toward Route 64, she noticed Deputy Cynthia Cooper on Route 250 heading in the opposite direction, siren blaring, lights flashing. Harry pulled off the two-lane road.

"Another wreck, I'll bet," Harry said to her passengers.

"Pretty bad." Mrs. Murphy, sharp-eyed, had noticed how grim Coop looked.

It occurred to Harry, the way things usually occurred to Harry — meaning it just popped into her head — that she didn't know what an IVAC unit was.

5

The straight corridors of lead pipes running overhead testified to the 1930s updating of the oldest section of the hospital. Like a metallic spiderweb, they led to the boiler room, a square cut deep down at the center of the old building. Smack in the middle of this deep square sat the enormous cast-iron boiler, as good as the day it was built in 1911.

Hunkered down, fingers touching the stone floor for balance, Rick Shaw, sheriff of Albemarle County, glanced up when his trusted deputy walked into the room.

She stopped a moment, surveyed the blood splattered on the wall ten feet away, then bent down on one knee next to her boss. "Jesus Christ."

Lying in front of her was the still-warm body of Hank Brevard. His throat had been cut straight across with such force that he was nearly decapitated. She could see his neckbone.

"Left to right." Rick pointed to the direction of the cut.

"Right-handed perp."

"Yep."

The blood had shot across the room when the victim was killed, his heart pumping furiously.

"Tracks?"

"No." Rick stood up. "Whoever did this must have come up behind him. He might not have much blood on him at all and then again even if he did, this is a hospital. Easy to dump your scrubs."

"I'll look around."

Coop hurried down the main corridor. She heard a door slam behind her, hearing the voices of the fingerprint and lab teams.

She pushed open grimy pea-green doors, each one guarding supplies, empty cartons, odds and ends. The old incinerating room was intact. Finally she found the laundry room for the old part of the hospital. Nothing there caught her eye.

Rejoining Rick she shrugged. "Nada." She paused a moment. "You know, I had a thought. I'll be back. But one quick thing. There may be laundry rooms for the newer sections of the hospital. We'll need to check them fast."

"Where are you going?"

"Incinerator."

She ran back down the corridor, opened

the door, and walked in. In the old days the incinerating room burned body parts. These days such things were considered biohazards so they were hauled out of the hospital and burned somewhere else. It seemed odd, trucks of gallbladders and cirrhotic livers rolling down Main Street to their final destination, but the laws made such incongruity normal.

She searched each corner of the room, then picked up the iron hook and gingerly opened the incinerator. A sheet of flame swept near her face. Instinctively she slammed the door shut. If there had been any evidence tossed in there, it was gone now.

"Damn!" She wiped her face, put the hook back on its hanger, and left the room.

Rick had returned to the corpse. Wearing thin plastic gloves like the ones worn in the hospital he went through Hank's pockets. A set of keys hung from the dead man's belt. In his left pocket he had $57.29. His right pocket contained his car keys and a folded sheet of notepaper, a grocery list. Rick put everything back in Hank's pockets.

"All right, guys. Do what you can." He stood up again and propelled Coop away from the others. "Let's get to Hank's office before we notify the hospital staff."

"Boss, who called you? And why isn't

anyone else here?"

"Bobby Minifee called me from his cell phone. I told him not to speak to anyone, to stay with the body. He's outside in the unmarked car with Petey."

Bobby Minifee was Hank's assistant.

Petey D'Angelo, a young officer on the force, showed a flair for his job. Both Rick and Coop, young herself at thirty-four, liked him.

"So you're hoping no one knows about this except for Bobby Minifee and whoever killed Hank?"

"Yeah. That's why I want to get to Hank's office. Bobby said it was at the northeast corner of the building. This is the center so we take that corridor." As they walked along in the dim underground light, Rick cursed. "Shit, this is like a maze from hell."

"You'd have to know your way around or you'd run into the Minotaur."

"I'll remember that." He vaguely remembered the Greek myth about the half-bull, half-man.

They arrived at an open door, the name Hank Brevard on a black sliding nameplate prominently displayed. The spacious office was jammed with file cabinets. Hank's desk, reasonably neat, had an old wooden teacher's swivel chair behind it and a newer, nicer chair in front for visitors.

Coop began flipping through drawers while Rick pulled out the file drawers.

"Records go back ten years. If this is only ten years I'd hate to see all of the records."

"I've got a pile of oil bills from Tiger Fuel. A picture of the wife and kids." She stopped. Who would get that awful job, telling them? She opened the long middle drawer. "Pencils, pens, a tiny light, paper clips. Ah . . ." She pulled the drawer out even farther. A few envelopes, lying flat, were at the rear. "Winter basketball league schedule. Repair bill for his car. A new alternator. Three hundred forty-nine dollars with labor. That hurts. And . . ." She turned. "You getting anything?"

"It will take half the force to go through these file cabinets and we'll do it, too, but no, nothing is jumping right out at me except the mouse droppings."

"Need Mrs. Murphy."

"You're getting as bad about that cat as Harry."

Coop opened the last letter; the end of the envelope had been slit. She took out the letter. "Sister Sophonisba will bring you good fortune." She laughed a low laugh. "Guess not." She glanced up at the date. "Guess he didn't make the twenty copies in time."

"What in the hell are you talking about?"

"A chain letter. Mail out twenty copies in three days. Well, it's past the three days."

Rick came over, snatched the chain letter, and read it. "'Ignore this letter at your peril.' Under the circumstances it's like a sick joke." He handed the letter back to Coop, who replaced it inside the envelope. "All right, let's find Sam Mahanes."

"Saturday night."

"H-m-m. I'll find Sam. You find out who's the head honcho Saturday night."

"Boss, when are we going to notify people?"

"Not until I talk to Sam and you talk to whoever. I think we're already too late. The killer's flown the coop."

"Or he's over our head." She looked up at the ceiling.

"There is that. I'll send Petey over to Lisa Brevard. He's going to have to learn to deliver the bad news. Might as well start now. I'll keep Bobby Minifee with me — for now."

"Rick, think Bobby could have done it?"

"I don't know. Right now I don't know much except that our killer is strong, very strong, and he knows where to cut."

6

Face as white as the snow that remained in the crevices and cracks of the county, Bobby Minifee clung to the Jesus strap above the window on the passenger side of the squad car.

Rick lit up a Camel, unfiltered, opening the window a crack. "Mind?"

"You're the sheriff," Bobby said.

"You need me to pull over?"

"No. Why?"

"You look like you're going to be sick."

A jagged intake of breath and Bobby shook his head no. At twenty-one, Minifee was good-looking. He worked nights at the hospital to make ends meet. During the day he studied at Piedmont Community College. A poor boy, he had hopes of going on to Virginia Tech at Blacksburg. He was bright and he wanted a degree in mechanical engineering. The more he studied the more he realized he liked fluid dynamics, waves, water, anything that flowed. He wasn't sure where this would lead him but right now he was considering a different kind of flow.

"Sheriff, you must see stuff like that all the time. Blood and all."

"Enough. Car wrecks mostly. Well, and the occasional murder."

"I had no idea blood could shoot like that. It was all over the wall."

"When the jugular is cut, the heart, which is close to the throat, remember, pumps it out like a straight jet. It's amazing — the human body. Amazing. Was he still bleeding like that when you found him?" Rick slowly worked his way into more questions. When he arrived on the crime scene he had gone easy on Bobby because the kid was shaking like a leaf.

"No, oozing."

"Do you think he was still alive when you found him?"

"No. I felt for his pulse."

"How warm was his wrist or his hand when you touched him?"

"Warm. Not clammy or anything. Like he just died."

"The blood was bright red?" Bobby nodded yes, so Rick continued. "Sure? Not caked around the edges, or clumping up on his neck?"

"No, Sheriff. The reddest red I've ever seen, and I could smell it." He shook his head as if to clear his brain.

"It's the smell that gets you." Rick slowed down for a stoplight. "I'd say you were a lucky man."

"Me?"

"You, Minifee, could be lying there with Hank. I'd guess you were within five minutes of seeing the killer. Did you hear a footfall?"

"No. The boiler is pretty noisy."

"Freight train. Those old cast-iron babies go forever, though. Our ancestors expected what they built to last. Now we tear stuff down and build structures and systems that decay in seven years' time." He stubbed out his cigarette in the ashtray. "Didn't mean to lecture."

"Takes my mind off —"

"When I drive you home I'll give you a few names of people you can talk to, people who specialize in this kind of shock. It is a shock, Bobby, and don't do the stupid testosterone thing and go it alone."

"Okay." His voice faded.

"Did you like Hank Brevard?"

"He was a hardass. You know what I mean? One of those guys who likes to make you feel stupid. He always knew more than I did or anybody did. A real negative kind of guy."

"So you didn't like him?"

Bobby turned to directly stare at Rick. "Funny, but I did. I figured here's a real loser. In his fifties, mad about young guys coming up. Used to shit on me all the time about my studies. 'An ounce of experience is worth a pound of book learning,' " Bobby imitated Hank. "I kind of felt sorry for him because he really knew his stuff. He kept on top of everything and he could fix just about anything. Even computers and he's not a computer guy. He had a gift."

"Being plant manager of a hospital isn't a small job."

"No, but he couldn't rise any higher." Bobby sighed.

"Maybe he didn't want to."

"He did. You should have heard him gripe about baseball player salaries or basketball. He felt plenty trapped."

"Insightful for a young man."

"What's age got to do with it?" Bobby turned back to gaze out the window. The night seemed blacker than when they had driven away from the hospital.

"Oh, probably nothing. I'm just used to young people being self-absorbed. But then think of what I see every day."

"Yeah, I guess."

"The other men who worked under Hank,

feel the same way you did?"

"I'm night shift. I don't know those guys."

"Can you think of anyone who might want to kill Hank?"

"He could really piss people off." Bobby paused. "But enough to kill him —" He shrugged. "No. I'd feel better if I could."

"Listen to me. When you return to work, stuff will fly through your head, when you first go back to that boiler room. Sometimes there's a telling detail. Call me. The other thing is, you might be scared for yourself. I know I would be. From my experience this doesn't look like a sicko killer. Sickos have signatures. Part of their game. Hank either crossed the wrong man or he surprised somebody."

"What could be down in the boiler room worth killing for?"

"That's my job." Rick coasted to a stop at Sam Mahanes' large, impressive home in Ednam Forest, a well-to-do subdivision off Route 250. "Bobby, come on in with me."

The two men walked to the red door, a graceful brass knocker in the middle. Rick knocked, then heard kids yelling, laughing in the background.

"I'll get it," a young voice declared, running feet heading toward the door.

"My turn," another voice, feet also running, called out.

The door swung open and two boys, aged six and eight, looked up in awe at the sheriff.

"Mommy!" The youngest scurried away.

"Hi. I'm Sheriff Shaw and we're here to see Daddy. Is he home?"

"Yes, sir." The eight-year-old opened the door wider.

Sally Mahanes, a well-groomed, very attractive woman in her middle thirties, appeared. "Kyle, honey, close the door. Hello, Sheriff. Hi, Bobby. What can I do for you?"

Kyle stood alongside his mother as his younger brother, Dennis, flattened himself along the door into the library.

"I'd like to see Sam."

"He's down in his shop. The Taj Mahal, I call it. Sam owns every gadget known to man. He's now building me a purple martin house and —" She smiled. "You don't need to know all that, do you?" She crossed over to the center stairwell, walked behind it, opened a door, and called, "Sam." Music blared up the stairs. "Kyle, go on down and get Daddy, will you?" She turned to Rick and Bobby. "Come on in the living room. Can I get you a drink or a bite to eat?"

"No, thanks." Rick liked Sally. Everyone did.

"No, thank you." Bobby sat on the edge of a mint-colored wing chair.

Sam, twenty years older than his wife, but in good shape and good-looking, entered the living room, his oldest son walking a step behind him. "Sheriff. Bobby?" He tilted his head a moment. "Bobby, is everything all right?"

"Uh — no."

"Boys, come upstairs." The boys reluctantly followed their mother's lead, Dennis looking over his shoulder. "Dennis. Come on."

Once Rick thought the children were out of earshot he quietly said, "Hank Brevard has been murdered in the boiler room of the hospital. Bobby found him."

Thunderstruck, Sam shouted, "What?"

"Right after sunset, I'd guess."

"How do you know he was murdered?" Sam was having difficulty taking this all in.

"His throat was cut clean from ear to ear," Rick calmly informed him.

Sam glanced to Bobby. "Bobby?"

Bobby turned his palms up, cleared his voice. "I came down the service elevator from the fourth floor. I checked the hot line for messages. None. So I thought I'd check the pressure of the boiler. Supposed to be cold tonight. I walked in and Hank was flat on his back, eyes staring up, and it's kind of strange but at first I didn't notice his wound. I noticed the blood on the wall. I thought maybe he threw a can of paint. You know, he had a temper. And then I guess I realized how bad it was and I knelt down. Then I saw his throat. I took his pulse. Nothing. I called the sheriff—"

Rick interrupted. "Sam, I ordered him not to call anyone else, not even you. I was there in five minutes. Coop took seven. He would have called you."

"I quite understand. Bobby, I'm very sorry this has happened to you. We'll get you some counseling."

"Thank you."

"Sam, running a hospital is a high-pressure job. I know you have many things on your mind, lots of staff, future building plans, but you did know Hank pretty well, didn't you?"

"Oh sure. He was there when I took over from Quincy Lowther. He was a good plant manager. Set in his ways but good."

"Did you like him?"

"Yes." Sam's face softened. "Once you got to know Hank, he was okay." A furrow crossed his brow, he leaned forward. "Have you told Lisa?"

"I have an officer over there right now."

"Unless you need to question her, Sally and I will go over."

"Pete will ask the basics if she's capable. I'll see her tomorrow. I'm sure she would be grateful for your comfort." Rick never grew accustomed to the grief of those left behind. "Do you have any idea who would kill Hank or why? Did he have a gambling problem? Was he having an affair? I know it's human nature to protect friends and staff but anything you know might lead me to his killer. If you hold back, Sam, the trail gets cold."

Sam folded his hands together. "Rick, I can't think of a thing. Bobby told you he had a hot temper but it flared up and then was over. We all shrugged it off. Unless he had a secret life, I really can't think of anyone or anything."

Rick reached in his shirt pocket. "Here. If you think of anything, tell me. Coop, too. If I'm not around, she'll handle it."

"I will." Sam shifted his gaze to Bobby. "Why don't you take off a few days — with pay. And" — he rose — "let me get those counselors' names for you."

"Sam, you get on over to Lisa. I'll give him some names." Rick stood up, as did Bobby.

"Right." Sam showed them to the door.

Rick drove Bobby home and as he pulled

into the driveway of his rented apartment he asked, "Who's in charge of night maintenance?"

"Me."

"Upstairs?"

"You mean, who stands in for Sam?"

"Yeah."

"Usually the assistant director, Jordan Ivanic."

Rick clicked on the overhead light, scribbled the name on his notepad, tore off the sheet. "Can't hurt."

"Thanks." Bobby opened the squad car door, stepped out, then bent down. "Do you ever get used to this?"

"No, not really."

On the way back to the hospital, Rick called Coop. She'd questioned Jordan Ivanic. Not much there except she said he had nearly passed out. The body had been removed thirty minutes ago and was on its way to the morgue. The coroner was driving in to get to work immediately. She had ordered Ivanic to sit tight until Rick got there and she hadn't called the city desk at the newspaper, although she would as soon as Rick gave her the okay. If she helped the media, they would help her. It was an odd relationship, often tense, but she knew she'd better do a good job with the media tonight.

"Good work." Rick sighed over his car phone. "Coop, it's going to be a long night."

"This one's out of the blue."

"Yep."

7

At ten o'clock Saturday evening, Harry, already snuggled in bed, Mrs. Murphy on her pillow, Pewter next to her, and Tucker on the end of the bed, was reading *Remembrance of Things Past*. This was one of those books she'd promised herself to read back in college and she was finally making herself do it. Amazed at Proust's capacity for detail and even more amazed that readers of the day had endured it, she plowed through. Mostly she liked it, but she was only halfway through Volume I.

The phone rang.

"Has to be Susan or Fair," Pewter grumbled.

"Hello." Harry picked up the receiver; the phone was on the nightstand by the bed.

"Har." Susan's voice was breathless. "Hank Brevard was found murdered at the hospital."

"Huh?" Harry sat up.

"Bobby Minifee found him in the boiler room, right after sunset. Throat slit. O-o-o."

Susan shuddered.

Susan, one of Crozet's leading younger citizens, was on the hospital board. Sam Mahanes, responsible and quick, had called every member of the board, which also included Mim Sanburne and Larry Johnson.

"Oh, I wish I hadn't picked on him." Harry felt remorse. "Even if he was a crab."

"You know, Harry, a little expression of grief might be in order here."

"Oh, balls, Susan. I did express grief — a little, your qualifier! Besides, I'm talking to you."

A light giggle floated over the line. "He was a downer. Still — to have your throat slit."

"A swift death, I assume."

The animals pricked their ears.

Susan paused a second. "Do you think people die as they lived?"

"Uh, I don't know. No. No. I mean how can you die as you lived if someone sneaks up behind you and s-s-s-t."

"You don't have to produce sound effects."

"And how can you die as you lived if you're propped up in a hospital bed, tubes running everywhere. That's a slow slide down. I'd hate it. Well, I guess most people in that position hate it."

"Yeah, but I wonder sometimes. What I'm getting at is even if you're on that deathbed, let's say, you would approach death as you approached life. Some will face it head-on, others will deny it, others will put on a jolly face."

"Oh that. Yeah, then I suppose you do — I mean, you do die as you lived. Makes Hank's death even stranger. Someone grabs him and that's the end of it. Swift, brutal, effective. Three qualities I wouldn't assign to Hank."

"No, but we'd assign them to his killer."

Harry thought a long time. "I guess so. What's so weird is why anyone would want to kill Hank Brevard other than to stop hearing him talk about how our country is a cesspool of political corruption, Sam Mahanes works him too hard, and let's not forget Hank's theories on the Kennedy assassination."

"Fidel Castro," Susan filled in.

"I count that as part of the Kennedy assassination." Harry changed the subject slightly. "When do you have a board meeting? I'm assuming you'll have an emergency one."

"Which Mim will take over as soon as Sam opens it."

"He'd damn well better smile when she

does it, too. She's one of the hospital's largest contributors. Anyway, imperious as Mim can be, she has good ideas. Which reminds me. I was going to call you tomorrow and tell you that Little Mim wants to run for mayor of Crozet."

"Tomorrow. You should have called me the minute you walked in the door," Susan chided her.

"Well, I kinda intended to but then I mopped the kitchen floor because it was a mud slide and then I trimmed Tucker's nails which she hates, the big baby."

"*I do,*" Tucker replied.

"Has Marilyn lost her senses?"

"I don't know. She pressured me a little bit but not in a bad way. She said her father had done a pretty good job but she and he were falling on opposite sides of the fence over the development of Crozet, especially where industry is concerned, and you know, she did make a good point. She said it's time our generation got involved."

"We have been slugs," Susan agreed. "So what are you going to do? Between a rock and a hard place."

"I said I'd think about it. She'll ask you, too. We're all going to have to make choices and publicly, too."

"M-m-m, well, let me call Rev. Jones so he

can get the Lutheran Church ladies in gear. Miranda will organize the Church of the Holy Light group. We'd better all get over to Lisa Brevard's tomorrow morning."

"Right. What time are you going?"

"Nine."

"Okay. I'll be there at nine, too. See you." Harry hung up the phone, informed her three animal friends of the bizarre event, then thought about the morning's task.

Sitting next to grief disturbed her. But when her mother and father had died within a year of each other, she had cherished those people who came to share that grief, brought covered dishes, helped. How selfish to deny yourself to another person in need because their sorrow makes you uncomfortable. People feel uncomfortable for different reasons. Men feel terrible because they can't fix it and men are raised to fix things. Women empathize and try to soothe the sufferer. Perhaps the categories don't break down that neatly along gender lines but Harry thought they did.

She reached over and set her alarm a half hour early, to five a.m.

Then she clicked off the light. "Who in the world would want to kill Hank Brevard?"

"Somebody very sure of himself," Mrs.

Murphy sagely noted.

"Why do you say that?" Pewter asked.

"Because he or she knew his way around the basement, probably he. He left the body. Humans who want to cover their tracks bury the body. At least, that's what I think. There's an element of arrogance in just leaving Hank crumpled there. And the killer either knew the schedule, the work routine, or he took the chance no one else would be in the basement."

"You're right," Tucker said.

"Will you guys pipe down? I need my beauty sleep."

"Try coma," Pewter smarted off.

The other two snickered but did quiet down.

8

The scale needle dipped. Tom Yancy, the coroner, lifted off the brain. His assistant wrote down 2 lb. 9 oz.

Both Rick and Coop had attended enough autopsies not to be so squeamish but Rick hated the part when the coroner sawed off the skullcap. The sound of those tiny blades cutting into fresh bone and the odor of the bone made him queasy. The rest of it didn't bother him. Most people got woozy when the body was opened from stem to stern but he could handle that just fine.

Each organ was lifted out of Hank Brevard.

"Liver's close to shot," Tom noted. "Booze."

"Funny. I never saw him drunk," Rick remarked.

"Well, it is possible to have liver disease without alcohol but this is cirrhosis. He drank."

"Maybe that's why he was so bitchy. He

was hungover most of the time," Coop said.

"He wasn't exactly beauty and light, was he?" Tom poked around the heart. "Look. The heart is disproportionate. The left side should be about one half the right. His is smaller. Chances are he would have dropped sooner rather than later since this pump was working too hard. Every body has its secrets."

After the autopsy, Tom washed up.

"The obvious?" Rick asked.

"Oh yeah. No doubt about it. Left to right as you noted. Back to the bone. The C-3 vertebra was even nicked with the blade where I showed you. Damn near took his head off. A razor-sharp blade, too. Nothing sloppy or jagged about it. Very neat work."

"A surgeon's precision." Coop crossed her arms over her chest. She was getting tired and hungry.

"I'd say so, although there are plenty of people who could make that cut if the instrument was sharp enough. People have been slitting one another's throats since B.C. It's something we're good at." Tom smiled wryly.

"But the assailant had to be powerful." Rick hated the chemical smells of the lab.

"Yes. There's no way the killer could be female unless she bench-presses two hundred and fifty pounds and some do, some do. But from the nature of the wound it was someone a bit taller than Hank. Otherwise the wound would have been a bit downward, unless he drove Hank to his knees, but you said there was no sign of struggle at the site."

"None."

"Then my guess, which I'm sure is yours, too, is the killer came up behind him, was Hank's height or taller, grabbed his mouth and cut so fast Hank barely knew what hit him. I suppose there's comfort in that."

"How long did it take him to die?"

"Two minutes, more or less."

"There'd be no shortage of suitable knives in the hospital," Coop said.

"Or people who know how to use them." Tom opened the door to the corridor.

Flames darted behind the glass front of the red enamel wood-burning stove. Tussie Logan hung up the phone in the kitchen.

When she returned to the living room, Randy Sands, her housemate and best friend, noticed her ashen face. "What's wrong?"

"Hank Brevard is dead."

"Heart attack?" Randy rose, walked over to Tussie, and put his arm around her shoulders.

"No. He was murdered."

"What?" Randy dropped his arm, turning to face her.

"Someone slit his throat."

"Good Lord." He sucked in his breath. "How primitive." He walked back to the sofa. "Come on, sit down beside me. Talking helps."

"I don't know what to say." She dropped next to him, which made his cushion rise up a little bit.

"Who just called to tell you?"

"Oh, Debbie, Jordan Ivanic's secretary. I guess we're all being called one by one. She said Sheriff Shaw or Deputy Cooper would be questioning us and —" She bit her lip.

"Not the most hospitable man but still." He put his arm around her again. "I'm sorry."

"You know, I was just in the post office with him and he was bitching and moaning about working a late shift because someone was sick or whatever. Half the time I tuned him out." She breathed in sharply. "Now I feel guilty as hell about it."

Randy patted her shoulder. "Everybody did that. He was boring."

A log popped in the stove.

Tussie flinched. "You never know. How trite." She rocked herself. "How utterly trite but it's true. Here I work in a hospital with these desperately sick children. I mean, Randy, we know most of them haven't a prayer but this shakes me."

"Working with terminally ill children is your profession. Having an associate or whatever you call Hank is quite another matter . . . having him murdered, I mean. Sometimes I open my mouth and I can't keep my tongue on track," he apologized.

"Start one sentence and bop into the second before you've finished the first." She smiled sadly. "Randy, I have to go back and work in that hospital and there's a killer loose." She shuddered.

"Now you don't know that. It could have been a random thing."

"A homicidal maniac goes to the hospital and selects Hank."

"Well," his voice lightened. "You know what I mean. It's got nothing to do with you."

"God, I hope not." She shuddered again and he kept patting her shoulder, keeping his arm around her.

"You'll be fine."

"Randy, I'm scared."

9

Once a human being reaches a certain age, death, while not a friend, is an acquaintance. Sudden death, though, always catches people off guard.

Lisa Brevard, in her early fifties, was stunned by her husband's murder. To lose him was bad enough, but to have him murdered was doubly upsetting. She knew his faults but loved him anyway. Perhaps the same could have been said of him for her.

After Harry left the Brevards' she, Susan, Miranda Hogendobber, and Coop had lunch at Miranda's, she being the best cook in Crozet.

"When does Tracy get back?" Coop asked Miranda about her high-school boyfriend, who had struck up a courtship with her at their reunion last year.

"As soon as he sells the house." She placed the last dish on the table — mashed potatoes — sat down, and held Harry's and Coop's hands. Coop held Susan's hand so the circle was complete. "Heavenly Father, we thank Thee for Thy bounty to us both in food and in friendship. We ask that Thou sustain and comfort Lisa and the family in their time of sorrow. In Jesus' name we pray. Amen."

"Amen," the others echoed, as did the animals, who quickly pounced upon their dishes on the floor.

"You look wonderful, Miranda." Susan was proud of Miranda, who had lost forty pounds.

"Men fall in love with their eyes, women with their ears." Miranda smiled.

Coop glanced up, fork poised in midair. "I never thought of that."

"The Good Lord made us differently. There's no point complaining about it. We have to accept it, besides" — Miranda handed the bowl to her left — "I wouldn't have it any other way."

"Wh-o-o-o." Harry raised her eyebrows.

"Don't start, Harry." Miranda shot her a glance, mock fierce.

"I hope Tracy sells that house in Hawaii fast." Harry heaped salad into her bowl.

"I do, too. I feel like a girl again." Miranda beamed.

They talked about Tracy and others in the town but the conversation kept slipping back to Hank Brevard.

"Cooper, are you holding back?" Harry asked.

"No. It takes us time to piece together someone's life and that's what we have to do with Hank. Whatever he was, whatever he did, someone wanted him dead. Big time."

"He couldn't have, say, surprised someone doing —" Susan didn't finish her sentence as Harry jumped in.

"In the boiler room of the hospital?"

"Harry, someone could have been throwing evidence into the boiler," Susan defended herself.

"Most likely the incinerator." Cooper then described the bowels of the hospital building to them. "So you see, given the corridors, whoever did this knew their way around."

"Someone who works there," Miranda said.

"Or someone who services equipment there. We have to run down every single contractor, repairman, delivery boy who goes in and out of that place."

"What a lot of work," Miranda exclaimed. "Like that old TV show, *Dragnet.* You do throw a net over everything, don't you?"

Cooper nodded. "And sooner or later, Miranda, something turns up."

And so it did, but not at all where they thought it would.

18

"Oh boy." Harry closed the post office door behind her just as Rob Collier pulled up to the front door. She hurried through and opened the front door. "Monday, Monday."

"I've got stuff for you," he sang out as he hauled canvas bags stuffed with mail.

"Valentine's Day. I forgot." She grimaced as he tossed two extra bags onto the mail-room floor.

"Just think of all the love in those bags," he joked.

"You're in a good mood."

"I already got my Valentine's Day present this morning."

"No sex talk, Rob, I'm too delicate."

He grinned at her, hopped back in the big mail truck, and took off in the direction of White Hall, where a small post office awaited him.

"Think Mom got any love letters?" Tucker tugged at one of the bags.

"I don't think she cares. She has to sort her mail the same as everybody

89

else's," Murphy replied.

"Saint Valentine. There ought to be a Saint Catnip or how about a Saint Tuna?" Pewter, having eaten a large breakfast, was already thinking about lunch at seven-thirty in the morning. *"I bet there wasn't even a real person called Valentine."*

"Yes, there was. He was a third-century martyr killed in Rome on the Flaminian Way under the reign of Claudius. There are conflicting stories but I stick to this one," Mrs. Murphy informed her gray friend.

"How do you know all that?" Pewter irritatedly asked.

"Whatever Harry reads I read over her shoulder."

"Reading bores me," Pewter honestly answered. *"Does it bore you, Tucker?"*

"No."

"Tucker, you can hardly read."

"Oh yes I can." The corgi glared at Murphy. *"I'm not an Afghan hound, you know, obsessed with my appearance. I've learned a few things in this life. But I don't get what a murdered priest has to do with lovers. Isn't Valentine's Day about lovers?"*

With a superior air, Murphy lifted the tip of her tail, delicately grooming it, and replied, *"The old belief was that birds pair off on February fourteenth and I guess since that was the day Valentine was murdered somehow that pairing became associated with him."*

"I'm sorry I'm late." Miranda bustled through the back door. "I overslept."

Harry, up to her elbows in mail, smiled. "You hardly ever do that."

They had spoken Sunday about the murder of Hank Brevard and, with that shorthand peculiar to people who have known one another a long time or lived through intense experiences together, they hopped right in.

"Accident?" Miranda placed packages on the shelves, each of which had numbers and letters on them so large parcels could be easily retrieved.

"Impossible."

"I guess I'm trying to find something —" A rap on the back door broke her train of thought.

"Who is it?" Harry called out.

"Miss Wonderful."

"Susan." Harry laughed as her best friend opened the door. "Help us out and make tea, will you? Rob showed up early and I haven't started a pot. What are you doing here this early, anyway?"

Susan washed out the teapot at the small sink in the rear. "Brooks' Volvo is in the shop so I dropped her at school. Danny's off on a field trip so I had to do it." Dan, her son, would be leaving for college this fall. "I swear that Volvo Ned bought her must be the prototype. What a tank but it's safe."

"What's the matter with it?" Miranda asked.

"I think the alternator died." She put tea bags in three cups, then came over to help sort mail until the water boiled. "You'd think most people would have mailed out their Valentine's cards before today."

"They did, but today" — Harry surveyed the volume of mail — "is just wild. There aren't even that many bills in here. The bills roll in here next week."

The teakettle whistled. "Okay, girls, how do you want your tea?"

"The usual," both called out, which meant Harry wanted hers black and Miranda wanted a teaspoon of honey and a drop of cream.

Susan brought them their cups and she drank one, too.

"Murphy, what are you looking at?"

"This Jiffy bag smells funny." She pushed it.

Pewter and Tucker joined her.

"Yeah." Pewter inhaled deeply. *"Addressed to Dr. Bruce Buxton."*

Puzzled, Tucker cocked her head to the right and then to the left. *"Dried blood. Faint but it smells like dried blood."*

The cats looked at one another and then back to Tucker, whose nose was unimpeachable.

"All right, you guys. No messing with government property." Harry snatched the bag, read the recipient's name, then placed it on the bookshelves, because it was too large for his brass mailbox. "Ned tell you anything?" she asked Susan.

"No. Client relationship."

Susan's husband, a trusted and good lawyer, carried many a secret. Tempted though he was at times, he never betrayed a client's thoughts or deeds to his wife.

"Is Bobby Minifee under suspicion?" Miranda put her teacup on the divider between the public space and the work space.

"No. Not really," Susan replied.

"Anyone seen Coop?" Harry shot a load of mail into her ex-husband's mailbox.

"No. Working overtime with all this." Susan looked on the back of a white envelope. "Why would anyone send a letter without a return address, the mail being what it is. No offense to you, Harry, or you, Miranda."

"None taken." Harry folded one sack,

now emptied. "Maybe they get busy and forget."

At eight on the dot, Marilyn Sanburne stood at the front door just as Miranda unlocked it.

"Good morning. Oh, Miranda, where did you get that sweater? The cranberry color complements your complexion."

"Knitted it myself." The older woman smiled. "We've got so much mail — well, there's some mail in your box but you'd better check back this afternoon, too."

"Fine." Little Mim pulled out her brass mailbox key, opened the box, pulling out lots of mail. She quickly flipped through it, then loudly exclaimed, "A letter from Blair."

"Great." Harry spoke quickly because Little Mim feared Harry had designs on the handsome model herself, which she did not.

"I also wanted you ladies to be the first to know that I've rented the old brick pharmacy building and it's going to be my campaign headquarters."

"That's a lot of space," Harry blurted out.

"Yes." Little Mim smiled and bid them good-bye.

They watched as she got into her car and opened Blair's letter. She was so intent upon reading it that she didn't notice her mother pull up next to her.

Mim parked, emerged well-dressed as always, and walked over to the driver's side of her daughter's car. Little Mim didn't see her mother, so Big Mim rapped on the window with her forefinger.

Startled, Little Mim rolled down the window. "Mother."

"Daughter."

A silence followed. Little Mim had no desire to share her letter, and she wasn't thrilled that her mother saw how engrossed she was in it.

Shrewdly, she jumped onto a subject. "Mother, I've rented the pharmacy."

"I know."

"How do you know?"

"Zeb Berryhill called your father and wondered if he would be upset and your father said he would not. In fact, he was rather looking forward to a challenge. So that was that."

"Oh." Little Mim, vaguely disappointed, slipped the letter inside her coat. She was hoping to be the talk of the town.

"It must be good."

"Mother, I have to have some secrets."

"Why? Nobody else in this town does," said the woman who had secrets going back decades.

"Oh, everyone has secrets. Like the person who killed Hank Brevard."

"M-m-m, there is that. Well, I'm off to a Piedmont Environmental Council meeting. Happy Valentine's Day."

"You, too, Mumsy." Little Mim smiled entirely too much.

As she drove off, Big Mim entered the post office just as Dr. Buxton pulled into the parking space vacated by her daughter. At that moment her irritation with her daughter took over the more pressing gossip of the day.

"Girls," Mim addressed them, "I suppose you've heard of Marilyn's crackbrained plan to oppose her father."

"Yes," came the reply.

"Not so crackbrained," Pewter sassed.

Bruce walked in behind her, nodded hello to everyone, opened his box, and almost made it out the door before Miranda remembered his package. "Dr. Buxton, wait a minute. I've got a Jiffy bag for you."

"Thanks." He joined Mim at the divider.

She placed her elbows on the divider. "Bruce, what's going on at the hospital? The whole episode is shocking."

"I don't know. He wasn't the most pleasant guy in the world but I don't think that leads to murder. If it did a lot more of

96

us would be dead." He looked Big Mim right in the eye.

"Was that your attempt at being subtle?" She bridled when people didn't properly defer to her.

"No. I'm not subtle. I'm from Missouri, remember?"

"Two points." Murphy jumped onto the divider, Pewter followed.

"Let me out," Tucker asked Harry, because she wanted to be right out there with Bruce and Mim.

"Crybaby." Harry opened the swinging door and the corgi padded out to the public section.

"You and Truman." Mim rapped the countertop with her long fingernails.

"Here we go." Miranda slid the bag across the counter.

"Ah." He squeezed the bag, examined the return address, which was his office at the hospital. "Huh," he said to himself but out loud. He flicked up the flat red tab with his fingernail, pulling it to open the top. He shook the bag and a large bloody scalpel fell out. "What the hell!"

11

Coop placed the scalpel in a plastic bag. Rick turned his attention to Dr. Bruce Buxton, not in a good mood.

"Any ideas?"

"No." Bruce's lower jaw jutted out as he answered the sheriff.

"Oh, come on now, Doc. You've got enemies. We've all got enemies. Someone's pointing the finger at you and saying, 'He's the killer and here's the evidence.' "

Bruce, a good four inches taller than Rick, squared his shoulders. "I told you, I don't know anyone who would do something like this and no, I didn't kill Hank Brevard."

"Wonder how many patients he's lost on the table?" Pewter, ever the cynic, said.

"He probably lost more due to bedside manner than incompetence," Mrs. Murphy shrewdly noted.

"He's not scared. I can smell fear and he's not giving off the scent." Tucker sniffed at Bruce's pants leg.

"You don't have to stop. You can still sort

the mail. But first tell me where you saw the bag," the sheriff asked Harry, Miranda, and Susan, now stuck because she had dropped in to help. He had interviewed Mim first so that she could leave.

"I saw it first," Tucker announced.

"You did not. I did," Pewter contradicted the bright-eyed dog.

"They don't care. If you gave these humans a week they wouldn't understand that we first noticed something peculiar." Murphy flopped on her side on the shelf between the upper and lower brass mailboxes.

"I saw the bag." Harry, feeling a chill, rolled up her turtleneck, which she had folded down originally. "Actually, Mrs. Murphy sniffed it out. Because she noticed it, I noticed it."

"What a surprise." Mrs. Murphy's long silken eyebrows twitched upward.

"Look, Sheriff, I've got to be at the hospital scrubbed up in an hour." Bruce impatiently shifted his weight from foot to foot.

"When will you be finished?" Rick ignored Bruce's air of superiority.

"Barring complications, about four."

"I'll see you at your office at four then."

"There's no need to make this public, is

there?" Bruce's voice, oddly light for such a tall man, rose.

"No."

"No need to tell Sam Mahanes unless it turns out to be the murder weapon and it won't."

Coop, sensitive to inflections and nuance, heard the suppressed anger when Bruce mentioned Sam Mahanes.

"Why are you so sure that isn't the murder weapon?" she asked.

"Because I didn't kill him."

"The scalpel could still be the murder weapon," she persisted.

"I heard that Hank was almost decapitated. You'd need a broad, long, sharp blade for that work. Which reminds me, the story was on all the news channels and in the paper. The hospital will be overrun with reporters. Are you sure you want to see me in my office?"

Rick replied, "Yes."

What Rick didn't say was that he wanted hospital staff to know he was calling upon Dr. Buxton. While there he would question other workers.

He couldn't be certain that the killer worked in the hospital. What he could be certain of was that the killer knew the layout of the basement.

Still, he hoped his presence might rattle some facts loose or even rattle the killer.

"Well, I'll see you at four." Bruce left without saying good-bye.

"Harry, what are you looking at?" Rick pointed at her.

"You."

"And?"

"You're good at reading people," she complimented him.

Surprised, he said, "Thanks" — took a deep breath — "and don't start poking your nose in this."

"I'm not poking my nose into it. I work here. The scalpel came through the mail." She threw up her hands.

"Harry, I know you." He nudged a mailbag with his toe. "All right then, you get back to work. Susan?"

"I dropped in for tea and to help. It's Valentine's Day."

"Oh, shit." He slapped his hand to his head.

"Shall I call in roses for your wife?" Miranda volunteered.

Rick gratefully smiled at her. "Miranda, you're a lifesaver. I'm not going to have a minute to call myself. The early days of a case are critical."

"I'd be glad to do that." Miranda moved

toward the phone as Rick flipped up the divider and walked out the front. "Coop," he called over his shoulder. "Start on the basement of the hospital today. In case we missed something."

"Roger," she agreed as she reached in her pocket for the squad car keys.

They had arrived at the post office in separate cars.

"Any leads?" Harry asked the big question now that Rick was out of the post office.

"No," Cynthia Cooper truthfully answered. "It appears to be a straightforward case of murder. Brutal."

"Doesn't that usually mean revenge?" Susan, having read too many psychology books, commented.

"Yes and no." She folded her arms across her chest. "Many times when the killer harbors an intense hatred for the victim they'll disfigure the body. Fetish killings usually involve some type of ritual or weirdness, say, cutting off the nose. Just weird. This really is straightforward. The choice of a knife means the killer had to get physically close. It's more intimate than a gun but it's hard to get rid of a gun. Even if the killer had thrown it in the incinerator, something might be left. A knife is easy to hide, easy to dispose of, and not so easy to figure out. What I mean by that is, in lieu of the actual weapon, there are a variety of knife types that could do the job. It's not like pulling a .45 slug out of a body. Also, a knife is quiet."

"Especially in the hands of someone who uses knives for a living." Murphy pounced on the third mailbag.

Cynthia, taller than the other women, reached her arms over her head and stretched. She was tired even though it was morning, and her body ached. She hadn't gotten much sleep since the murder.

Miranda hung up the phone, having ordered flowers for Rick's wife. "Did I miss anything? You girls talking without me?"

"No. No suspects," Harry told her.

" 'Be sure your sin will find you out.' Numbers, thirty-second chapter." She reached into the third mailbag to discover that Murphy had wriggled inside. "Oh!" She opened the drawstring wider. "You little stinker."

"Ha. Ha." Murphy backed farther into the mass of paper.

"Harry, if I get a day off anytime soon I'm coming out to your place." Coop smiled.

"Sure. If it's not too cold we can go for a ride. Oh, hey, before you go — and I know you must — have you heard that Little Mim is going to run against her father for the mayor's office?"

"No." Cynthia's shoulders cracked, she lowered her arms. "They'll be playing happy families at Dalmally." She laughed.

"Well." Harry shrugged, since the Sanburnes were a law unto themselves.

"Might shake things up a bit." Cynthia sighed, then headed for the door.

"I expect they've been shaken up enough already," Miranda wisely noted.

Harry made a quick swing to the hospital to find Larry Johnson. Although semi-retired, he seemed to work just as hard as he had before taking on Dr. Hayden McIntire as a partner.

She spied him turning into a room on the second-floor corridor.

She tiptoed to the room. No one was there except for Larry.

He looked up. "My article for the newsletter." He snapped his fingers. "It's in a brown manila envelope in the passenger seat of my car. Unlocked."

Harry looked at the TV bolted into the ceiling, at the hospital bed which could be raised and lowered. Then her attention was drawn to the IVAC unit, an infusion pump, a plastic bag on a pole. A needle was inserted usually into the patient's arm and the machine could be programmed to measure out the appropriate dose of medicine or solution.

"Larry, if I'm ever taken ill you'll be sure to fill my drip with Coca-Cola."

"Well, that's better than vodka — and I've seen alcohol sneaked into rooms in the most ingenious ways." He rolled the unit out of the way.

"Got any ideas?" She didn't need to say about the murder.

"No." He frowned.

"Nosy."

"I know." He smiled at her. "I apologize for not running my newsletter article to the post office. I'm a little behind today."

"No problem."

She left, found his red car easily, grasped the manila envelope, and drove home. Cindy Green, editor of the newsletter, would pick it up at the post office tomorrow.

If nothing else, the great thing about working at the post office was you were central to everybody.

12

"Intruder! Intruder!" Tucker barked at the sound of a truck rolling down the driveway.

Murphy, her fabulously sensitive ears forward, laconically said, *"It's Fair, you silly twit."*

Murphy, like most cats, could identify tire sounds from a quarter of a mile away. Humans always wondered how cats knew when their mate or children had turned for home; they could hear the different crunching sounds. Humans could tell the difference between a big truck and a car but cats could identify the tire sounds of all vehicles.

Within a minute, Fair pulled up at the back door. Murphy jumped on the kitchen windowsill to watch him get out of the truck, then reach back in for a box wrapped in red paper with a white bow.

He glanced up at the sky, then walked to the porch, opened the door, stopped at the back kitchen door, and knocked. He opened the door before Harry could yell, "Come in."

"It's me."

"I know it's you." She walked out of the living room. "Your voice is deeper than Susan's."

"Happy Valentine's Day." He handed her the red box.

She kissed him on the cheek. "May I open it now?"

"That's the general idea." He removed his coat, hanging it on a peg by the back door.

"Wormer! Thanks." She kissed him again.

He'd given her a three-month supply of wormer for her horses. That might not be romantic to some women but Harry thought it was a perfect present. "I have one for you, too."

She skipped into the living room, returning with a book wrapped in brown butcher paper yet sporting a gleaming red ribbon and bow. "Happy Valentine's Day back at you."

He carefully opened the present, smoothing the paper and rolling up the ribbon. A leather-bound book, deep rich old tan with a red square between two raised welts on the spine, gave off a distinctive aroma. He opened to the title page. The publication date was in Roman numerals.

"Wow. 1792." He flipped through the pages. "Ever notice how in old books, the ink on the page is jet black because the letter was cut into the page?"

"Yeah. The best." She stood next to him admiring the book, an old veterinary text printed in London.

"This is a beautiful present." He wrapped his arms around her, kissing her with more than affection. "You're something else."

"Just what, I'd like to know." Pewter, ready for extra crunchies, was in no mood for romance.

"I've got corn bread from Miranda, if you're hungry."

"I am!"

"Pewter, control yourself." Harry spoke to the now very vocal Pewter, who decided to sing a few choruses from *Aïda* at high register.

Harry poured out crunchies.

"Yahoo." The cat dove in.

"Anything to shut her up." Harry laughed.

"She's got you trained." He pulled two plates out of the cupboard as Harry removed the tinfoil from the corn bread.

As they sat and ate she told him what had happened at the post office with Bruce Buxton.

After hearing the story, Fair shook his head. "Sounds like a cheap trick."

"Bruce doesn't win friends and influence

people," Harry truthfully remarked.

"Arrogant. A lot of doctors are like that, or at least I think they are. Then again, a lot of vets are that way. I don't know what there is about medical knowledge that makes a man feel like God but Bruce sure does."

"You've got a big ego but you keep it in check. Maybe that's why you're such a good equine vet. Not good, really, the best." She smiled at him.

"Hey, keep talking." He beamed.

"Come to think of it, I don't know anyone that really does like Bruce. Too bad they couldn't have seen his face when he opened the Jiffy bag. Whoever sent it would have been thrilled with their success. 'Course if they could see him in the hunt field, they'd have a giggle, too."

Bruce liked the excitement of the chase, the danger of it, but in truth he was a barely adequate rider, as was Sam Mahanes. It was one more place where they could get in each other's way.

"Don't you wonder what Hank Brevard did to get himself killed? I mean, there's another guy not exactly on the top of anyone's 'A' list." Fair cut a bigger piece of corn bread. "Still, you didn't want to kill him. Now I could see someone doing in Bruce. Being around him is like someone rubbing salt in your wound. Murder is — dislocating."

"For the victim." Harry laughed at him.

"You know what I'm trying to say. It calls everything you know into question. What would push you to kill another human being?"

"Yeah, we were talking about that at volleyball." She pressed her lips together and raised her eyebrows, her face a question. "Who knows?"

"Did you think Hank Brevard was smart?" Fair asked Harry. He trusted her reactions to people.

"M-m-m, he knew how to cover his ass. I'm not sure I would call him smart. I guess he was smart about mechanical things or he wouldn't have been plant manager. And I suppose he'd be pretty efficient, good at scheduling maintenance checks, that sort of thing."

"Yeah," Fair agreed.

"No sense of culture, the arts, enjoying people."

"Cut and dried. I think the only people really upset at his death are his wife and family." Fair stood up and walked to the window. "Damn, this weather is a bitch. This afternoon the mercury climbed to fifty-two degrees and here comes the snow."

"What's my thermometer read?" She had an outdoor thermometer on the kitchen window, the digital readout on the inside of the window.

"Twenty-nine degrees Fahrenheit."

"Let's hope it stays snow. I'm over it with the ice."

"Me, too. Those farm roads don't always get plowed and horses get colic more in the winter. Of course, if people would cut back their feed and give them plenty of warm water to drink I'd have fewer cases and they wouldn't have large vet bills. I can't understand people sometimes."

"Fair, it takes years and years to make a horseman. For most people a horse is like a living Toyota. God help the poor horse."

He looked back at her, a twinkle in his eyes. "Some horses know how to get even."

"Some people do, too."

13

The next day proved Fair's theory. The snow, light, deterred no one from foxhunting that morning. Foxhunting — or fox chasing, since the fox wasn't killed — was to Virginia what Indiana U. basketball was to the state of Indiana. Miranda happily took over the post office, since the mail lightened up after Valentine's Day. She felt Harry needed an outlet, since all she did was work at the post office and then work at the farm. As foxhunting was her young friend's great love, she liked seeing Harry get out. She also knew that Fair often hunted during the week and she still nurtured the hope that the two would get back together.

Cold though the day was when Harry first mounted up, the sun grew hotter and by eleven o'clock the temperature hit 47 degrees Fahrenheit. As the group rode along they looked at the tops of the mountains, each tree outlined in ice. As the sun reached the top of the mountains the crests exploded into millions of rainbows, glittering and brilliant.

At that exact moment, a medium-sized red fox decided to give everyone a merry chase.

Harry rode Tomahawk. Fair rode a 17.3 Hanoverian, the right size for Fair's height at six four and then some in his boots. Big Mim had so many fabulous horses Harry wondered how she chose her mount for the day. Little Mim, always impeccably turned out like her mother, sat astride a flaming chestnut. Sam Mahanes, taking the morning off, grasped his gelding, Ranulf, with a death grip, tight legs and tight hands. The gelding, a sensible fellow, put up with this all morning because they were only trotting. Once the fox burst into the open and the field took off flying, though, Sam gripped harder.

Coming into the first fence, a slip fence, everything was fine, but three strides beyond that was a stiff coop and the gelding had had quite enough. He cantered to the base of the jump, screeched on the brakes. Sam took the jump. His horse didn't. Harry, riding behind Sam, witnessed the sorry spectacle.

Sam lay flat on his back on the other side of the coop.

Harry hated to miss the run but she tried

to be helpful so she pulled up Tomahawk, turning back to Sam, who resembled a turtle.

Dismounting, she bent down over him. "You're still breathing."

"Just. Wind knocked out of me," Sam gasped, a sharp rattle deep in his throat. "Where's Ranulf?"

"Standing over there by the walnut tree."

As Sam clambered up, brushed off his rear end, and adjusted his cap, Harry walked over to the horse, who nickered to Tomahawk. "Come on, buddy, I'm on your side." She flipped the reins over his head, bringing him back to Sam. "Sam, check your girth."

"Oh, yeah." He ran his fingers under the girth. "It's okay."

"There's a tree stump over there. Make it easy on yourself."

"Yeah." He finally got back in the saddle. "We'll have a lot of ground to make up."

"Don't worry. I'll get us there. Can you trot?"

"Sure."

As they trotted along, Harry was listening for hounds. She asked, "Ever been to Trey Young's?"

"No."

"He's a good trainer."

Still miffed because of his fall, which he blamed completely on his horse, Sam snapped, "You telling me I can't ride?"

Harry, uncharacteristically direct with someone to whom she wasn't close, fired back, "I'm telling you you can't ride that horse as well as you might. I take lessons, Sam. Ranulf is a nice horse but if you don't give with your hands and you squeeze with your legs, what do you expect? He's got nowhere to go but up or he'll just say, 'I've had enough.' And that's what he said."

"Yeah — well."

"This isn't squash." She mentioned his other sport. "There's another living creature involved. It's teamwork far more than mastery."

Sam rode along quietly. Ranulf loved this, of course. Finally, he said, "Maybe you're right."

"This is supposed to be fun. If it isn't fun you'll leave. Wouldn't want that." She smiled her flirtatious smile.

He unstiffened a little. "I've been under a lot of pressure lately."

"With Hank Brevard's murder, I guess."

"Oh, before that. That just added to it. Hospital budgets are about as complicated as the national budget. Everybody has a pet toy they want, but if everyone got what they wanted when they wanted it, we'd be out of business and a hospital is a business, like it or not."

"Must be difficult — juggling the egos, too."

"Bunch of goddamned prima donnas. Oh, you probably haven't heard yet. The blood on the blade sent to Bruce was chicken blood." He laughed a rat-a-tat laugh. "Can you believe that?"

Rick Shaw had contacted Sam when the blade arrived in the mail. When the lab report came back Rick called Bruce Buxton first and Sam second.

"Fast lab report."

"I guess chicken blood is easy to figure." Sam laughed again. "But who would do a fool thing like that? Sending something like that to Buxton?"

"One of his many fans," Harry dryly replied.

"He's not on the top of my love list but if you needed knee surgery, he'd be on top of yours. He's that good. When they fly him to operate on Jets linebackers, you know he's good."

She held up her hand. They stopped and listened. In the distance she heard the Huntsman's horn, so she knew exactly where to go.

"Sam, we're going to have to boogie."

"Okay."

They cantered over a meadow, the powdery snow swirling up. A stone wall, maybe two and a half feet, marked off one meadow from another.

Harry called to Sam, "Give with your hand. Grab mane. Never be afraid to grab mane." Taking her own advice she wrapped her fingers around a hunk of Tomahawk's mane and sailed over the low obstacle. She looked back at Sam and he reached forward with his hands, a small victory.

Ranulf popped over.

"Easy." Harry smiled.

The two of them threaded their way through a pine forest, emerging on a snowy farm road. Harry followed the hoofprints until they crossed a stream, ice clinging to the sides of the bank in rectangular crystals.

"Up over the hill." Sam pointed to the continuing tracks.

"Hounds are turning, Sam. We're smack in the way. Damn." She looked around for a place to get out of the way and hopefully not turn back the fox into the hounds, a cardinal sin in foxhunting.

Sam, not an experienced hunter, really thought they should charge up the hill but he deferred to Harry. After all, she'd been doing this since she was tiny.

She pushed Tomahawk into the woods, off the old farm road. They climbed over a rocky outgrowth and stopped about forty yards beyond that. No sooner had they reached their resting point than the red fox sauntered into view, loping onto the farm road. He crossed, hopped onto a log, trotted across that, scampered along, and then, for reasons only he knew, he flipped on the afterburners and was out of there before you could count to ten.

Within two minutes the first of the hounds, nose to the ground, reached the farm road.

Sam started to open his mouth.

"No," Harry whispered.

He gulped back his "Tally Ho," which would have only disturbed the hounds. "Tally Ho" was sometimes called out when a fox was seen but only if the witness was sure it was the hunted fox, and not a playful vagrant. Also, if hounds were close, the human voice could disturb them, making their task even more difficult. Yet it was human nature to want to declare seeing the fox.

In about five minutes, the Huntsman, the person actually controlling the hounds, who had been battling his way through a nasty briar patch, emerged onto the road.

"Okay, Sam, turn your horse in the direction in which you saw the fox, take off your cap, arm's length, and now you can say 'Tally Ho.' Hounds are far enough away."

Excited, Sam bellowed, "Tally Ho!"

The Huntsman glanced up, winked at Harry, and off he rode, following his hounds, who were on the line.

In another two minutes the field rode up, Harry and Sam joining them in the rear. Sam, being an inexperienced hunter, needed to stay in the back out of other people's way.

They ran a merry chase until the red fox decided to disappear and in that maddening way of foxes, he vanished.

Ending on a good note, the Huntsman, after conferring with the Master, the person in charge of the hunt, called it a day.

Riding back, Sam thanked Harry.

Little Mim came alongside Harry as Sam rode up to Larry Johnson to chat. "Think he'll ever learn?"

"Yeah. At least he's not a know-it-all. He doesn't like advice but eventually it sinks in."

"Men are like that," Little Mim remarked.

"Jeez, Marilyn, think of the women we

know like that, too."

"You mean my mother?"

Harry held up her hand. "I didn't say your mother."

"Well, I mean my mother." Little Mim glanced over her shoulder to make certain Mother wasn't within earshot.

She wasn't. Big Mim at that very moment was pressing Susan Tucker to join the Garden Club, which was supposed to be a great honor, one Susan devoutly wished to sidestep.

Back at the trailers, people shared flasks, hot tea, and coffee. Susan brought Mrs. Hogendobber's orange-glazed cinnamon buns. The mood, already high, soared.

"Gee, I hate to go back to work." Harry laughed.

"Isn't it a shame we couldn't have been born rich?" Susan said in a low voice, since a few around them had been, like Big Mim and Little Mim.

"Breaks my heart."

"What'd Fair give you for Valentine's?"

"Wormer. Ivermectin."

"Hey, that's romantic." Susan, a hint of light sarcasm in her voice, laughed.

"I gave him a vet book from 1792."

"Hey, that *is* romantic." Susan handed Harry a mug of hot tea. "You know, this new thermos I bought is fabulous. We've been out for two and a half hours. I put the tea in the thermos a good hour before that and it's piping hot."

"Yeah. I'll have to get one."

Sam walked over. "Harry, thank you again."

"Sure." She offered him a sip of tea. He held up his flask.

"A wee nip before returning to drudgery." He bowed, said "Ladies," then walked back to his trailer.

Susan looked at Harry. Neither one said anything. They neither liked nor disliked Sam. He was just kind of there.

Larry Johnson, carrying a tin of chocolate-covered wafers, came over. "Ladies. Don't worry about the calories. I'm a doctor and I assure you any food eaten standing up loses half its caloric value."

They laughed, reaching in for the thin delicious wafers.

"How's the mood at the hospital?" Susan asked.

"Good. Hank's death may not be hospital related." He paused. "But as you know I'm semi-retired so I'm not there on a daily basis."

"Semi-retired." Harry laughed. "You work as hard as you did when I was a kid."

Larry had an office in his home. Years ago he had taken on a partner, Hayden McIntire, vowing he would retire, but he hadn't.

"That was good of you to nurse Sam along," Larry complimented Harry. "Soon you'll be in Tussie Logan's class. She's wonderful with children." He laughed low. "I kind of regard Sam in that light."

"You didn't see me stop to help him." Susan ate another chocolate-covered wafer. "The run was too good."

Larry, in his early seventies, was in great shape thanks to hunting and walking. "A straight-running fox, joy, pure joy. But you know, I think he doubled back. He was so close, then —" He snapped his fingers.

"Fox magic." Susan smiled, checked her watch, and sighed, "I'd better get home."

"Well, back to work for me." Harry finished off her tea.

14

"Mom!" the animals cried when Harry bounced through the back door of the post office.

"Hi," she called out.

"Oh, Harry, I'm so glad you're here. Look." Miranda handed her an envelope, opened. "Susan left this for you. She forgot to give it to you at the breakfast."

Harry checked the addressee, Mrs. Tucker. "H-m-m." She slid out the letter and read it aloud:

"Dear Susan,

As you know, I will be running for the office of mayor of our great town of Crozet.

I need your support and the help of all our friends. I hope that you and Harry will throw your weight behind my campaign.

My top two priorities are keeping Crozet's rural character intact and working closely with the Albemarle Sheriff's Department to decrease crime.

Please call me at your earliest convenience.

Yours truly, Marilyn Sanburne."

Harry rattled the paper a bit. "Call her? She can nab any of us in the street. Waste of postage."

"It is rather formal but I don't think staying neutral is as easy as you do. And if we waffle too long we will gain her enmity," Miranda sensibly said.

"The thing is, did Little Mim get the support of the party?" Harry was surprised that Little Mim would write Susan. It seemed so distant.

"No. Not yet. Called Rev. Jones. He's on the party's local steering committee. He said that yes, they voted to support Marilyn at their monthly meeting, which was Saturday. They wouldn't make the vote public until the state steering committee gave them the okay. Herb said they would probably hear from them in Richmond today. He didn't anticipate any problems. After all, Jim Sanburne, as a Republican, has run unopposed for nearly twenty years. The Democrats ought to be thrilled with their candidate. Not only is someone challenging Jim, it's his own daughter."

Mrs. Murphy rubbed against her mother's

124

leg. *"We checked in your mailbox, Mom. You only have bills."*

She reached down, scooping up the beautiful tiger cat. "Mrs. Murphy, you are the prettiest girl."

"Ha," came a croak from Pewter, reposing on her side on the small kitchen table in the rear. She wasn't supposed to be on the table but that never stopped her.

"Jealous." Harry walked over to rub Pewter's ears.

"I'm not jealous."

"Are, too," Murphy taunted her friend.

"Am not." Pewter stuck out her amazingly pink tongue, hot pink.

Murphy wiggled out of Harry's arms, pouncing on Pewter. They rolled over and over until they fell off the table with a thud, shook themselves, and walked in opposite directions as though this was the most natural event in the world.

"Cats." Tucker cocked her head, then looked up at Harry. *"Mom, I don't like these chain letters. Something's not right."*

Harry knelt down. "You are the best dog in the universe. Not even the solar system but the universe." She kissed her silky head.

"Gag me." Pewter grimaced, then turned and walked over to sit beside Mrs. Murphy, their kitty spat forgotten as quickly as it

125

flared up. *"Obsequious."*

"Dogs always are." Murphy knowingly nodded, but Tucker could have cared less.

Within the hour Coop drove up and ducked into the front door of the post office just as rain began to fall. "Is this weather crazy or what?" she said as she closed the door behind her.

"Find anything out?" Miranda flipped up the divider to allow her in the back.

"Yes." Cynthia stepped through, removed her jacket, and hung it on the Shaker peg by the back door. "Crozet Hospital is in turmoil. Jesus, what a petty place it is. Backstabbers."

"Well, I'm sorry to hear that. I guess a lot of businesses are like that." Mrs. Hogendobber was disappointed. "No suspects?"

"Not yet," Coop tensely replied.

"Oh great. There's a killer on the loose."

"Harry." Mrs. Murphy spoke out loud. *"You humans rub shoulders with killers more than you imagine. I'm convinced the human animal is the only animal to derive pleasure from murder."*

As though picking up on her cat's thoughts, Harry said aloud, "I wonder if Hank's killer enjoyed killing him."

"Yes," Cooper said without hesitation.

"Power?" Harry asked.

"Yes. No one likes to talk about that aspect of murder. The Lord giveth and the Lord taketh away. No one has the right to take another human life."

"Miranda, people may read their Bible but they don't follow the precepts," Cooper told her.

"You know, the post office is in the middle of everything. Action Central, sort of." Harry's eyes brightened. "We could help."

"No, you don't." Cooper's chin jutted out.

"Yeah." Mrs. Murphy fluffed her tail. *"A little skulking about is good for a cat."*

"Which cat?" Pewter grumbled.

Cynthia Cooper waggled her finger at Harry and Miranda. "No. No. And no."

15

A meeting that evening brought together the faithful of St. Luke's Lutheran Church, presided over by the Reverend Herbert C. Jones. While Harry considered herself a lapsed Lutheran she adored the Rev, as she called him. She liked that the Lutheran church — as well as the other churches in the area — hummed, a hive of activity, a honeycomb of human relationships. If someone was sickly, the word got out and people called upon him or her. If someone struggled with alcoholism, a church member who was also in Alcoholics Anonymous invariably paid a call.

The other major denominations, all represented, cooperated throughout major crises such as when someone's house burnt down. It wasn't necessary that the assisted person be a member of any church. All that mattered was that they lived in Crozet or its environs.

Reverend Jones, warm and wise, even pulled together the Baptist and Pentecostal churches, who had often felt slighted in the past by the "high" churches.

Mrs. Hogendobber, a devout member of the Church of the Holy Light, proved instrumental in this new area of cooperation.

Tonight the meeting concerned food deliveries and medical services for those people unable to shop for themselves and who had no families to help them. Often the recipients were quite elderly. They had literally outlived anyone who might be related to them. In other cases, the recipient was a mean old drunk who had driven away family and friends. The other group involved AIDS patients, most of whom had lost their families, self-righteous families who shrank into disapproval, leaving their own flesh and blood to die alone and lonely.

Harry especially felt a kinship with this group since many were young. She had expected to meet many gay men but was shocked to discover how many women were dying of the insidious disease, women who had fooled around with drugs, shared needles, or just had the bad luck to sleep with the wrong man. A few had been prostitutes in Washington, D.C., and when they could no longer survive in the city they slipped into the countryside.

Harry, well educated, was not an unsophisticated person. True, she chose country life over the flash and dash of the city, but she hardly qualified as a country bumpkin. Then again few people really did. The bumpkin was one of those stereotypes that seemed to satisfy some hunger in city people to feel superior to those not in the city. Still, she realized through this service how much she didn't know about her own country. There was an entire separate world devoted to drugs. It had its rules, its cultures, and, ultimately, its death sentence.

Sitting across from her in the chaste rectory was Bruce Buxton. Insufferable as he could be, he gave of his time and knowledge, visiting those that needed medical attention. How Herb had ever convinced him to participate puzzled her.

"— three teeth. But the jaw isn't broken." BoomBoom Craycroft read from her list of clients, as the group called their people.

Herb rubbed his chin, leaned back in his seat. "Can we get her down to the dentist? I mean can she get away from him and will she go if you take her?"

BoomBoom, becoming something of an expert on domestic violence, said, "I can try. He's perverse enough to knock out the new teeth if she gets them."

Bruce spoke up. He'd been quiet up to now. "What about a restraining order?"

"Too scared. Of him and of the system."
BoomBoom had learned to understand the
fear and mistrust the very poor had of the
institutions of government and law enforcement. She'd also learned to understand that
their mistrust was not unfounded. "I'll see if
I can get her out of there or at least get her to
the dentist. If I can't, I can't."

"You're very persuasive." Herb put his
hand on his knee as he leaned forward in
the chair a bit. His back was hurting.
"Miranda."

"The girls and I" — she meant the choir
at the Church of the Holy Light — "are
going to replace the roof on Mrs. Weyman's
house."

"Do the work yourself?" Little Mim
asked. Though an Episcopalian and not a
Lutheran, she attended for two reasons:
one, she liked Herb, and two, it irritated her
mother, who felt anything worth doing had
to be done through the Episcopalian
Church.

"Uh — no. We thought we'd give a series
of concerts to raise money for the roof and
then perhaps we could find some men to do-
nate their labor. We're pretty sure we can
come up with the money for materials."

"Here I had visions of you on the roof,
Miranda." Herb laughed at her, then turned

to Bruce, moving to the next topic on the agenda. "Any luck?"

Before Bruce could give his report they heard the door to the rectory open and close. Larry Johnson, removing his coat as he walked from the hall to the pleasant meeting room, nodded at them.

"Late and I apologize."

"Sit down, Larry, glad you could make it. Bruce was just about to give his report about the hospital cooperating with us concerning our people who can't pay for medical services."

Larry took a seat next to Miranda. He folded his hands, gazing at Bruce.

Bruce's pleasant speaking voice filled the room. "As you can imagine, the administration sees only problems. Both Sam and Jordan insist we could be liable to lawsuits. What if we treated an indigent patient who sued, that sort of thing. Their second area of concern is space. Both say Crozet Hospital lacks the space to take care of paying patients. The hospital has no room for the non-paying."

Little Mim raised her hand. Bruce acknowledged her.

"While I am not defending the hospital, this is true. One of my goals as a board member and your next mayor" — she paused to smile reflectively — "will be to raise the money *privately* for a new wing to be built."

"Thank you." Herb's gravelly voice was warm. He was amused at her campaigning.

"It is true," Bruce agreed, "but if we could bring people in on the off hours, before eight a.m. or after three p.m., we might at least be able to use equipment for tests. I know there is no way we will get hospital beds. Which brings me to the third area of concern voiced by the administration, the use of hospital equipment. The increased wear and tear on equipment, whether it's IVAC units, X-ray machines, whatever, will raise hospital operating costs. The budget can't absorb the increases." He breathed in. "That's where we are today. Obviously, Sam and Jordan don't want to give us a flat no. They are too politically astute for that. But there is no question in my mind that they evidence a profound lack of enthusiasm for our purpose."

The room fell silent, a silence punctuated when the door to the rectory was again opened and closed. The sound of a coat being removed, placed on the coatrack was heard.

Tussie Logan, face drawn, stepped into the room. "Sorry."

"Come on in. We know your time isn't always your own." Herb genially beckoned to her. "Bruce has just given us his progress report."

"Or lack thereof," Bruce forthrightly said. "Tussie, you look tired."

Bruce slid his chair over so she could wedge in between himself and BoomBoom.

"One of my kids, Dodie Santana, the little girl from Guatemala, had a bad day."

"We're sorry." Herb spoke for the group.

"We'll do a prayer vigil for her," Miranda volunteered.

"Thank you." Tussie smiled sadly. "I'm sorry. I didn't mean to interrupt."

"I'm glad you did." Larry lightened the mood. "It means I'm not the last one to the meeting."

"Back to business then." Herb turned to Bruce. "Can we get access to the hospital's insurance policy?"

"Yes. I don't think Sam would refuse that," Bruce replied.

"But who would understand it?" Larry said, half in jest. "I can't even understand the one Hayden and I have for the practice."

"I believe Ned Tucker will help us there." Herb watched as both Cazenovia and Elocution paraded into the room. "Harry?"

"I'll call him." She volunteered to ring up

Susan's husband, a man well liked by all except those who crossed him in court.

"Bruce and I have spoken about this," Tussie joined in, "and — there's no way to delicately put this. Jordan Ivanic fears poor patients will steal — not just drugs, mind you, which would be most people's first thought, oh no, he thinks they'll steal toilet paper, pencils, you name it."

"He said that?" Harry was upset.

Cazzie jumped in her lap, which made her feel better. Elocution headed straight for Herb.

"Yes. Flat out said it." Tussie tapped her foot on the floor.

"My experience is the biggest thieves are the rich." Bruce rubbed his chin, perceived the frown on Little Mim's face, and hastened to add, "Think of Mike Milken, all those Wall Street traders."

"Well, I think I'd better call upon Sam and Jordan." Herb petted his youngest cat, who purred loudly.

"Meow." Elocution closed her eyes.

Bruce said, "I've been able to secure the cooperation of at least one physician in each department. Our problem now is convincing Sam Mahanes to use a portion of the hospital, even a room, to initially screen these people.

"He did voice one other small concern." Bruce's voice was filled with sarcasm. "And that is the paying patients. He didn't feel they should be around the charity cases. It would engender hard feelings. You know, they're paying and these people aren't. So he said if we could find space and if we could solve the liability problem, where are we going to put people so they wouldn't be visible?"

"Ah." Herb exhaled.

Miranda shifted in her seat, looked down at the floor, took a deep breath, then looked at the group. "Bruce, you weren't born and raised here so I don't expect you to know this but sequestering or separating the poor gets us awfully close to segregation. In the old days the waiting rooms in the back were always for colored people. That was the proper and polite term then, and I tell you no white person ever went through the back door and vice versa. It brings back an uneasy feeling for me and I expect it does for those of us in this room old enough to remember. The other problem is that a goodly number of our people are African-American or Scotch-Irish. Those seem to be the two primary ethnic groups that we serve and I couldn't tell you why. Anyway, I think Sam needs to be —" She looked at Herb and shrugged.

"I know." Herb read her perfectly. After all, Sam was a Virginian and should know better, but one of the problems with Virginians was that many of them longed for a return to the time of Thomas Jefferson. Of course, none of them ever imagined themselves as slaves or poor white indentured servants. They always thought of themselves as the masters on the hill.

The group continued their progress reports and then adjourned for tea, coffee, and Miranda's baked goods.

BoomBoom walked over to Harry. "I'm glad we're working together."

"It's a good cause." Harry knew BoomBoom wanted to heal the wounds and she admitted to herself that BoomBoom was right, although every now and then Harry's mean streak would kick up and she wanted to make Boom squirm.

"Are you going to work on Little Mim's campaign?"

"Uh — I don't know but I know I can't sit in the middle. I mean, I think Jim's a good mayor." She grabbed another biscuit. "What about you?"

"I'm going to do it. Work for Little Mim. She's right when she says our generation needs to get involved and since Big Mim will sit this out we won't offend her."

"But what about offending Jim?" Harry asked as Cazenovia rubbed her leg.

"Some ham biscuit please."

Harry dropped ham for the cat.

"He won't be offended. I think he's going to enjoy the fight. Really, he's run unopposed for decades." BoomBoom laughed.

Bruce, his eye on BoomBoom — indeed, most men's eyes were on BoomBoom — joined them. "Ladies."

"Our little group has never had anyone as dynamic as you. We are so grateful to you." BoomBoom fluttered her long eyelashes.

"Oh — thank you. Being a doctor isn't always about money, you know."

"We are grateful." Harry echoed Boom-Boom's praise minus the fluttering eyelashes. "Oh, I heard about the chicken blood on the blade. I'm sorry. Whoever did that ought to be horsewhipped."

"Damn straight," he growled.

"What?" BoomBoom's eyes widened.

This gave Harry the opportunity to slip away. Bruce could tell BoomBoom about his experience and she could flirt some more.

"Harry." Herb handed her a brownie.

When his back was turned from the table, both cats jumped onto it. People just picked up the two sneaks and put them back on the floor.

"M-m-m, this thing could send me into sugar shock." She laughed.

He lowered his voice as he stood beside her. "I'm very disturbed by Sam's attitude. I think some of the problem may be that it was Bruce who asked. Sam can't stand him, as you know."

"He'll talk to you."

"I think so." He picked up another brownie for himself. "There goes the diet. How are things with you? I haven't had any time to catch up with you."

"Pretty good."

"Good." His gravelly voice deepened.

"Rev, do me a favor. I know Sam will talk to you — even more than he'll talk to Rick Shaw or Coop. Ask him flat out who he thinks killed Hank Brevard. Something doesn't add up. I don't know. Just —"

"Preys on your mind." He dusted off his fingers. "I will."

"I asked Bruce before the meeting started what he thought about Brevard," Harry continued. "He said he thought he was a royal pain in the ass — and maybe now the hospital can hire a really good plant manager. Pretty blunt."

"That's Bruce." Herb put his arm around

her reassuringly, then smiled. "You and your curiosity."

Tussie, her back to Herb, reached for a plate, took a step back, and bumped into him. "Oh, I'm sorry."

"Take more than a little slip of a girl like you to knock me down."

"He's right. Tussie, you're getting too skinny. You're working too hard," Harry said.

"Runs in the family. The older we get, the thinner we get."

"Sure doesn't run in my family," Miranda called out from the other side of the table, worked her way around the three-bean salad, and joined them.

"Do you think poor patients will steal?" Harry asked Tussie.

"No," she said with conviction.

"Aren't hospitals full of drugs?" Miranda paused, then laughed at herself. "Well, that's obvious but I mean the drugs I read about in the paper — cocaine, morphine."

"Yes and those drugs are kept under lock and key. Any physician or head nurse signs in, writes down the amount used and for what patient, the attending physician then locks the cabinet back up. That's that."

"But someone like Hank Brevard would know how to get into the drug cabinets, storage." Harry's eyebrows raised.

"Well — I suppose, but if something was missing, we'd know." Tussie's lower lip jutted out ever so slightly.

"Maybe. But if he was smart, he could replace cocaine with something that looks like it, powdered something, powdered milk of magnesia even."

Slightly irritated, Tussie gulped down a bite of creamy carrot salad. "We'd know when the patient for whom the drug was prescribed didn't respond."

"Oh hell, Tussie, if they're sick enough to prescribe cocaine or morphine, they're probably on their way out. I bet for a smart person who knows the routine, who is apprised of patients' chances, it would be like stealing candy from a baby." Harry didn't mean to be argumentative; the wheels were turning in her mind, that was all.

"You watch too much TV." Tussie's anger flashed for a second. "If you'll excuse me I need to talk to BoomBoom."

Harry, Miranda, and Herb looked at one another and shrugged.

"She's a little testy," Miranda observed.

"Pressure," Herb flatly stated.

"I guess. Guess I wouldn't want to be working where someone was murdered. See, Miranda, imagine a murder at the post office — The body stuffed in the mailbag." Harry's voice took on the cadence of a radio announcer's: "The front and back door locked, a fortune in stock certificates jammed into one of the larger, bottom post-boxes."

"Harry, you're too much." Miranda winked at her.

"And remember what I said about your curiosity, young lady. I've known you all your life and you can't stand not knowing something." Herb put his arm around her.

16

It was that curiosity that got Harry in trouble. After the meeting she cruised by the hospital when she should have driven home. The puddles from the melted ice glistened like mica on the asphalt parking lot.

Impulsively, she turned into the parking lot, drove around behind the hospital to the back delivery door, which wasn't far from the railroad tracks. She paused a moment before continuing around the corner to the back door into the basement.

She parked, got out, and carefully put her hand on the cold doorknob. Slowly she turned it so the latch wouldn't click. She opened the door. Low lights ran along the top of the hallway. The dimness was creepy. Surely, the hospital didn't have to save money by using such low-wattage bulbs. She wondered if Sam Mahanes really was a good hospital director or if they were all cheap where the public couldn't observe.

She tiptoed down the main corridor which ran to the center of the building, the oldest part of the complex, built long before the War Between the States. She counted halls off this main one but wished like Hansel and Gretel she had dropped bread crumbs, because if she ducked into some of these offshoot halls she wouldn't find her way out quickly. Bearing that in mind, she kept to the center hall corridor.

If she'd thought about it, she would have waited for this nighttime exploration until she could bring Mrs. Murphy, Pewter, and Tucker. Their eyes and ears were far better than her own, plus Tucker's sense of smell was a godsend. However, she'd taken them home after work, whipped off her barn chores, and hopped over to the rectory for the meeting.

She thought she heard voices somewhere to her right. Instinctively she flattened against the wall. She wanted to find the boiler room. The voices faded away, men's voices. A closed door was to her right.

Stealthily she crept forward. A flickering light to her right told her a room lay ahead. The voices sounded farther away, and then — silence.

The door behind her opened. She hurried away, slipping into the boiler room. She'd found her goal. Again, she flattened against the wall listening for the footfall but the boiler gurgling drowned out subtle sounds.

She quickly noted that another exit from the boiler room lay immediately in front of her on the other side of the room.

Glancing around she took a deep breath, walked to the boiler. The chalk outline of Hank's body had nearly worn away. She knelt down, then looked at the wall. Though it was scrubbed, a light bloodstain remained visible. Shuddering at the picture of blood spurting from Hank's throat, jetting across the room, she started to rise.

Harry never made it to her feet. A clunk was the last thing she heard.

17

Sheriff Rick Shaw and Deputy Cynthia Cooper hit the swinging doors of the emergency room so hard they nearly popped off their hinges.

"Where is she?" Rick asked a startled ER nurse.

The young woman wordlessly pointed to yet another set of doors and Rick and Cynthia blasted through them.

A woozy Harry, covered with a blanket, lay on a recovery-room bed. A quiet night at the hospital, no other patients were in the room.

Jordan Ivanic, a sickly smile on his face, greeted the officers. "Why does everything happen on my watch?"

"Just lucky, I guess," Dr. Bruce Buxton growled at him. Bruce considered Jordan a worm. He had little love for any administrative type but Jordan's whining and worrying curdled his stomach.

"Well?" Rick demanded, staring at Bruce.

He pointed to the right side of Harry's

head. "Blow. Blunt instrument. We've washed the blood off and cleaned and shaved the wound. I've taken X rays. She's fine. She's stitched up. A mild concussion at the worst."

"Harry, can you hear me?" Cynthia leaned down, speaking low.

"Yes."

"Did you see who hit you?"

"No, the son of a bitch."

Her reply made Cooper laugh. "You'll be just fine."

"Who found her?" Rick asked Jordan.

"Booty Weyman. New on the job and I guess he just happened to be checking the boiler room. We don't know how long she was there. We don't know exactly what happened either."

"I can tell you what happened," Rick snapped. "What happened was someone hit her on the head."

"Perhaps she fell and struck her head." Jordan tried to find another solution.

"In the boiler room? The only thing she could have hit her head on is the boiler and then we'd see burns. Don't pull this shit, Ivanic." Rick rarely swore, considering it unprofessional, but he was deeply disturbed and surges of white-hot anger shot through him. "There's something wrong in this hospital. If you know what it is you'd better come clean because I am going to turn this place upside down!"

Jordan held up his hands placatingly. "Now Sheriff, I'm as upset about this as you are."

"The hell you are."

This made Bruce laugh.

"Dr. Buxton." Cynthia leaned toward the tall man. "When did you get here?"

"I came a little bit after the meeting at the rectory, the God's Love group, you know. Herb's group."

"Yes." She nodded.

"Stopped at the convenience store. So I guess I got here about eight forty-five."

"Did you go to the boiler room yourself?" Rick asked the doctor.

"No. She was brought to me. When Booty Weyman found her, he had the sense to call for two orderlies. Scared to death." Bruce remembered Booty's face, which had been bone white.

"Well, if you won't be needing me I'll go back to my office." Jordan moved toward the door.

"Not so fast." Rick stopped him in his tracks. "I want the blueprints to the hospital. I want every single person's work schedule. I don't care who it is, doctors, receptionists, maintenance workers. I want the records for every delivery and trash removal for the last year and I want all this within twenty-four hours."

"Uh." Jordan's mind spun. "I'll do my best."

"Twenty-four hours!" Rick raised his voice.

"Is that all?" Jordan felt like he was strangling on his voice, which got thinner and higher the more nervous he became.

"No. Have you had any patients die under mysterious or unexplained circumstances?"

"Certainly not!" Jordan held his hands together.

"You would say that." Rick got right in his face.

"Because it's true. And I remind you, Sheriff," Jordan found a bit of courage to snap back, "whatever has occurred here has occurred in the basement. There are no patients in the basement."

"Get out." Rick dismissed him with a parting shot. "Twenty-four hours, on my desk."

"I'm glad he left before he peed his pants," Bruce snorted.

"I did not pee my pants," Harry thickly said.

"Not you, Harry. Just relax." Cooper

reached for her hand.

Rick whispered to Bruce, "Do you think Harry is in danger?"

"No. Her pulse is strong. She's strong. She's going to have a tender spot on her head." He pointed to the three tiny, tight stitches. "These will drive her crazy."

"The blow was that hard?" Cynthia carefully studied the wound.

"No. If it was that hard, Deputy, we'd have seen a fracture in the skull. Whoever hit her knew just how hard to hit her, which is interesting in and of itself. But the skin on the skull is thin and tears quite easily. Also, as you know, the head bleeds profusely. If I hadn't stitched up what was a relatively small tear, the wound would have seeped for days. She might scratch it, infecting it or tearing it further. Something like this doesn't throb as much as it stings and itches." He smiled warmly. He had a nice smile, and it was a pity he didn't smile more often.

"Do you have any idea what she was doing here? Did she mention coming to the hospital at the meeting?" Cynthia asked.

"No."

Rick sighed, a long, frustrated sigh. "Mary Minor Haristeen can be damned nosy."

"Drugs." Harry tried to raise her voice but couldn't.

"What?" Cooper bent low.

"Drugs. I bet you someone is stealing drugs."

Bruce sighed. "It's as good an explanation as any other." He rubbed his hands together.

"I'd like to keep her here overnight for observation."

"I'll bring her home and stay with her," Cynthia declared.

"You said she was in no danger." Rick, understanding Cynthia's concern, stared at Bruce.

Bruce cupped his chin in his hand. "From a medical point of view, I don't think she is. She might suffer a bit of dizziness or nausea. Occasionally vision will be impaired. Again, I don't think the blow was that hard."

"She has a hard head." Rick smiled ruefully.

"You got that right, Sheriff." Bruce smiled back at him.

18

"Ow." Harry touched her stitches as Cynthia Cooper drove her home in her own truck.

As they walked through the kitchen door the two cats and dog ran up to their human, all talking at once. She knelt down, petting each one, assuring them that she was fine.

"We can skip breakfast, Mom, if you feel punk," Tucker volunteered.

"No, we can't." Pewter meowed so loudly that Cynthia laughed, walked over to the kitchen counter, and opened a can of food. "I'll do that."

"Harry, sit down. I can feed the cats and dog."

"Thanks."

Mrs. Murphy, now on Harry's lap, licked her face. *"We were scared. We didn't know where you were."*

"Yes, don't leave us. You need a brave dog to guard you." Tucker's lovely brown eyes shone with concern.

Harry rose to make a pot of coffee. Mrs. Murphy walked beside her.

153

"Sit down. I'll do it." Cynthia laughed to herself. Harry had a hard time accepting help. "Besides, I need to know what happened and your full concentration is necessary."

"I can concentrate while I make the coffee."

"All right." Coop put out the food as Pewter danced on her hind legs.

She then put down Tucker's food.

"Thank you." Tucker dove in.

"Okay. I went to the God's Love meeting. Regular cast of characters. On the way home I thought, why not cruise the hospital." Harry noticed Mrs. Murphy sticking to her like glue. "Murphy, I'm fine. Go eat." The tiger cat joined Pewter at the food bowl.

"I'm with you so far." Coop smiled, wondering how Harry would explain nosing around the basement.

"Well, I zipped into the parking lot and I don't know, the idea occurred to me that I might go around the back. I did that and then, uh, no one was around so I thought, 'Why not just take a peek?' I wasn't being ghoulish. I just wanted to see the room where Hank was killed."

"What time was this?"

"Um, eight-thirty or nine."

"Go on." Cynthia began frying eggs.

"Okay. I parked the truck. I got out. The door was unlocked. I opened it. Boy, the lights are dim down there. Cheapskates. Well, I walked down the hall. I passed a closed door on my right and up ahead, a wash of light spilled out onto the hallway and I heard voices. Low. Sounded like men's voices. I froze. I couldn't hear too much because I was outside the boiler room. Anyway, I kind of slid down, peeked into the room and no one was there. They left but I don't know how. I mean I noticed doors in there but I didn't hear any open or close. I tiptoed over to the chalk marks for Hank's body. Not much of them left. I knelt down and I looked over to the wall. At least I think that was the wall where the blood splashed. The light is pretty good in the boiler room. There's discoloration on that wall. I started to get up and — that's all I remember."

"Whoever hit you, hit you hard enough to knock you out but not hard enough to do damage, real damage. That tells me something."

"Oh?"

"Yes." Coop slid the eggs onto a plate Harry handed to her. "Either your assailant is a medical person who knows his stuff, or your assailant knew you and didn't want you dead. Or both. Everyone who knows you

155

knows you can't resist a mystery, Harry. But the fact remains that the assailant was merciful, if you can stand the term, given your stitches."

"Ah." Harry hadn't thought of that, but then she hadn't had time to think of anything.

"Merciful, hell," Tucker growled. *"Wait until I sink my fangs into his leg."*

"I'll scratch his eyes out," Mrs. Murphy hissed.

"I'll regurgitate on him," Pewter offered.

"Gross!" Mrs. Murphy stepped back from the food bowl as Pewter pretended to gag.

"Ha ha," Pewter giggled.

"Lot of talk around here," Harry teased her animals.

Coop, now sitting at the table, leaned across it slightly. "Harry, just what in the hell did you think you would find?"

Harry put down her fork, her eyes brightened. "I asked myself — what goes on in a hospital? Life or death. Every single day. Right?"

"Right." Coop shook pepper on her eggs.

"What if there is an incompetent doctor or technician? One false move on the anesthesiologist's part and —" She snapped her fingers to signify the patient dying instantly. "One misapplied medication to a critically

156

ill patient or one angel of death." Noticing Coop's noncomprehension she hastened to explain. "A nurse who wants to ease patient suffering or who decides old people can just die and get out of the way. There are hundreds of secrets at a hospital and I would imagine hundreds of potential lawsuits. We all know doctors cover for one another."

"Yes." Cynthia thoughtfully chewed for a moment. "But given that they have to work together and cooperate closely, I suppose that's natural. Cops cover for one another, too."

"But you see where I was heading. I mean what if there's a problem person, an inadequate physician?"

"I understand. I'm still trying to link this to Hank Brevard."

"Yeah, me, too. The head of maintenance wouldn't exactly be in the know if the problems were medical." She paused. "Unless he had to hide evidence or bury it or he was stealing drugs."

"Be pretty damn hard to cart a body or bodies out of the hospital. Or down into the basement. Now, drugs, that's another matter."

"Then, too, people do just fall into things. Pop up at the wrong place at the wrong time." Harry jabbed at her eggs.

"True."

"Or maybe Hank had a problem. Gambling. Just an example. They nailed him at work. It might not have anything to do with the hospital but I think it does. If he owed money I'd think a killer would shoot him somewhere else. There are easier ways to get rid of somebody than the way he was killed."

Coop reached for the toast. "That's what I think, too. Rick isn't saying much. But we're all traveling down the same path."

"I even thought it might have something to do with harvesting body parts. A patient dies. Okay, now how would the family know if the liver or kidneys have been removed?"

"The undertaker would certainly know if there'd been an autopsy but — he wouldn't necessarily know if any body parts or organs had been removed."

"If the family requests an autopsy, and most do, it would be so easy. And in some hospitals aren't autopsies a matter of course?"

"I don't know. They aren't in Crozet." Coop tapped her fork on the side of the plate, an absentminded gesture.

"Let's go with my thesis. Organs. A healthy kidney is worth five thousand dollars. In any given week a hospital the size of Crozet, a small but good place, will have, I would think, at least three people die with healthy organs. I mean that's not far-fetched. A black market for body parts."

"No, I guess it isn't far-fetched. We can clone ourselves now. So much for reproduction." Her light eyes twinkled.

"Don't worry. Old ways are the best ways."

The two women laughed.

"Where to hide the organs before shipping them out?" Cynthia knew how Harry thought.

"I've seen those containers. They're not big. They're packed with dry ice. They'd be pretty easy to stash away in the basement. A nurse or doctor might find that kidney upstairs but who goes into the basement? Hank was in on it. The key is in the basement. Maybe it really was part of the Underground Railroad once. There'd be lots of places to hide stuff in then."

"Well, it's a theory. However, I don't think organs last very long. And donor types need to match. Still, it's something to investigate."

"And I can help."

"There she goes again." Tucker shook her head.

"What I want from you is: keep your mouth shut. Don't you dare go back into that hospital without me. Whoever hit you knows you, I think. You show up again and the blow might be —" Coop's voice trailed off.

"Is Rick mad at me?"

"Of course. He'll get over it."

"Who found me?"

"Booty Weyman, new on the job. Poor kid. Scared him half to death."

"Who stitched me up?"

"Bruce Buxton — and for free."

Surprised, she said, "That was nice of him." Glancing at the old railroad clock on the wall, Harry said, "I've got to feed horses, turn out, and get to work."

"You feel good enough to go to work?"

"Yeah. It hurts but it's okay. I'll stuff myself with Motrin."

"How about if I help you feed? One other little thing, don't tell people where you were or what you were doing. You've got until you walk into the post office to come up with a good story. The last thing we need on this case is to draw everyone's attention to the basement. It's much better if the killer or killers get a little breathing room. Whatever they are doing, if indeed it does involve the hospital, let them get back to it. Rick is even delaying talking to Sam about this for twenty-four hours. The trick is to get everyone to let down, relax."

"You need someone on the inside."

"I know."

"Larry Johnson still goes to the hospital. He's true blue."

"Larry is in his seventies. I need a younger man," Coop replied.

"Old Doc might be in his seventies but he's tough as nails and twice as smart. I'd put my money on him any day of the week."

"Well — I'll talk to Rick."

"The other thing is, Larry's a deep well. Whatever goes in doesn't come out."

"That's true. Well, come on, girl. If you're going to work we'd better get cracking in the barn."

"Hey, Coop, thanks. Thanks for everything."

"You'd do the same for me."

As the humans pulled on their coats, Mrs. Murphy said to her friends, *"She's right about one thing. A hospital is life and death."*

19

"What happened to you?" Miranda practically shouted when Harry walked through the back door at work.

Harry trusted Miranda, a well-founded trust, so she told her everything as they sorted the mail, fortunately light that morning.

"Oh, honey, I hope you haven't stirred up a hornet's nest." The older woman was quick to grasp the implications of what Harry had done.

In fact, Miranda's mind clicked along at a speedy pace. Most people upon meeting her beheld a pleasant-looking woman somewhere in her early sixties, late fifties on a good day. She used to be plump but she'd slimmed down quite a bit upon reigniting the flame with her high-school beau. She wore deep or bright colors, had a real flair for presenting herself without calling undue attention to herself, the Virginia ideal. But most people who didn't really know Mrs. George Hogendobber had slight insight into

162

how bright she was. She always knew where the power in the room resided, a vital political and social survival tool. She was able to separate the wheat from the chaff. She also understood to the marrow of her bones that actions have consequences, a law of nature as yet unlearned by a large portion of the American population. She'd happily chat about her garden, cooking, the womanly skills at which she excelled. It was easy for people to overlook her. Over the years of working together, Harry had come to appreciate Miranda's intelligence, compassion, and concern. Without being fully conscious of it she relied on Miranda. And for Miranda's part, she had become a surrogate mother to Harry, who needed one.

Naturally, the cats and dog understood Miranda perfectly upon first introduction. In the beginning Miranda did not esteem cats but Mrs. Murphy set her right. The two became fast friends, and even Pewter, a far more self-indulgent soul, liked Miranda and vice versa.

Pewter couldn't understand why humans didn't talk more about tuna. They mostly talked about one another so she often tuned out. Or as she put it to herself, tuna-ed out.

Nobody was tuning out this morning though. The animals were worried and simultaneously furious that Harry had taken such a dumb chance. Furthermore, she had left them home. Had they been with her, the crack on the head would have never happened.

As the morning wore on, everyone who opened a postbox commented on the square shaved spot on Harry's head and the stitches. Her story was that she clunked herself in the barn. Big Mim, no slouch herself in the brain department, closely examined the wound and wondered just what could do that.

Harry fibbed, saying she'd hung a scythe over the beam closest to the hayloft ladder and when she slid down the ladder — she never climbed down, she'd put a foot on either side of the ladder and slide down — she forgot about the scythe. The story was stupid enough to be believable.

After Mim left, Miranda wryly said, "Harry, couldn't you have just said you bumped your head?"

"Yeah, but I had to bump it on something hard enough to break skin." She touched the spot. "It hurts."

"I'm sure it does and it's going to keep hurting, too. You promise me you won't pull a stunt like that again?"

"I didn't think it was such a stunt."

"You wouldn't." Miranda put her hands on her hips. "Now look here, girlie. I know you. I have known you since you came out of the womb. You don't go around that hospital by yourself. A man's been murdered there."

"You're right. I shouldn't have gone alone."

Right before lunch Bruce Buxton walked in. "How's my patient?"

"Okay."

He inspected his handiwork. "A nice tight stitch if I do say so myself."

As luck would have it, Sam Mahanes dropped in. As no one had thought to tell Bruce to keep his mouth shut, he told Sam what happened to Harry.

"You stitched her up, discharged her, and didn't inform me?" Sam was aghast, and then wondered why Rick Shaw hadn't told him immediately.

"I'm telling you now," Bruce coolly responded, secretly delighted at Sam's distress.

"Buxton, you should have been on the phone the minute this happened. And whoever was down there" — he waited for a name to be forthcoming but Bruce was not about to finger Booty Weyman so Sam continued — "should have reported to me, too."

"First off, I gave the order to the orderlies that carried her up, to the nurse, to shut up. I said that I'd talk to you. I'm talking to you right now. I was going to call you this morning." He checked his watch. "In twenty minutes to be exact. Don't blow this out of proportion."

"I don't see how it could be any worse." Sam's jaw clapped shut.

"Oh, trust me, Sam Mahanes. It could be a lot worse."

This comment so enraged the hospital director that he turned on his heel, didn't even say good-bye to the ladies, and strode out of the post office, slamming the door hard behind him.

28

Sam, still angry, cut off Tussie Logan as she was trying to back into a space in the parking lot reserved for staff.

He lurched into his space, slammed the door, and locked his car as she finally backed in, avoiding his eyes.

Tussie knew the director's rages only too well. She didn't want to cross him and she didn't want her new Volkswagen Passat station wagon scratched.

Larry Johnson, who had been driving behind Sam at a distance, observed the incident.

Sam strode toward the hospital without a hello or wave of acknowledgment.

After parking, Larry stepped out of his car as Tussie reached into hers, retrieving her worn leather satchel.

"Good morning, Dr. Johnson." She put her arm through the leather strap while closing her car door.

"Morning, Tussie. He damn near knocked you out of the box."

"One of his funks."

"I don't remember Sam being such a moody man." The older doctor fell into step next to Tussie.

"The last month, I don't know, maybe it's been longer. He's tense, critical, nothing we do is right. Maybe he's having problems at home."

"Perhaps, but Sally seems happy enough. I've always prided myself on being able to read people but Sam eludes me."

"I know what you mean." She turned up the collar of her coat, an expensive Jaeger three-quarter-length that flowed when she walked. "I guess you've seen everything and everybody in this burg."

"Oh — some," he modestly replied. "But you still get surprised. Hank Brevard. I wouldn't think he could have aroused enough passion in another person to kill him."

"Maybe he got the better of someone in a car deal." She said this with little conviction.

Hank had put his mechanical skills to work in fixing up old cars and trucks. His hobby became an obsession and occasionally a source of income, as he'd repair and sell a DeSoto or Morgan.

"God knows, he had his own car lot. This last year he must have gone on a buying spree. I don't remember him having so many cars. I'd love to buy the 1938 Plymouth. No such luck." Larry laughed.

"I bet once the dust settles, Lisa will sell his collection."

"Ah, Tussie, even if she did, I couldn't afford the Plymouth."

"Maybe you could. You've got to treat yourself every now and then. And what we do is draining. There are days when I love it as much as my first day out of nursing school and there are other days when I'm tired of being on my feet."

"Tussie, you're a wonderful nurse."

"Why, thank you, Doctor."

He smiled. "Here we are." He opened the front door. "Into the fray." He paused a moment, then said, "If you see anything off track, please tell me. In confidence. If there is something wrong here we've got to get to the bottom of it. This is too good of a hospital to be smeared with mud."

Surprised, she shrank back a moment, caught herself, and relaxed. "I agree. I'm a little touchy right now. A little watchful."

"We all are, Tussie. We all are."

21

Four medium-sized smooth river stones anchored the corners of the large blueprint that covered Sheriff Shaw's desk. He leaned over with a magnifying glass, puffing away like a furnace on his cigarette. The smoke stung his eyes as he took the cigarette out, peered closely, then stuck the weed back in his mouth.

Cynthia, also smoking, stood next to him. She told herself she was smoking in self-defense but she was smoking because that little hit of nicotine coated her frayed nerve endings.

He pointed a stubby finger at the boiler room, put down the magnifying glass, and placed his left forefinger on the incinerator room. This meant his cigarette dangled from his mouth, a pillar of smoke rising into his eyes.

Coop took the cigarette out of his mouth, putting it in an ashtray.

"Thanks." He breathed deeply. "The two easiest spots to destroy evidence."

"Right but I don't think that's our problem."

"Oh?" His eyebrows arched upward. "I wouldn't mind finding the damned knife."

She shook her head. "That's not what I mean. We aren't going to find the knife. It's burned to a crisp or he could have taken it right back up to where those things are steamed or boiled or whatever they do. Fruitless."

"I like that word, fruitless." He reached for his cigarette again with his right hand but kept his left forefinger square on the incinerator room. "What's cooking in your brain?"

"You know, Harry had some good ideas last night."

"Oh." He snorted. "This I've got to hear."

"She thought maybe someone is pirating body parts, organs."

He paused a long time, lifted up his left finger. "Uh-huh."

"Or stealing drugs."

He stubbed out his cigarette, which he'd smoked to a nub. "The other angle is that his killer was an enemy and knew this would be the best place to find him. The killer knew his habits but then most killers do know the habits of their victims. Until Harry got clunked on the head I was not

171

convinced the crime was tied to the hospital. Now I am."

"Me, too," Cooper agreed. "Now the trick is to find out what is at the hospital. What doesn't add up for me about Hank is — if he were in on a crooked deal, wouldn't he have lived higher on the hog? He didn't appear to live beyond his means."

Rick rubbed his chin. "Maybe not. Maybe not. Wait for retirement and then whoosh." He put his hands together and fluttered his fingers like a flyaway bird.

"He was in a position to take kickbacks from the fuel company, the electrical supply company, from everybody. For instance, those low-wattage lightbulbs. I noticed that when we answered Bobby Minifee's call. How do we know he didn't charge for a hundred watts but put in sixty? Now I went over those records and know that he didn't but I mean, for example. He was in the perfect position to skim."

"Wouldn't have been killed for that, I wouldn't reckon. But if he was corrupt it would have been damned hard to pin down. Those records, he could have falsified them, tossed the originals in the incinerator." He rubbed his palms together. "Right now, Coop, we're grasping at straws. We've got a hundred theories and not one hard piece of evidence."

"Let's go back to the basement. Don't tell Sam Mahanes when we're there. Call and tell him our people will be there next Tuesday. Then you and I go in Monday night. Someone might be tempted to move something out. But even if that isn't the case we'd be down there without Sam or anyone knowing except for the maintenance man on duty and we can take care of him."

"That's not a bad idea."

"A light hammer might help. To tap walls."

Rick smiled. She was good. She was good.

22

The sunset over the Blue Ridge Mountains arced out like a pinwheel of fire, oriflamme radiating from the mountaintops, an edge of pink gold on each spoke.

Harry paused at the creek dividing her property from the property of her neighbor, Blair Bainbridge. The sky overhead deepened from robin's-egg blue to a blue-gray shot through with orange. She never tired of nature's palette.

As she watched the display, so did Rick Shaw and Cynthia Cooper. They had parked an unmarked car along the railroad tracks near the hospital just below the old switching station, a smallish stone house, finally abandoned by the C & O Railroad in the 1930s.

"Something," Rick murmured.

"Yeah." Coop watched the sky darken to velvety Prussian blue, one of her favorite colors.

One by one lights switched on, dots of life. Drivers turned on their headlights and

Crozet's residents hurried home for supper.

"When's the last time you went to a movie?" Rick asked.

"Uh — I don't know."

"Me, too. I think I'll surprise the wife tomorrow night and take her to a movie. Dinner."

"She'll like that."

He smiled. "I will, too. I don't know how I had the sense to pick her and I don't know why she married me. Really."

"You're a — well, you know, you're a butch kind of guy. Women like that."

He smiled even bigger. "You think?"

"I think."

He pulled out a Camel, offered her one, then lit up for both of them. "Coop, when you going to find what you're looking for? You still thinking about Blair Bainbridge?"

She avoided the question. "I meant to ask you the other day, when did you switch to Camels? You used to smoke Chesterfields."

"Oh," he exhaled. "I thought if I tried different brands" — he inhaled — "I might learn to hate the taste."

"Marlboro."

"Merit." He grimaced.

"Kool."

"I hate menthol."

"Dunhill. Red pack."

"Do you know any cop can afford Dunhills?"

"No. Shepheard's Hotel. Another good but real expensive weed."

"You must be hanging out with rich folk."

"Nah — every now and then someone will offer me a cigarette. That's how I smoked a Shepheard's Hotel."

"M-m-m, what's the name of that brand, all natural, kind of thirties look to the pack, an Indian logo. Where did I see those?" he pondered.

She shrugged. "I don't know." A beat. "Viceroy."

"Pall Mall. You're too young to remember."

"No, I'm not. Winstons."

He waited, took a deep drag. "I go to the convenience store. I ask for cigarettes, I see all those brands stacked up and now I can't think of any more."

"Foreign ones. Gauloises. French. Those Turkish cigarettes. They'll knock your socks off."

He grunted, then brightened. "Virginia Slims."

"Lucky Strike."

"Good one. And I note you haven't answered my question about Blair Bainbridge."

Blair Bainbridge worked as a model, flying all over the world for photo shoots. Little Mim Sanburne more or less claimed him but he was maddeningly noncommittal. Many people thought he was the right man for Harry, being tall and handsome, but Blair and Harry, while recognizing one another's attractiveness, had evolved into friends.

"Well, he is drop-dead gorgeous," she sighed.

"Have I ever spoken to you about your personal life?" He turned toward her, his eyebrows quizzically raised.

"No." She laughed. "Because I don't have a personal life."

"Yeah, well, anyway, you and I have been on this force a good long time. You're in your thirties now. You're a good-looking woman."

"Thanks, boss." She blushed.

He held up his hand, palm facing her. "Don't waste your time on a pretty man. They're always trouble. Find a guy who works hard and who loves you for you. Okay, maybe he won't be the best-looking guy in the world or the most exciting but you know, for the long run you want a doer, not a looker."

She gazed out the window, touched that

he had thought about her life away from work. "You're right."

"That's all I have to say on the subject except for one more little thing. He has to meet my approval."

They both laughed as the darkness gathered around them. They got out of the car and walked up the railroad tracks to the hospital, slipping down over the embankment at the track.

They opened the back door. Each carried a flashlight and a small hammer. Both had memorized the blueprints.

Wordlessly, they walked down the main corridor to the boiler room. The boiler room sat smack in the middle of the basement. The thick back wall of the room was almost two and a half feet of solid rock, an effective barrier should the boiler ever blow up. The other three walls each had corridors coming into the boiler room.

The only other hallway not connecting into the boiler room was one along the east side of the building at the elevator pool. But in the middle of that east hallway, intersecting it perpendicularly, the east corridor ran into the boiler room.

Offices and storage rooms were off of each of these corridors. The incinerator room was not far from the boiler room.

Coop tapped the solid wall behind the boiler. No empty sound hinted at a hidden storage vault. The two prowled each corridor, noted the doors that were locked, and checked every open room.

The silence downstairs was eerie. Every now and then they could hear the elevator doors open and close, the bell ringing as the doors shut. They heard a footfall and then nothing.

The opened rooms contained maintenance items for the most part. Each corridor had mops, pails, and waxers strategically placed so they could be easily carried to the elevators. A few rooms, dark green walls adding to the gloom, contained banks of ancient file cabinets.

As they quietly walked along, the linoleum under their feet squeaked. Back at the oldest part of the building, the floors were cut stone.

"Three locked doors. Let's find Bobby Minifee." Rick checked his watch. They'd been in there for two and a half hours.

Bobby hadn't taken over Hank Brevard's old office until that morning. The Sheriff's Department had crawled over every inch, every record. Satisfied that nothing had escaped the department's attention, the office was released for use.

"Bobby." Rick knocked on the open door.

Startled, he looked up and blinked. "Sheriff."

"We need your help."

"Sure." He put down the scheduling sheet he was working on.

"Bring all your keys."

"Yes, sir." Minifee lifted a huge ring full of keys.

The three walked to the first locked door, which was between Hank's office and a storage room full of paper towels and toilet paper.

After fumbling with keys, Bobby found the right one. The door swung open and he switched on the light. Shelves were jammed with every kind of lightbulb imaginable.

"Hank made us keep this locked because he said people would lift the bulbs. They're expensive, you know, especially the ones used in the operating room."

"People would steal them."

Bobby nodded yes. "Hank used to say they'd steal a hot stove and come back for the smoke. I never saw much of it myself." He politely waited while Rick and Cooper double-checked the long room, tapping on walls.

"Okay. Next one," Rick commanded.

The second locked room contained stationery and office supplies.

"Other hot items?" Coop asked.

"Yep. It's funny but people think taking a notebook isn't stealing."

"Everyone's got that problem, I think." The sheriff flipped up a dozen bound legal pads. "If I had a dollar for every pen that's walked off my desk I'd have my car paid for."

The third room, much larger than the others and quite well lit, contained a few pieces of equipment — one blood-infusion pump, one oscillator, two EEG units.

"Expensive stuff." Rick whistled.

"Yes. Usually it's shipped out within forty-eight hours to the manufacturer or the repair company. For a hospital this size, though, we have few repairs. We're lucky that way." Bobby walked through the room with Rick and Cynthia. "Hank took care of that. He was very conscientious about the big stuff. He'd call the manufacturer, he'd describe the problem, he'd arrange for the shipping. He'd be at the door for the receiving. You couldn't fault him that way."

"Huh," was all Rick said.

"Where do you keep the organ transplants?"

Bobby's eyes widened. "Not here."

"You don't receive them at the shipping

door?" Coop asked.

"Oh, no. The organ transplants are hand-walked right into the front door, the deliverer checks in at the front desk, and then they are delivered immediately to the physician. They know almost to the minute when something like that is coming in. Most of the time the patient is ready for the transplant. They'd *never* let us handle something like that."

"I see." Rick ran his forefinger over the darkened screen of an oscilloscope.

"Let's say someone has a leg amputated. What happens to the leg?" Coop asked.

Bobby grimaced slightly. "Hank said in the old days the body parts were burned in the middle of the night in the incinerator. Now stuff like that is wrapped up, sealed off, and picked up daily by a company that handles hazardous biological material. They burn it somewhere else."

"In the middle of nowhere, I'd guess, because of the smell," Coop said.

"No." Rick shook his head. "They use high heat like a crematorium. It's fast." He smiled smugly, having done his homework.

"I'm glad. I wouldn't throw arms and legs into the incinerator." Bobby shuddered.

"People were tougher in the old days." Rick wanted another cigarette. "Well, thank you, Bobby. Keep it to yourself that we were here."

"Yes, sir."

Rick clapped him on the back. "You doing okay?"

"Yeah." He shrugged.

"Notice any change in the routine here?" Coop clicked off her flashlight as Bobby walked them to the back door by the railroad tracks.

"No. Not down here. I'm duplicating Hank's routine. He'll be hard to replace. We're not as efficient right now. At least, that's what I think."

"Anyone coming down here who usually doesn't come down?"

"Sam and Jordan made separate appearances. But now that things have settled a little it's business as usual — no one cares much about our work. If something isn't done we hear about it but we don't receive compliments for doing a good job. We're kind of invisible." A slight smirk played on Bobby's lips.

"Has anyone ever offered you drugs? Uppers. Downers. Cocaine?"

"No. I haven't even been offered a beer." The corners of his mouth turned up. Dimples showed when he smiled.

Rick opened the back door. "Well, if anything pops into your head, no matter how small it seems, you call me or Coop."

"I will."

The temperature had dropped below freezing. They climbed up the bank to the tracks.

"Ideas?"

"No, boss. Wish I had even one."

"Yeah, me, too."

It had never occurred to them to tap the floors in the basement.

That same Monday evening, Big Mim and Larry Johnson dined at Dalmally. Jim Sanburne was at a county commissioners' meeting in Old Lane High School, now the county offices, in Charlottesville. Little Mim was ensconced in her cottage.

The two dear friends chatted over fresh lobster, rice, vegetables, a crisp arugula salad, and a very expensive white Chilean wine.

"— his face." Larry laughed.

"I haven't thought of that in years." Mim laughed, remembering a gentleman enamored of her Aunt Tally.

He had tried to impress the independent lady by his skill at golf. They were playing in a foursome during a club tournament. He was in the rough just off the green, which was surrounded by spectators. The day being sultry, ladies wore halter tops or camp shirts and shorts. The men wore shorts and short-sleeved shirts, straw hats with bright ribbon bands.

The poor fellow hit a high shot off the rough which landed right in the ample bosom of Florence Taliaferro. She screamed, fell down, but the golf ball was not dislodged from its creamy resting place.

No one knew of a rule to cover such an eventuality. He couldn't play the ball but he was loath to drop a ball and take a penalty shot. His contentious attitude so soured the caustic Tally that the moment they turned in their cards, she never spoke to him again.

Larry cracked a lobster claw. "I'm amazed at what flutters through my mind. An event from 1950 seems as real as what's happening this moment."

"Y-e-s." She drew out the word as the candlelight reflected off her beautiful pearls.

Larry knew Mim always dined by candlelight; the loveliness of the setting proved that Mim needed luxury, beauty, perfect proportion.

Gretchen glided in to remove one course and bring out another. She and Big Mim had been together since girlhood. Gretchen's family had worked for Mim's parents.

"What do you think about my daughter opposing my husband?"

"Ah-ha! I knew you had an agenda."

"She shouldn't do it," Gretchen piped up.

"Did I ask you?"

"No, Miss Mim, that's why I'm telling you. I have to get a word in edgewise."

"You poor benighted creature," Big Mim mocked.

"Don't you forget it." Gretchen disappeared.

Larry smiled. "You two would make a great sitcom. Hollywood needs you."

"You're too kind," Mim replied, a hint of acid in her tone.

"What do I think? I think it's good for Marilyn but it creates stress for the residents of Crozet. No one ever wants to offend a Sanburne."

"There is that," Mim thoughtfully considered. "Although Jim has been quite clear that he doesn't mind."

"It still makes people nervous. No one wants to be on the losing side."

"Yes." Mim put down her fork. "Should I tell her to stop?"

"No."

"I can't very well suggest to Jim that he step down. He's been a good mayor."

"Indeed."

"This is a pickle."

"For all of us." He chewed a bit of lobster, sweet and delicious. "But people will pay attention to the election; issues might get discussed. We've gotten accustomed to apathy — only because Jim takes care of things."

"I suppose. Crozet abounds with groups. People do pitch in but yes, you're right, there is a kind of political apathy. Not just here. Everywhere."

"People vote with their feet. They're bored, with a capital B."

"Larry," she leaned closer. "What's going on at Crozet Hospital? I know you know more than you're telling me and I know Harry didn't cut her head on a scythe."

"What's Harry got to do with it?"

"There's no way she could stay away from the murder site. She's been fascinated with solving things since she was tiny. Now really, character is everything, is it not?" He nodded assent so she continued. "I'd bet my earrings that Harry snuck over to the hospital and got hurt."

"She could have gotten hurt sticking her nose somewhere else. What if she snuck around Hank Brevard's house?"

"I *know* Mary Minor Haristeen."

A ripple of silence followed. Then Larry sighed. "Dear Mim, you are one of the most intelligent women I have ever known."

She smiled broadly. "Thank you."

"Whether your thesis is correct or not I really don't know. Harry hasn't said anything to me when I grace the post office with my presence." He was telling the truth.

"But you have been associated with the hospital for, well, almost fifty years. You must know something."

"Until the incident I can't say that I noticed anything, how shall I say, untoward. The usual personality clashes, nurses grumbling about doctors, doctors jostling one another for status or perks or pretty nurses." He held up his hand. "Oh yes, plenty of that."

"Really." Mim's left eyebrow arched upward.

"But Mim, that's every hospital. It's a closed world with its own rules. People work in a highly charged atmosphere. They're going to fall for one another."

"Yes."

"But there has been an increase of tension and it predates the dispatch of Hank Brevard. Sam Mahanes has lacked discretion, shall we say?"

"Oh."

"People don't want to see that sort of thing — especially in their boss or leader."

"Who?"

"Tussie Logan."

"Ah."

"They avoid one another in a theatrical manner. But Sam isn't always working during those late nights." He held up his left palm, a gesture of questioning and appeasement. "Judge not lest ye be judged."

"Is that meant for me?"

"No, dear. We've gracefully accommodated one another's faults."

"It was me, not you."

"I should have fought harder. I've told you that. I should have banged on this front door and had it out with your father. But I didn't. And somehow, sweetheart, it has all worked out. You married and had two good children."

"A son who rarely comes home," she sniffed.

"Whose fault is that?" he gently chided her.

"I've made amends."

"And he and his wife will finally move down from New York some fine day. Dixie claims all her children. But whatever the gods have in store for us — it's right. It's right that you married Jim, I married Annabella, God rest her soul. It's right that we've become friends over the years. Who is to say that our bond may not be even

189

stronger *because* of our past. Being husband and wife might have weakened our connection."

"Do you really think so?" She had never considered this.

"I do."

"I shall have to think about it. You know, I cherish our little talks. I have always been able to say anything to you."

"I cherish them as well."

A car drove up, parked, the door slammed, the back door opened.

Jim slapped Gretchen on the fanny. "Put out a plate for me, doll."

"Sexual harassment."

"You wish," he teased her.

"Ha. You'll never know."

He strode into the dining room. "Finished early. A first in the history of Albemarle County."

"Hooray." Mim smiled.

Jim clapped Larry on the back, then sat down. "Looks fabulous."

"Wait until you taste the rice. Gretchen has put tiny bits of orange rind in it." Mim glanced up as Gretchen came into the room.

"Isn't that just perfect."

"Of course. I prepared it." Gretchen served Jim rice, vegetables, then tossed salad for him.

The small gathering chattered away, much to Larry's relief. Had he continued to be alone with Mim she would have returned to her questions about the hospital.

Mim had to know everything. It was her nature, just as solving puzzles was Harry's.

And Larry did know more than he was telling. He could never lie to Mim. He was glad he didn't have to try.

23

Each day of the week grew warmer until by Saturday the noon temperature rose into the low sixties. March was just around the corner bringing with it the traditional stiff winds, the first crocus and robin, as well as hopes of spring to come. Everybody knew that nature could and often did throw a curveball, dumping a snowstorm onto the mountains and valley in early April, but still, the days were longer, the quality of light changed from diffuse to brighter, and folks began to think about losing weight, gardening, and frolicking.

Hunt season ended in mid-March, bringing conflicting emotions for Harry and her friends. They loved hunting yet they were thrilled to say good-bye to winter.

This particular Saturday the hunt left from Harry's farm. Given the weather, over forty people turned out, quite unusual for a February hunt.

As they rode off, Mrs. Murphy, Pewter, and an enraged Tucker watched from the barn.

"I don't see why I can't go. I can run as fast as any old foxhound." Tucker pouted.

"You aren't trained as a foxhound." Mrs. Murphy calmly stated the obvious, which she was forced to do once a year when the hunt met at Harry's farm.

"Ha!" The little dog barked. *"Walk around, nose to the ground. Pick up a little scent and wave your tail. Then you move a bit faster and finally you open your big yap and say, 'Got a line.' How hard is that?"*

"Tail," Pewter laconically replied.

"How's zat?" The dog barked even louder as the hounds moved farther away, ignoring her complaints.

"You haven't got a tail, Tucker. So you can't signal the start of something mildly interesting." The tiger was enjoying Tucker's state almost as much as Pewter, who did have the tiniest malicious streak.

"You don't believe that, do you?" She was incredulous, her large dog eyes imploring.

"Sure we do." The two cats grinned in unison.

"I could run after them. I could catch up and show my stuff."

"And have a whipper-in on your butt." Pewter laughed, mentioning the bold out-riders responsible for seeing that hounds behaved.

"Wouldn't be on my butt. Would be on a hound's," Tucker smugly replied. *"I think Mom should whip-in. She'd be good at it. She's got hound sense, you know, but only because I taught her everything she knows — about canines."*

"Pin a rose on you," Pewter sarcastically replied.

Tucker swept her ears back for a second, then swept them forward. *"You don't know a thing about hunting unless it's mice and you aren't doing so hot on that front. And then there's the bluejay who dive-bombs you, gets right in front of you, Pewter, and you can't grab him."*

"Oh, I'd like to see you tangle with that bluejay. He'd peck your eyes out, mutt." Pewter's temper flared.

"Hey, they hit a line right at the creek bed." Mrs. Murphy, a keen hunter of all game, trotted out of the barn, past Poptart and Gin Fizz, angry at not hunting themselves. She leapt onto the fence, positioning herself on a corner post.

Tucker scrambled, slid around the corner of the paddock, then sat down. Pewter, with far less enthusiasm, climbed up on a fence post near Mrs. Murphy.

"Tally Ho!" Tucker bounded up and down on all fours.

"That's the Tutweiler fox. He'll lead them straight across the meadows and dump them about two miles away. He always runs through the culvert there at the entrance to the Tutweiler farm, then jumps on the zigzag fence. I don't know why they can't get his scent off the fence but they don't." Mrs. Murphy enjoyed watching the unfolding panorama.

"How do you know so much?" Tucker kept bouncing.

"Because he told me."

"When?"

"When you were asleep, you dumb dog. I hunt at night sometimes. By myself since both of you are the laziest slugs the Great Cat in the Sky ever put on earth."

"Hey, look at Harry. She took that coop in style." Pewter admired her mother's form over fences.

"She would have taken it better with me," a very sour Gin Fizz grumbled. *"Why she bothers with Tomahawk, I'll never know. He's too rough at the trot and he gets too close to the fence."*

As Gin was now quite elderly, in his middle twenties, but in great shape, the other animals knew not to disagree with him.

Poptart, the young horse Harry was

bringing along, respectfully kept quiet. A big mare with an easy stride, she couldn't wait for the day when she'd be Harry's go-to hunter. She listened to Gin because he knew the game.

As the animals watched, Miranda drove up with church ladies in tow. She cooked a hunt breakfast for Harry once a year and Harry made a nice donation to her Church of the Holy Light. Each lady emerged from the church van carrying plates of food, bowls of soup, baskets of fresh-baked breads and rolls. Although called a breakfast, hunters usually don't get to eat until twelve or one in the afternoon, so the selection of food ranged from eggs to roasts to biscuits, breads, and all manner of casseroles.

The enticing aroma of honey-cured Virginia ham reached Tucker's delicate nostrils. She forgot to be upset about the hounds. Her determination to trail the hounds wavered. Her left shoulder began to lean toward the house.

"I bet Miranda needs help," Tucker said in her most solicitous tone.

"Sure." Murphy laughed at her while observing Sam Mahanes lurch over a coop. *"That man rides like a sack of potatoes."*

Sam was followed by Dr. Larry Johnson, who rode as his generation was taught to ride: forward and at pace. Larry soared over the coop, top hat not even wobbling, big grin on his clean, open face.

"Amazing." Pewter licked a paw, rubbing it behind her ears.

"Larry?" Murphy wondered.

"Yes. You know humans would be better off if they didn't know arithmetic. They count their birthdays and it weakens their mind. You are what you are. Like us, for instance." Pewter out of the corner of her eye saw Tucker paddle to the back door. *"Do you believe her?"*

"She can't help it. Dogs." Murphy shrugged. *"You were saying?"*

"Counting." Pewter's voice boomed a bit louder than she had anticipated, scaring Poptart for a minute. *"Sorry, Pop. Okay, look at you and me, Mrs. Murphy. Do we worry about our birthdays?"*

"No. Oh boy, there goes Little Mim. She just blew by Mother. That'll set them off. Ha." Murphy relished that discussion, since Harry hated to be passed in the hunt field.

"Tomahawk's too slow." Gin Fizz, disgruntled though he may have been, was telling the truth. *"She needs a Thoroughbred. Of course, Little Mim can buy as many hunters as she wants and the price is irrelevant. Mom has to make her own*

horses. *She does a good job, I think."* Gin loved Harry.

"But I'm only half a Thoroughbred," Poptart wailed. *"Does that mean we'll be stuck in the rear?"*

Gin Fizz consoled the youngster. *"No. You can jump the moon. As the others fall by the wayside, you'll be going strong as long as you take your conditioning seriously. But on the flat, well, yes, you might get passed. Don't worry. You'll be fine."*

"I don't want to be passed," the young horse said fiercely.

"Nobody does." Gin Fizz laughed.

"Am I going to get to finish my thought or what?" Pewter snarled. She liked horses but herbivores bored her. Grass eaters. How could they eat grass? She only ate grass when she needed to throw up.

"Sorry." Gin smiled.

"As I was saying," Pewter declaimed. *"Humans count. Numbers. They count money. They count their years. It's a bizarre obsession with them. So a human turns thirty and begins to fret. A little fret. Turns forty. Bigger. Is it not the dumbest thing? How you feel is what matters. If you feel bad, it doesn't matter if you're fifteen. If you feel fabulous like Larry, what's seventy-five? Stupid numbers. I really think*

they should dump the whole idea of birth-days. They wouldn't know any better then. They'd be happier."

"They'd find a way to screw it up." Murphy looked over at her gray friend. *"They fear happiness like we fear light-ning. I don't understand it. I accept it, though."*

"They're so worried about something bad happening that they make it happen. I truly believe that." Pewter, for all her con-centration on food and luxury, was an intel-ligent animal.

"Yeah, I think they do that all the time and don't know it. They've got to give up the idea that they can control life. They've got to be more catlike."

"Or horselike." Gin smiled wryly.

"They've got to eat some meat, Gin. I mean they're omnivores," Pewter replied.

"I'm not talking about food, I'm talking about attitude. Look at us. We have good food, a beautiful place to live, and someone to love and we love her. It's a per-fect life. Even if we didn't have a barn to live in, it's a perfect life. I don't think horses were born with barns anyway. Harry needs to think more like a horse. Just go with the flow." Gin used an old term from his youth.

"Uh — yeah," Pewter agreed.

Harry may not have gone with the flow but she certainly followed her fox. Just as Mrs. Murphy predicted, the Tutweiler fox bolted straightaway. Two miles later he scurried under a culvert, hopped onto a zigzag fence to disappear, ready to run another day.

The hounds picked up a fading scent but that fox didn't run as well as the Tutweiler fox. He dove into his den. After three hours of glorious fun, the field turned for home.

Harry quickly cleaned up Tomahawk, turning him out with Poptart and Gin Fizz, who wanted to know how the other horses behaved on the hunt.

Her house overflowed with people, reminding her of her childhood, because her mother and father had loved to entertain. She figured most people came because of Mrs. Hogendobber's cooking. The driveway, lined with cars all the way down to the paved road, bore testimony to that. Many of the celebrants didn't hunt, but the tradition of hunt breakfast was, whoever was invited could come and eat whether they rode or not.

Bobby Minifee and Booty Weyman attended, knowing they would be welcome. The Minifees were night hunters so Bobby would pick a good hillock upon which to observe hounds. Night hunters did just that, hunted at night on foot. Usually they chased raccoons but most hunters enjoyed hunting, period, and Bobby and Booty loved to hear the hounds.

Sam Mahanes had parted company with his horse at a creek bed and didn't much like Bruce Buxton reminding him of that fact.

Big Mim Sanburne declared the fences were much higher when she was in her twenties and Little Mim, out of Mother's earshot, remarked, "Must have been 1890."

Everyone praised Miranda Hogendobber, who filled the table with ham biscuits, corn bread, smoked turkey, venison in currant sauce, scrambled eggs, deviled eggs, pickled eggs, pumpernickel quite fresh, raw oysters, salad with arugula, blood oranges, mounds of almond cake, a roast loin of pork, cheese grits and regular grits, potato cakes with applesauce, cherry pie, apple pie, devil's food cake, and, as always, Mrs. Hogendobber's famous cinnamon buns with an orange glaze.

Cynthia Cooper, off this Saturday, ate herself into a stupor, as did Pewter, who couldn't move from the arm of the sofa.

Tussie Logan and Randy Sands milled about. Because they lived together people assumed they were lovers but they weren't.

They didn't bother to deny the rumors. If they did it would only confirm what everyone thought. Out of the corner of her eye, Tussie observed Sam.

Tucker snagged every crumb that hit the floor. Mrs. Murphy, after four delicious oysters, reposed, satiated, in the kitchen window. Eyes half closed, she dozed off and on but missed little.

"Where's Fair today?" Bruce Buxton asked Harry.

"Conference in Leesburg at the Marion Dupont Scott Equine Medical Center. He hates to miss any cooking of Mrs. Hogendobber's and the Church of the Holy Light but duty called."

"I think I would have been less dutiful." Bruce laughed.

"Mrs. H.," Susan Tucker called out. "You said you and the girls had practiced 'John Peel.' "

"And so we have." A flushed, happy Miranda held up her hands, the choir ladies gathered round, and she blew a note on the pitch pipe. They burst into song about a famous nineteenth-century English foxhunter, a song most kids learn in second grade. But the choir gave it a special resonance and soon the assemblage joined in on the chorus.

Mrs. H., while singing, pointed to Larry Johnson, who came and stood beside her. The choir silenced as he sang a verse in his clear, lovely tenor and then everyone boomed in on the chorus again.

After the choir finished, groups sporadically sang whatever came into their heads, including a medley of Billy Ray Cyrus songs, Cole Porter, and various nursery rhymes, while Ned Tucker, Susan's husband, accompanied them on the piano.

Many of the guests, liberally fueling themselves from the bar, upped the volume.

Tucker, ears sensitive, walked into Harry's bedroom and wiggled under the bed.

Pewter finally moved off the sofa arm but not to the bedroom, which would have been the sensible solution. No, she returned to the table to squeeze in one more sliver of honey-cured ham.

"You're going to barf all over the place." Mrs. Murphy opened one eye.

"No, I'm not. I'll walk it off."

"Ha."

Coop grabbed another ham biscuit as people crowded around the long table. Larry Johnson, uplifted from the hunt and three desert-dry martinis, slapped the deputy on the back.

"You need to hunt with us."

"Harry gets after me. I will. Of course, I'd better learn to jump first."

"Why? Sam Mahanes never bothered." He couldn't help himself and his laughter sputtered out like machine-gun fire.

It didn't help that Sam, talking to Bruce, heard this aspersion cast his way. He ignored it.

"Harry would let you take lessons on Gin Fizz. He's a wonderful old guy." Susan volunteered her best friend's horse, then bellowed over the din. "Harry, I'm lending Gin Fizz to Coop."

"What a princess you are, Susan," Harry yelled back.

"See, that's all there is to it." Larry beamed. "And by the way, I'll catch up with you tomorrow."

Before Coop could whisper some prudence in his ear — after all, why would he need to see her — he tacked in the direction of Little Mim, who smiled when she saw him. People generally smiled in Larry's company.

Mrs. Murphy had both eyes open now, fixed on Coop, whose jaw dropped slightly ajar.

Miranda walked up next to the tall blonde. "I don't know when I've seen Larry

Johnson this happy. There must be something to this hunting."

"Depends on what you're hunting." Mrs. Murphy looked back out the window at the horses tied to the vans and trailers. Each horse wore a cooler, often in its stable colors. They were a very pretty sight.

24

Miranda stayed behind to help Harry clean up, as did Susan Tucker. The last guest tottered along at six in the evening, ushered out by soft twilight.

"I think that was the most successful breakfast we've had all year. Thanks to you." Harry scrubbed down the kitchen counters.

"Right," Susan concurred.

"Thank you." Miranda smiled. She enjoyed making people happy. "When your parents were alive this house was full of people. I remember one apple blossom party, oh my, the Korean War had just ended and the apple trees bloomed like we'd never seen them. Your father decided we had to celebrate the end of the war and the blossoms, the whole valley was filled with apple fragrance. So he begged, borrowed, and stole just about every table in Crozet, put them out front under the trees. Your mother made centerpieces using apple blossoms and iris, now that was beautiful. Uncle

Olin, my uncle, he died before you were born, brought down his band from up Winchester way. Your dad built, built from scratch, a dance floor that he put together in sections. I think all of Crozet came to that party and we danced all night. Uncle Olin played until sunup, liberally fueled by Nelson County country waters." She laughed, using the old Virginia term for moonshine. "George and I danced to sunrise. Those were the days." She instinctively put her hand to her heart. "It's good to see this house full of people again."

"They step on my tail," Pewter grumbled, rejoining them from the screened-in porch and, hard to believe, hungry again.

"Because it's fat like the rest of you." Mrs. Murphy giggled.

"Cats don't have fat tails," Pewter haughtily responded.

"You do," Murphy cackled, then jumped on the sofa, rolled over, four legs in the air, and turned her head upside down so she could watch her gray friend, who decided to stalk her.

Pewter crouched, edged forward, and when she reached the sofa she wiggled her hind end, then catapulted up in the air right onto the waiting Murphy.

"Banzai. Death to the Emperor!" Pewter,

who had watched too many old movies, shouted.

The cats rolled over, finally thumping onto the floor.

"What's gotten into you two?" Harry laughed at them from the kitchen.

"You know, I've heard people say that animals take on the personality of their owner," Miranda, eyes twinkling, said.

"Is that a fact?" Harry stepped into the living room as the cats continued their wrestling match with lots of fake hissing and puffing.

"Must be true, Harry. You lie on the sofa and wait for someone to pounce on you." Susan laughed.

"Humor. Small, pathetic, but an attempt at humor nonetheless." Harry loved it when her friends teased her.

"Is that true?" Miranda appeared scandalized. "You're a sex bomb?" The words "sex bomb" coming out of Miranda's mouth seemed so incongruous that Harry and Susan burst out laughing and were at pains to explain exactly why.

Tucker, dead asleep in the hallway to the bedroom, slowly raised her head when the cats broke away from one another, ran to her, and jumped over her in both directions. Then Pewter bit Tucker's ear.

"Pewts, that was mean." Mrs. Murphy laughed. *"Do the other one."*

"Ouch." Tucker shook her head.

"Come on, lazybones. Let's play and guess what, there are leftovers," an excited, slightly frenzied Pewter reported before she tore back into the living room, jumped on the sofa, launched herself from the sofa to the bookcases, and miraculously made it.

Mrs. Murphy followed her. Once she and Pewter were on the same shelf, they had a serious decision to make: which books to throw on the floor.

Harry, sensing their plan, rushed over. "No, you don't."

"Yes, we do." Mrs. Murphy pulled out *The Eighth Day* by Thornton Wilder.

Crash.

"I will smack you silly." Harry reached for the striped devil but she easily eluded her human.

Pewter prudently jumped off but not before knocking off a silver cup Harry had won years before at a hunter pace. As the clanging rang in her ears, the cat spun out, slid around the wing chair, bolted into the kitchen where Miranda was putting Saran Wrap over the remains of the honey-cured ham, stole a hunk of ham, and crouched under the kitchen table to gnaw it.

"I've seen everything." Miranda shook her head.

"Wild." Susan knelt down as Tucker walked into the kitchen. "Aren't you glad you're not a crazy kitty?"

"Got her a piece of ham," Tucker solemnly stated.

Harry surveyed the house. "We did a good job."

Mrs. Murphy joined Pewter under the table.

"I'm not giving you any. I stole this myself with no help from you."

"I'm not hungry."

"Liar," Pewter said.

Harry peered under the table. "Radical."

"That's us." Murphy purred back.

Harry examined the ham before Miranda put it in the refrigerator. "She tore a hunk right off of there, didn't she?"

"Before my very eyes. Little savage."

"Might as well cut the piece smooth." Harry lifted up the corner of the Saran Wrap and sliced off the raggedy piece. She divided it into three pieces, one for each animal. "Hey, anyone want coffee, tea, or something stronger? The coffee's made. Will only take me a second to brew tea."

"I'd like a cuppa." Miranda wrapped the

last of the food, then she reached into the cupboard, bringing down the loose Irish tea that Harry saved for special occasions. "How about this?"

"My fave." She turned to Susan. "What will you have?"

"Uh, I'll finish off the coffee and sit up all night. Drives Ned nuts when I do it but I just feel like a cup of coffee. Hey, before I forget, is that possum still in the hayloft?"

"Yeah, why?"

"I saved the broken chocolate bits for him."

"He'll like that. He has a sweet tooth."

"I don't know how Simon" — Mrs. Murphy called the possum by his proper name — *"can eat chocolate. The taste is awful."*

"I don't think it's so bad." Tucker polished off her ham. *"Although dogs aren't supposed to eat it. But it tastes okay."*

"You're a dog." Murphy shook her head in case any tiny food bits lingered on her whiskers. She'd follow this up with a sweep of her whiskers with her forearm.

"So?"

"You'll eat anything whether it's good for you or not."

Tucker eyed Mrs. Murphy, then turned her sweet brown eyes onto Pewter. *"She*

213

eats anything."

"I don't eat celery," Pewter protested vigorously.

As the animals chatted so did the humans. The hunt was bracing, the breakfast a huge success, the house was cleaned up, the barn chores done. They sat and rehashed everything that had happened in the hunt field for Miranda's benefit as well as their own. Then all shared what they'd seen and heard at the party, laughing over who became tipsy, who insulted whom, who flirted with whom (everybody flirted with everybody), who believed it, who didn't, who tried to sell a horse (again, everybody), who tried to buy a horse (half the room), who tried to weasel recipes out of Miranda, various theories about Hank Brevard, and who looked good as well as who didn't.

"I heard only twenty people attended Hank's funeral." Miranda felt badly that a man wasn't well liked enough to pack the church. It is one's last social engagement, after all.

"As you sow so ye shall reap." Harry quoted the Bible not quite accurately to Miranda, which made the older woman smile.

"Some people never learn to get along with others. Maybe they're born that way."

Susan lost all self-restraint and took the last cinnamon bun with the orange glaze.

"Susan Tucker," Harry said in a singsong voice.

"Oh, I know," came the weak reply.

"You girls have good figures. Stop worrying." Miranda reached down to scratch Tucker's head. "I wonder about that. I mean how it is that some people draw others to them and other people just manage to say the wrong thing or just put out a funny feeling. I'm not able to say what I mean but do you know what I mean?"

"Bad vibes," Harry simply said, and they laughed together.

"These aren't bad vibes but Little Mim was working the party. She's really serious about being mayor." Susan was amazed because Little Mim had never had much purpose in life.

"Maybe it would be good," Harry said thoughtfully. "Maybe we need some fresh ideas.

"But we can't go against her father. He's a good mayor and he knows everybody. People listen to Jim." Harry wondered how it would all turn out. "I don't see why he can't take her on as vice-mayor."

"Harry, there is no vice-mayor," Miranda corrected her.

"Yeah," she answered back. "But why can't we create the position? If we ask for it now either as a fait accompli or charge the city council to create a referendum, it's a lot easier than waiting until November."

"Oh, ladies, all you have to do is tell Jim your idea and he'll appoint her. You know the city council will back him up. Besides, no one wants to see a knock-down-drag-out between father and daughter — not that Jim would fight, he won't. But we all know that Little Mim hasn't much chance. Your solution is a good one, Harry. Good for everybody. The day will come when Jim can't be mayor and this way we'd have a smooth transition. You go talk to Jim Sanburne," Miranda encouraged her.

"Maybe I should talk to Mim first." Harry drained her teacup.

"There is that," Susan said, "but then Jim hears it first from his wife. Better to go to him first since he is the elected official and on the same day call on her. She can't be but so mad."

"You're right." Harry looked determined, scribbling the idea on her napkin.

The phone rang. They sat for a moment.

"I'll get it." Mrs. Murphy jumped onto the counter, knocking the wall phone receiver off the hook.

"Her latest trick." Harry smiled, got up, and picked up the phone. "Hello." She paused. "Coop, I can't believe it." She paused again. "All right. Thanks." She turned to her friends, her face drained white. "Larry Johnson has been shot."

"Oh my God." Miranda's hands flew to her face. "Is he — ?" She couldn't say the word.

25

The revolving blue light from Rick's squad car cast a sad glow over the scene. Cynthia stood with him behind the three barns at Twisted Creek Stables. The parking lot for trailers and vans was placed behind the barns, out of sight. Those renting stalls could use the space for their rigs.

Larry Johnson, who lived in town, boarded his horse here. He'd always boarded horses, declaring he wasn't a farm boy and he wasn't going to start now. He'd boarded his horses ever since he started his practice after the war.

Facedown in the grass, one bullet in his back, another having taken off part of the back of his skull, he'd been dead for hours. How long was hard to say, since the mercury was plummeting. He was frozen stiff.

He would have lain there all night if Krystal Norton, a barn worker, hadn't come to the back barn to bring up extra feed. She thought she heard a motor running behind the barn, walked outside, and sure enough,

Larry's truck was parked, engine still humming. She didn't notice him until she was halfway to the truck to cut the motor.

"Krystal," Cynthia sympathetically questioned, "what's the routine? What would Larry have done after the hunt breakfast?"

"He would drive to the first barn, unload his horse, put him in his stall, and then drive back here, unhitch his trailer, and drive home in his truck."

"And he'd unloaded his horse?"

"Yes." Krystal wiped her runny nose; she'd been sobbing both from shock and because she loved Dr. Johnson. Everybody did.

"Nobody noticed that he hadn't pulled out?" Cynthia led Krystal a few steps away from the body.

"No. We're all pretty busy. There's people coming and going out of this hack barn all the time." She used the term "hack barn," which meant a boarders' barn.

"You didn't hear a pop?"

"No."

"Sometimes gunfire sounds like a pop. It's not quite like the movies." Coop noticed a pair of headlights swerving into the long driveway and hoped it was the whiz kids, as she called the fingerprint man, the photographer, and the coroner.

"We crank up the radio." Krystal hung her head, then looked at the deputy. "How can something like this happen?"

"I don't know but it's my job to find out. How long have you worked here?"

"Two years."

"Krystal, go on back to the barn. We'll tell you when you can go home but there's no need to stand out here in the cold. This has been awful and I'm sorry."

"Is there some — some deranged weirdo on the loose?"

"No," Cynthia replied with authority. "What there is is a cold-blooded killer who's protecting something, but I don't know what. This isn't a crime of passion. It's not a sex crime or theft. I don't believe you are in danger. If you get worried though, you call me."

"Okay." Krystal wiped her nose again as she walked back into the barn.

The headlights belonged to Mim Sanburne's big-ass Bentley. She slammed the door and sprinted over to Larry Johnson. She knelt down to take him up in her arms.

The sheriff, gently but firmly, grabbed her by the shoulders. "Don't touch him, Mrs. Sanburne. You might destroy evidence."

"Oh God." Mim sank to her knees,

putting her head in her hands. She knelt next to the body, saw the piece of skull missing, the hole in his back.

Rick motioned Coop to come on over fast.

Cynthia's long legs covered the distance between the barn and the parking lot quickly. She knelt down next to Mim. "Miz Sanburne, let me take you back to your car."

"No. No. I want to stay with him until they take him away."

Another pair of headlights snaked down the driveway. Miranda Hogendobber stepped out of her Ford Falcon, which still ran like a top. Behind her in Susan's Audi station wagon came Susan, Harry, and the two cats and dog.

Rick squinted into the light. "Damn."

Coop, voice low, whispered, "They can help." She tilted her head toward Mim.

"Help with what?" Mim cried. "He's gone! The best man God ever put on this earth is gone."

Miranda hurried over, acknowledged Rick, and then knelt down next to Mim. She shuddered when she saw Larry's frozen body. "Mim, I'm going to take you to my place."

"I can't leave him. I left him once, you know."

Miranda did know. Friends since birth, they shared the secrets of their generation, secrets hardly suspected by their children or younger friends who always thought the world began with their arrival.

Taking a deep breath, Miranda put her cheek next to Mim's. "You did what you had to do, Mimsy. And your mother would have killed you."

"I was a coward!" Mim screamed so loud she scared everyone.

Susan and Harry hung back. They wouldn't come forward until Miranda got Mim out of there.

"Make a wide circle so the humans don't notice," Mrs. Murphy told Pewter and Tucker. *"We need to inspect the body before other humans muck it up."*

"I'm not big on dead bodies." Pewter turned up her nose.

"It's not like he's been moldering out here for days," Murphy snapped. *"Follow me."*

The three animals walked in a semicircle, reaching the back of the two-horse trailer. They scrunched under the trailer, wriggling out by the body but careful not to move too quickly.

"Come on, Mim, you can't stay here. This can't get in the papers. I'll take care of you."

Miranda struggled to lift up Mim, who was dead weight even though she was elegant and thin. Coop gently held Mim's right arm, pulling her up along with Miranda's efforts.

"I don't care. I don't care who knows."

"You can make that decision later," Miranda wisely counseled.

Mim glanced over her shoulder at the fallen man. "I loved him. I don't care who knows it. I loved him. He was the only man I ever truly loved, and I threw him aside. For what?"

"Those were different times. We did what we were told." Miranda tugged.

Mim turned to Cynthia. "I don't know if you know what love is but I did. If you do fall in love, don't lose it. Don't lose it because someone tells you he isn't a suitable husband."

"I won't, Mrs. Sanburne." Coop asked Miranda, "What car?"

"Hers. I'll drive. Ask Harry to bring my car home later."

"Yes." Coop helped fold Mim into the passenger seat. Her eyes were glassy. She looked ahead without seeing.

Miranda turned on the ignition, found the seat controls, moved the seat back, then reached over to grasp Mim's left hand. "It's going to be a long, long night, honey. I don't know how to use that thing." She indicated the built-in telephone. "But if you call Jim or Marilyn, I'll tell them we're having a slumber party. Just leave it to me."

Wordlessly, Mim dialed her home number, handing the phone to Miranda.

As they drove back down the drive, they passed the coroner driving in.

Tucker, nose to the ground, sniffed around the body. Rick noticed and shooed her away. The cats climbed into the two-horse trailer tack room.

Although the night was dark they could see well enough. No spent shells glittered on the floor of the trailer. A plastic bucket, red, with a rag and a brush in it sat on the floor of the small tack room. The dirty bridle still hung on the tack hook, a bar of glycerin soap on the floor.

"Guess he was going to clean his bridle and saddle before going home," Pewter speculated.

"I don't smell anything but the horse and Larry. No other human was in here." Mrs. Murphy spoke low. *"Although Tucker is better at this than we are."*

Tucker, chased off again by Rick, hopped into the tack room. *"Nothing."*

"Check in here," Pewter requested.

With diligence and speed, the corgi moved through the trailer. *"Nothing."*

"That's what we thought, too." Mrs. Murphy jumped out of the open tack room door, breaking into a run away from the parking lot and the barns.

"Where's she going?" Tucker's ears stood straight up.

Pewter hesitated for a second. *"We'd better find out."*

Harry didn't notice her pets streaking across the paddock. She and Susan walked over to Larry's body.

"I'll kill whoever did this!" Harry started crying.

"I didn't hear that." Rick sighed, for he, too, admired the older man.

"He brought me into this world." Susan cried, too. "Of all people, why Larry?"

"He got too close." Coop, not one to usually express an opinion unsolicited, buttoned up her coat.

"This is my fault." A wave of sickening guilt washed over the sheriff. "I asked him to keep his eyes and ears open at the hospital and he did. He sure did."

"If only we knew. Boss, he kind of said something at Harry's breakfast today. He'd had a little bit to drink, a little loud. He said —" She thought a moment to try and accurately quote him. " 'Yes,' he said, 'I'll catch up with you tomorrow.' "

"Who heard him?" Rick was glad when Tom Yancy pulled up. He trusted the coroner absolutely.

"Everyone," Harry answered for her. "It wasn't like he had a big secret. He didn't say it that way. He was happy, just — happy and flushed."

"Harry, I want a list of everyone who was at your breakfast this morning," Rick ordered.

"Yes, sir."

"Go sit in the car to get warm and write it out. Susan, help her. A sharp pencil is better than a long memory." He pointed toward Susan's station wagon.

The two women walked back to Susan's vehicle as Tom Yancy bent down over the body. He, too, was upset but he was professional. His old friend Dr. Larry Johnson would have expected nothing less of him.

Mrs. Murphy stopped on a medium-sized hill about a quarter of a mile from the barn.

"What?" Tucker, whose eyes weren't as good in the dark, asked.

"Two places the killer could stand. On top of the barn. On top of this hill — or he could have been flat on his stomach."

"How do you figure that?" Pewter asked.

"Powder burns. No powder burns or

Tucker would have mentioned it. He had to have been killed with a high-powered rifle. With a scope — easy."

"Shooting from here would be easier than climbing on the roof of one of the barns," Pewter suggested. "And the killer could hide his car."

The three animals stared behind them where an old farm road meandered into the woods.

"It would have been simple. Hide the car, walk to here. Wait for your chance. Someone who knew his routine." Tucker appreciated Mrs. Murphy's logic.

"Yeah. And it's hunting season. People carry rifles, handguns. There's nothing unusual about that." Pewter ruffled her fur. She wasn't a kitty who enjoyed the cold.

"We'd better go back before Harry starts worrying." Mrs. Murphy lifted her head to the sky. The stars shone icy bright as they only do in the winter. "Whoever this guy is, he's able to move quickly. He was at the breakfast. He heard Larry. I guarantee that."

"Do you think it's the same person who hit Mother over the head?" Pewter asked.

"Could be." Mrs. Murphy loped down the hill.

"That doesn't give me a warm and fuzzy feeling." Tucker felt a sinking pit in her stomach.

26

The fire crackled in Miranda's fireplace, the Napoleon clock on the mantel ticked in counter rhythm to the flames. Mim reclined on the sofa, an afghan Miranda had knitted decades ago wrapped over her legs. A cup of hot cocoa steamed on the coffee table. Miranda sat in an overstuffed chair across from Mim.

"I hope he didn't suffer."

"I don't think he did." Miranda sipped from her big cup of cocoa. She enjoyed cocoa at night or warm milk and hoped the substance might soothe her friend a little bit.

"Miranda, I've been a fool." Mim's lovely features contracted in pain.

Mim could pass for a woman in her middle forties and often did. Rich, she could afford every possible procedure to ensure that beauty. She'd grown distant and haughty with the years. She was always imperious, even as a child. Giving orders was the breath of life to Mim. She had to be in the center of everything and those who knew and loved her accepted it. Others loathed it. The people jockeying for power in their groups, the developer ready to rip through the countryside, the errant politician, promising one thing and delivering another or nothing, Mim was anathema to them.

Her relationship with her daughter alternated between adversarial and cordial, depending on the day, for Mim was not an effusive mother. Her relationship with her son, married and living in New York City, had transformed from adulation to fury to coldness to gradual acceptance of him. The fury erupted because he married an African-American model and that just wasn't done by people of Mim's generation. But Stafford displayed that independence of spirit exhibited and prized by his mother. Over time and with the help of Mary Minor Haristeen, a friend to Stafford, Mim confronted her own racism and laid it to rest.

Her aunt, Tally Urquhart, flying along in her nineties, said to Mim constantly, "Change is life." Sometimes Mim understood and sometimes she didn't. Usually she thought change involved other people, not herself.

"You haven't been a fool. You've done a lot of good in this life," Miranda truthfully told her.

Mim looked at her directly, light eyes bright. "But have I been good to myself? I want for nothing. I suppose in that way I've been good to myself but in other ways, I've treated myself harshly. I've suppressed things, I've put off others, I've throttled my deepest emotions." She patted a tear away with an embroidered linen handkerchief. "And now he's gone. I can never make it up to him."

The years allowed Miranda to be brutally direct. "Would you? He was in his seventies. Would you?"

Mim cried anew. "Oh, I wish I could say yes. I wish I had done a lot of things. Why didn't you tell me?"

"Tell you? Mim, no one can tell you anything. You tell us."

"But you know me, Miranda. You know how I am."

"It's been a long road, hasn't it? Long and full of surprises." She breathed in deeply. "If it was meant to be, it was meant to be. You and Larry." She gazed into the fire for a moment. "What a long time ago that was. You were beautiful. I envied you, your beauty. Never the money. Just the beauty. And he was handsome in his naval uniform."

"Somewhere along the way we grew old." Mim dropped a bejeweled hand on her breast. "I'm not quite sure how." She sat up. "Miranda, I will find who killed Larry. I will pursue him to the ends of the earth like the harpies pursued Orestes. With God as my witness, I swear it."

"The Lord will extract His vengeance. You go about your business, Mimsy. Whoever did this wouldn't stop at killing you either. They hit Harry on the head."

"Yes, her story sounded fishy."

Miranda shut her eyes. It had popped out of her mouth, and after she'd promised Harry not to tell. "Oh, me. Well, the cat's out of the bag. Harry snooped in the basement of the hospital and someone cracked her on the noggin. It's supposed to be a secret and I, well, you can keep a secret — obviously."

"Funny, isn't it? We live cheek by jowl, everyone knows everyone in Crozet, and yet each of us carries secrets — sometimes to the grave."

"People say we should be honest, we should tell the truth, but they aren't ready to hear it," Miranda sagely noted.

"Mother certainly wasn't," Mim simply said.

"Well, dear, Jim Sanburne was quite a payback."

A slight smile played over Mim's lips.

"Damn near killed her. Aunt Tally understood but then Aunt Tally understands
more than the rest of us. She keeps reminding me, too."

"Why *did* you marry Jim?"

"He was big, handsome, a take-charge
guy. An up-and-comer as Dad would say. Of
course, he came from the lower orders. That
killed Mother but by then I'd learned."

"What?"

"I'd learned to just go ahead. The hell
with everybody. I knew she wasn't going to
cut me out of the will."

"But did you love him?"

A long, long silence transpired; then Mim
leaned back. "I wanted to be in love. I
wanted, well, I wanted the things you want
when you're young. I never loved Jim the
way I loved Larry. He's a different sort of
man. You know, those early years I'd see
Larry driving to work at the hospital,
driving back to his private practice, at the
country club with Bella. At first the sight of
him hurt me because I was wrong. I knew I
was wrong. But he always said he forgave
me. I was young. I wasn't quite twenty, you
know, when I fell in love with Larry. He was
so kind. I think a little part of me died when
he got married but I understood. And —"
She opened her hands as though they might

have contained treasure. "What could I do?"

"Love never dies. The people die but love is eternal. I believe that with all my heart and soul. And I believe God gives us chances to love again."

"If you envy me my looks, I envy you your faith."

"You can't reason your way to faith, Mim. You just open your heart."

"As we both know, I haven't been too good at that. I sometimes wonder if I would have been a more loving woman had I rebelled earlier against my family and married Larry. I think I would have. I closed off. I became guarded. I lost myself along the way. Now I've lost him. You see, even though we weren't lovers anymore, even though we lived separate lives, I knew he was there. I knew he was there." She cried harder now. "Oh, Miranda, I loved him so."

Miranda rose from her chair to sit on the edge of the sofa. She took Mim's hand in both of hers. "Mimsy, he knew you loved him."

"In time, Jim knew, too. I think that's why he redefined the word 'unfaithful' — well, that and the fact that he wearied of me bossing him around. It's rather difficult for a man when the wife has all the money. I think it's difficult in reverse, too, but the culture supports it, plus we've been raised to be simpletons. Really." Mim's modulated voice wavered. "That, too, was one of the things I loved about Larry. He respected my mind."

"It's like that Amish saying, 'We grow too soon old and too late smart.'" Miranda smiled. "But Jim grew out of it or he grew old. I don't know which."

"Breast cancer. Scared both of us. I believe that's when Jim came back to me, realized he loved me and maybe we'd both been foolish. Well, that's all behind me. My cancer hasn't recurred in five years' time nor has Jim's unfaithfulness." She smiled slightly. She sighed. "What did Jim say when you spoke to him? I don't remember. I know you told me but I don't even remember you driving me here."

"He said to call him if you needed him. He was going straight to Twisted Creek Stables." She let go of Mim's hand, reached over to the coffee table, and brought up Mim's cup. "This really will make you feel a little better."

Mim drank, handed the cup back to Miranda. "Thank you."

"I wouldn't want to be in Sheriff Shaw's shoes right now."

"I mistakenly assumed this had nothing to do with us." She made a dismissive gesture with her hand. "When Hank Brevard was found with a slit throat I thought it was brutal, but Hank lacked the fine art of endearing himself to others. That someone would finally kill him didn't seem too far-fetched. One had only to find the reason. But now — everything's different now."

"Yes." Miranda nodded.

"I think of death as an affront. I know you don't. You think you'll join up with Jesus. I hope you're right."

" 'For I have no pleasure in the death of anyone, says the Lord God; so turn and live.' Ezekiel, chapter eighteen, verse thirty-two. Turn and live," Miranda emphasized.

"You've changed, too, Miranda."

"I know. After George's death the church was my comfort. Perhaps I tried too strenuously to comfort others." A smile played on her lips. "It all takes time."

"And Tracy." Mim mentioned Miranda's high-school boyfriend, who had returned to her life but was currently in Hawaii selling his home.

"I feel alive again. And you will, too. We need to think of something to do to honor Larry, something he would have loved."

"I thought I'd establish a scholarship at

the University of Virginia Medical School in his name — for family practice."

"Jim?"

"He'll like the idea. Jim's not mean-spirited."

"I know that." Miranda smiled. "Do you think you could ever talk to him about those years?"

Mim shook her head no. "Why? You know, Miranda, I believe there are some things best left unsaid in a marriage. And I think every woman knows that."

"Mim, I think every man knows that, too."

"I always think they know less than we do, most of them anyway."

"Don't fool yourself." Miranda got up and threw another log on the fire. "More cocoa?"

"No."

"Do you think you can sleep? The spare bedroom is toasty."

"I think I can." Mim threw off the afghan and stood up. "I take you for granted, Miranda. I think I've taken many people for granted. You're a good friend to me. Better than I am to you."

"I don't think like that, Mim. There's only love. You do for the people you love."

"Well." This was hard for Mim. "I love you."

"I love you, too."

The old friends embraced. Miranda led Mim to the spare bedroom.

"Miranda, whoever killed Larry had no conscience. That's the real danger."

27

While most of the residents of Crozet spent the night in shock and tears, Sheriff Shaw worked like a demon, as did Cynthia Cooper.

Once Larry's body was loaded on the ambulance, Shaw and Cooper sped on their way to Sam Mahanes.

They knocked on the door.

Sally opened it. "Sheriff Shaw, Coop, come on in."

They could hear the boys upstairs in the bathroom, splashing and shouting.

"Sorry to disturb you, Sally, but it's important."

"I know that." She smiled genuinely, revealing broad, even teeth. "He's in his shop."

"We'll just go on down." Rick had his hand on the doorknob.

"Fine." She turned back, heading up the stairs, since the water noise was taking on a tidal wave quality.

"Sam," Rick called to him.

The tall director, bent over a workbench,

his hands gripping a tiny soldering iron, finished the small seam, then turned off the implement. "Rick, had to finish this or it'd be ruined."

Rick and Cynthia admired the thin wooden box with inlaid gold and silver.

"Beautiful." Coop admired his work.

"Thank you. Keeps me sane."

Rick scoped the shop. Sam had the best woodworking equipment, soldering equipment, even a small, very expensive lapidary saw. "Back door?"

"Sometimes I slip in to escape the boys. I love 'em but I need to get away. Dennis is at the age where he wants to pick up everything. I lock the doors. I think when they're a little older I'll let them work with me."

"Good idea." Rick smiled. As there was no place to sit down, he suggested going upstairs.

Once settled in the library Rick got to the point. "Sam, Larry Johnson was shot twice and killed at Twisted Creek Stables."

"What?"

"As soon as we finished examining the body and the scene of the murder I drove to you. I wanted to talk to you before the reporters get to you."

"Thank you," Sam said.

"And I wanted to reach you before your

phone started ringing off the hook." Rick noticed how pale Sam's face was, so pale from the shock that his cheeks looked like chalk. "Level with me, Sam. Do you know what's going on at your hospital? Any idea?"

"I don't. Nothing makes sense to me and — this may not be related to Crozet Hospital."

"No, but I have to take into consideration that Larry's murder might be connected to events there."

Cynthia discreetly flipped open her notepad.

"Yes — of course." Sam swallowed hard.

"We've considered black-market traffic in organs."

"Good God, Rick, you can't be serious."

"I have to think of anything worth killing for and money surely seems to be number one on the list."

"There's no selling of kidneys and livers. I'd know about it."

"Sam, maybe not. Hypothetical situation. You've got a young intern on the take. A person dies — someone in fairly good condition — the intern harvests the kidney, packs it up, and sends it off."

"But we have records of pickups and deliveries. Besides, families often request autopsies. If a kidney were missing we'd know.

The family would know. There'd be hell to pay and lawsuits until kingdom come."

"What if the person responsible for the autopsies is in on it, too?"

Sam's brow furrowed, he ran his forefinger across the top of his lip, a nervous gesture. "The more people involved, the more opportunity for mistakes or loose talk."

"If there is a ring, Hank Brevard would have been in a good position to reap the benefits. He could ship organs out of there without anyone knowing."

"The pickup would know."

"The pickup gets a cut. You don't know how many trucks go down to the back door or to loading and unloading. But the back door is my guess there because it's simply a service entrance for the workers. All someone has to do is walk in, go to Hank's office or wherever the organs are stored, and walk out. They could be in a carton, surrounded by a plastic bag filled with dry ice — any number of unobtrusive carriers."

"For one thing, Sheriff, we know who uses operating rooms. I don't think it's possible. Just not possible."

"The patients are dead, Sam. They could cut them and sew them in a broom closet, in a bathtub. All they'd need is water to wash the blood, then zip the body back up in a body bag and off to the morgue — or they could cut them up at the morgue."

"Procedures in the morgue are as strict as in the operating room. Sheriff, I understand you need to consider every angle but this one is just not possible."

"What about fraud? Double-billing — ?"

Sam shrugged. "Over time that, too, would show up. And we have few complaints in that department — other than shock at medical costs, but no, that's out."

"Has anyone been acting peculiar? Anyone attracting your attention?"

"No." Sam held out his hands as if in supplication. "Apart from Hank Brevard's death, everything is routine. The trains run on time. I can't think of anyone behaving in an untoward manner. Bruce is hostile towards me but he's always hostile towards me." Sam smirked slightly.

Rick persisted. "Are there other ways to create illicit profit, if you can stand that phrase? Something specific to hospitals of which Coop and I might be unaware?"

"Drugs. That's obvious. We keep them under lock and key but a clever head nurse or doctor can find ways to pilfer."

"Enough to make a lot of money?"

"We'd notice fairly soon but enough to

make one quick, big hit. It's possible to do that and get away with it."

"Do you think any of your staff is on drugs?" Rick kept his face impassive.

"Yes. It's part of the hospital business. It takes some time to find them out but there's usually a nurse, a doctor, an orderly taking uppers or downers. The doctor creates false dosages for a patient. Again, we'll sniff it out but it takes some time — and I hasten to add it's part of our culture."

"How often has this happened at the hospital?"

Sam hesitated. "I think I ought to have the hospital lawyer here for this conversation."

"For Christ's sake, Sam, Larry Johnson is dead and you're worried about hospital liability! I'm not going to the press with this but I've got to know and if you don't tell me I'll dig it out and in the process uproot other things as well. It will get everyone in an uproar. How often has this happened?"

"Last year we found two people stealing Darvocet, codeine-based pills, Quaaludes. We fired them. End of story." He took a deep breath. "As I said, drug abuse is as American as apple pie."

"Once fired from a hospital that person will never work in a hospital again unless he or she goes to Honduras — am I right?"

"And they might not even get work in Central America. They'd have to go where people were so desperate they didn't care about their records from anywhere else. It definitely would be a career killer."

"All those years of medical school, all those bills — for nothing." Rick folded his hands together, leaning forward. "Other ways to steal or make money?"

"Oh, patient jewelry, wallets, and credit cards."

"Equipment?"

Sam exhaled. "No. Who would they sell it to? Also, we'd notice it immediately."

"Was Hank Brevard a good plant manager?"

"Yes. We discussed that before. He was conscientious. Apart from his obvious personality flaw that he was resistant to new technology. He wanted to do everything the way it always had been done."

"Remind me, had he ever been disciplined during his career at Crozet Hospital?" Rick glanced over at Coop.

"No. Well." Sam opened his hands, palms upward. "I'd routinely meet with him and request he, uh, lighten up. But no, Hank was no trouble."

"Ever hear about affairs?"

"Hank?" Sam's eyebrows shot upward. "No."

"Gambling?"

"No. Sheriff, we've been over this."

"You're right. Was Larry Johnson off the rails at any time?"

"I beg your pardon?"

"Did people feel he was too old to practice? Was he carried for old times' sake?"

"No. Quite the contrary. He was a G.P., of course." Sam abbreviated General Practitioner. "So he wasn't a glamour boy but he was a good, solid doctor and always open to new procedures, medical advances. He is, I mean was, a remarkable human being."

"Could he have been stealing drugs?"

"Absolutely not." Sam's voice raised. "Never."

"Sam, I have to ask these questions."

"There is no blemish on that man's record."

"Then I must respectfully suggest he got too close to whoever is blemished."

"The murder of Larry Johnson may not be related to Crozet Hospital. You're jumping to conclusions."

"Perhaps but you see, Sam, he was my man on the inside." The color drained from Sam's face as Rick continued, "I believe the murders are related and I will prove it."

"You should have told me."

"What if you're in on it?" Rick said bluntly.

"Thank you for the vote of confidence." Sam's face now turned red, and he fought back his anger.

"Or Jordan Ivanic. He's in a position to pull strings — excuse the worn phrase."

"Jordan." Sam's lips pursed together. "No. He's a man devoid of all imagination. He does everything by the book."

"You don't like him?"

"Oh, he's one of those men who can't think on his own. He has to find a precedent, a procedure, but he's honest. We aren't the best team personality-wise but Jordan isn't a criminal."

"He has three speeding tickets in two years' time. Had to take a driver's course mandated by the state."

"That doesn't make him a criminal." Sam's patience was wearing thin.

"Did you know about the tickets?"

"No. Sheriff, why would I know? You're grasping at straws. You assume my hospital, and I do think of it as my hospital, is a hotbed of crime. You connect two murders which while heinous may not be connected. As for Larry Johnson being your spy, that still doesn't prove his murder's connected to

the hospital. He may have had a secret life."
Sam's eyes blazed.

"I see." Rick stared at his shoes for a moment, then looked up at Sam. "What about the hospital killing people through negligence?"

"I resent that!"

"It happens." Rick raised his voice. "It happens every day all over America. It has to have happened at your hospital, too."

"I won't discuss this without a lawyer." Sam's jaw hardened.

"Well, you just do that, Sam. You'd better hire a public-relations firm, too, because I won't rest until I find out everything, Sam, everything and that means just who the hell was killed at your hospital because some bozo forgot to read their chart, gave the wrong medicine, or the anesthesiologist screwed up. Shit happens even in Crozet Hospital!" Rick stood up, his face darkening. Coop stood up, too. "And I'll have your ass for interfering with a law-enforcement officer in the prosecution of his duties!"

Rick stormed out, leaving an angry Sam sitting in the library with his mouth hanging wide open.

Coop, wisely, slipped behind the wheel of the squad car before Rick could do it. She had no desire to peel out of the Mahanes' driveway, then careen down the road at eighty miles an hour. Rick drove fast anyway; angry, he flew.

He slammed the passenger door.

"Where to?"

"Goddamned Jordan Ivanic, that's where. Maybe that smart bastard will tell us something."

She headed toward the hospital, saying nothing because she knew the boss. The misery over Larry's death swamped him and this was his way of showing it. Then again, he had a good reason to be livid. Someone was killing people and making him look like a jerk.

"Boss, this is a tough case. Go easy on yourself."

"Shut up."

"Right."

"I'll nail Sam Mahanes. I will fry him. I will slice and dice him. You know patients have died from stupidity. It happens!"

"Yes, but Sam's job is to protect the reputation of the hospital. Covering up one or two mistakes is one thing, covering up a rash of them is something else — and Larry would have known, boss. Doctors may be able to keep secrets from patients and patient families but not from one another, not for long, anyway."

"Larry would have known." Rick lit a cigarette. "Coop, I'm stuck. Everywhere I turn there's a wall." He slammed his fist into the dash. "I know this is about the hospital. I know it!"

"Any one of our ideas could provoke someone to kill."

"You know what really worries me?" He turned his face to her. "What if it's something else? What if it's something we can't imagine?"

No sooner had Rick Shaw and Cynthia Cooper pulled out of the driveway than Sam Mahanes made a beeline to his shop, grabbed his cell phone, and dialed Tussie Logan.

"Hello."

"Tussie."

"Oh, hello." Her voice softened.

"I'm glad you're home. Have you heard the terrible news about Larry Johnson?"

"No."

"He was found shot at Twisted Creek Stables."

"Larry Johnson." She couldn't believe it.

"Listen, Tussie, Sheriff Shaw and that tall deputy of his are going to be all over the hospital. We're going to have to cool it for a while."

A long pause followed. "I understand."

28

The streets, alleys, and byways leading to the Lutheran Church were parked solid. The funeral service slated to start at eleven a.m. brought out all of Crozet, much of Albemarle County, plus the friends and family flying in from places Virginians often forgot, like Oklahoma.

At quarter to eleven some people were frantically trying to find places to park. Sheriff Shaw figured this would happen. He instructed the two officer escorts for the funeral cortege to ignore double-parking and parking in a No Parking zone. He did not waive the rules on parking by a fire hydrant.

Businesses opened their parking lots to everyone. The crush of people was so great that over two hundred had to file into the offices and hallways of the church, the church itself being full. At eleven there were still over seventy-five people standing outside, and the day turned crisp, clear, and cold.

The Reverend Herbert C. Jones, anticipating this, hung up speakers outside as well as in the hallways. Yesterday had been Ash Wednesday, so he wore his Lenten vestments.

Herb had known Larry all his life. He pondered over his eulogy, pondered over the life of a good man being snuffed out so violently. As a man of God he accepted the will of God but as a friend, a human of great feeling, he couldn't help but question.

The upper-management staff of Crozet Hospital filled the left-hand, front side of the church. Behind Sam Mahanes, Jordan Ivanic, Dr. Bruce Buxton, and others were those support people who worked with Larry over the years, Tussie Logan, other nurses, secretaries, people who had learned to love him because he valued them. Larry hadn't had an ounce of snobbery in his soul.

On the right-hand side of the church, at the front, sat distant relatives, nephews and nieces and their children. Larry's brother, a lawyer who had moved to Norman, Oklahoma, after World War II, was there. Handsome people, the Johnsons shared many of Larry's qualities: down-to-earth, respectful, hardworking. One great-nephew in particular looked much like Larry himself at twenty-five.

When Mim Sanburne saw this young man she burst into tears. Both Jim and Little

Mim put their arms around her, but this reminder in the flesh, this genetic recall, tore at her heart. Larry was irretrievably gone and with him, Mim's youth and passion.

Harry, Susan, and Miranda sat together near the front on the right-hand side of the church. All three women wore hats, as was proper. In Harry's case the hat also served to cover the stitches.

The walnut casket, closed, sat at the nave, down below the altar. The scent of the massed floral arrangements overpowered those in the front. For those in the rear the sweet odors brought hopes of the not-too-distant spring, an exquisite season in the Blue Ridge Mountains.

The murmur of voices hushed when Herb opened the door behind the lectern. Two acolytes were already seated, one by the lectern, the other by the pulpit. When Herb entered, the congregation stood. He walked to the center, held his hands up, and the congregation was seated.

As the service for the dead progressed, those who knew the good reverend felt the force of his deep voice, felt the genuine emotion. By the time he read his sermon, liberally sprinkled with pawprints from his cats, people knew this was the greatest sermon Herb had ever given.

He eschewed the usual easy words about the deceased being with the angels. He spoke of a life well lived, of a life spent in service to others, of a life devoted to easing pain, to healing, to friendship. He spoke of foxhunting and fly-fishing, Larry's favorite pastimes. He recalled his record in the Navy, his youthful practice, his rapport with people. He argued with God, Herb did.

"Lord, why did you take Thy faithful servant when we have such need of him here on earth?" He read Psalm 102. " 'Hear my prayer, O Lord; let my cry come to Thee! Do not hide thy face from me in the day of my distress! Incline thy ear to me; answer me speedily in the day when I call! For my days pass away like smoke and my bones burn like a furnace. My heart is smitten like grass, and withered; I forget to eat my bread.' "

As Herb continued with the psalm, Mrs. Hogendobber quietly recited it with him, her memory of the Good Book being a source of comfort to her and astonishment to others.

At the end of the service, Herb asked that people join hands and repeat the prayers with him. "Larry spent his life bringing people together. Whoever is on your right, whoever is on your left, remember that Dr.

Larry Johnson has brought you together even in death."

After the service the church doors opened. People slowly left the church, almost unwilling to go because the emotions holding them there were so powerful.

Mim, in control now, walked to the car. From here the group would wind its way to the cemetery just southwest of town.

Harry reached her truck, stepped on the running board to get in, and noticed a dead chicken, its neck broken, in the bed of the truck.

She reached over, picking it up. There was nothing special about it except that it was tossed deliberately in the back of her truck.

She had an old canvas tarp which she pulled over the bird. It wouldn't do to drive to the entombment with feathers flying.

She knew in her bones this was a cheap warning.

29

Mrs. Murphy's tail stuck out from under the canvas in the back of the truck.

"Throw it down to me," Tucker's bright eyes implored her kitty friend.

"No way, José." The tiger cat sank her fangs in one red leg, backing out, pulling the heavy chicken with her.

Pewter, also sitting in the bed of the truck, called out, *"We aren't stupid, Tucker."*

"I just want to sniff it. I can tell you how long it's been dead."

"Liar." Murphy inspected the corpse. *"Been dead since this morning."*

"It's cold. Maybe it's freezing up," Tucker called from the ground.

"Maybe." Murphy hopped over the side of the truck, softly landing on the ground.

Pewter chose the less athletic route. She carefully eased herself over the closed tailgate, her hind paws touching the bumper. Then she dropped down on her front paws and jumped off to the ground.

The animals heard the story of the funeral

and the dead chicken when Harry and Miranda returned to work. The post office front door was always unlocked but the back door and the counter divider could be locked. There was a pulldown door, like a garage door, which pulled to the counter divider, locking from the back side. Because stamps were valuable, Miranda and Harry had wrapped up everything tight before leaving for the funeral. It wasn't that anyone had ever stolen anything from the post office other than rubber bands and pencils but the murders inspired them to caution. Then, too, they had put the cats and dog in the locked portion along with a big bowl of water and crunchies on the small table out of Tucker's reach. As there was an animal door in the back of the post office, Harry had locked that, too.

Usually when humans returned, the animals bolted outside, but they wanted to hear the events. Once Harry told about the chicken they bolted and now they sat, fur ruffled against the cold with the northwest wind kicking up. Harry planned on taking the chicken home to feed the fox living on her land.

"I say we go to the hospital." Tucker was resolute. *"It's a fifteen-minute jog."* Tucker cut time off the trip to make it

more attractive.

"We'll last five minutes. You know how fussy humans are at hospitals. Insulting, really. We're cleaner than they are. All those humans with diseases." Pewter shuddered in distaste.

"We won't go in the front door." Tucker knew Pewter was trying to get out of the walk in the cold to the hospital.

"Oh." The gray cat ducked underneath the truck to escape the wind. It was a good idea but the wind whipped underneath the truck as well as swirling around it.

"We go to the back door."

"Tucker, the back door is closed." Pewter didn't like this idea one bit.

"The loading dock isn't," Murphy thought out loud. *"We could slip in there and work our way to the basement."*

"What if we get locked in? We could starve in there."

"Pewter." Mrs. Murphy maliciously smiled. *"You could eat cast-off body parts. How about a fresh liver?"*

"I hate you," Pewter spit.

"Well, fine, you big weenie. You stay here and we'll go." Tucker wanted to get over there.

"Oh sure, and hear from you two for the next eleven years about what a fat chicken

I am." She thought about the chicken a moment, then continued, *"Besides, you don't know everything. I see things you miss."*

"Then shut up and come on. Time's a-wasting. Harry will be out of here at five and it's already one-thirty." Mrs. Murphy looked down both sides of the road, then scampered across heading north toward the hospital, the wind in her face.

The three animals stayed off the road, dashing through lawns, hopping creeks, and eluding the occasional house dog upset because three animals crossed his or her lawn.

They reached the hospital by two-ten. To test their luck they hurried to the back door first. The doorknob was reachable but the cats couldn't turn it.

By now they were cold so they ran around the side of the building to the loading dock, one level up from the back door. It was child's play to elude the humans working the dock. There was only one truck and one unloader. Neither noticed the animals. Once inside the building, grateful for the warmth, the three headed away from the dock.

Murphy led them to an elevator pool.

"We can't take that," Tucker said.

"I know but stairwells are usually near elevator pools so start looking, genius."

Her voice was sarcastic.

Sure enough, the stairwell was tucked in the corner, the door unlocked. Tucker, a strong dog for her size, pushed it open and the animals sped downstairs, opening the unlocked door with a red BASEMENT neatly painted across it.

They had landed on the east side of the building, site of the elevator bank.

"Come on, let's get out of here before someone steps off that thing." Murphy turned left, not out of any sense of where she was going but just to escape possible detection. They raced past storage rooms, finally arriving at the boiler room, the hub of all corridors.

"Oh." Pewter saw the blood on the wall; most of it had been washed off, but enough had stained into the old stone wall that she could see it.

The three sat down for a moment, considering where Hank Brevard's body had been crumpled.

"This is where Mom got hit on the head. In this room." Tucker put her nose to the ground but all she could smell was oil from the furnace.

"She should never have come in here by herself," Pewter complained. *"She has no fear and that isn't always a good thing."*

"Boy, you'd think the hospital could af-ford better lights." The dog noted the low wattage.

"That's why we're here." Mrs. Murphy systematically checked out each corner of the room. *"Let's go outside."*

"Which door?" Tucker asked.

"The one in the opposite direction. We came in from the east. Let's go west."

"I hope you remember because it all looks the same to me." The basement gave Pewter the creeps.

"Wimp."

"I'm not a wimp." Pewter smacked Murphy, who smacked her back.

"Girls," Tucker growled.

The cats stopped following the dog as she pushed open the door, which wasn't latched. A hallway led to the end of the building. The light from the small square in the door was brighter than the lights over-head.

"Is that the door we first tried?" Pewter asked.

"Yes. It's the only door downstairs on the west side."

They slowly walked down the hall, the storage rooms appearing as innocuous to them as they had to the humans. Satisfying themselves that nothing was amiss in that hall, they returned to the boiler room and went down the southerly corridor, the one which contained the incinerator.

Tucker sniffed when they entered the room. *"This incinerator could destroy a multitude of sins."*

"And does, I'm sure," Pewter said.

"Nothing in here." Tucker had thoroughly sniffed everything.

They returned to the corridor, poking their heads in rooms. Hearing voices, they ducked into a room that had empty cartons neatly stacked against the wall.

Bobby Minifee and Booty Weyman walked by. Bobby had been promoted to Hank's job and Booty had moved up to day schedule. Engrossed in conversation, they didn't even glance into the storage room.

Tucker put her nose to the ground once the men passed. The cats heard them turn toward the boiler room.

"Someone's been here recently." Tucker moved along the cartons.

"That doesn't mean anything. People have probably been in each of these rooms for one thing or another." Pewter was getting peckish.

Tucker paid no attention to her. Murphy knew her canine friend well enough to put her own nose to the ground. She could smell

262

shoes, one with leather soles, one with rubber.

"Hands." Tucker stopped over a spot on the old slate floor. *"I can smell the oil on their hands. They've been here today."*

"Hands on the floor?" Pewter's gray eyebrows shot upward, for the dog was sniffing where the wall met the floor.

"Yes." Tucker kept sniffing. *"Here, just above the floor."*

"Pewter, look for a handle or something," Murphy ordered her.

"In the wall?"

"Yes, you dimwit!"

"I'm not a dimwit." Pewter declined to further the argument because she, too, was intrigued.

The animals sniffed the walls. Murphy, claws out, tapped and patted each stone, part of the original foundation.

"Hey." Pewter stopped. *"Do that again."*

The two cats strained to hear. Murphy rapped her claws harder this time. A faint hollow sound rewarded her efforts.

"Flat down," Tucker whispered as Bobby and Booty returned, but once again the two men didn't look toward the room full of boxes.

When they passed, the dog came over to the cats. She sniffed the wall as high up as

263

she reached. *"Yes, here. Human hands."*

"Let's push it," Murphy said and the three leaned against the square stone.

A smooth, soft sliding sound rewarded their efforts, then a soft clink surprised them. The floor opened up. One big slate stone slid under another one, revealing a ladder. It was dark as pitch down there.

"Tucker, you stay here. Pewter, you with me?" Murphy climbed down the ladder.

Wordlessly, Pewter followed. Once down there their eyes adjusted.

"It's a bunch of machines." Pewter was puzzled.

"Yeah, those drip things. They don't look broken up."

"Get out of there. Someone's coming!" Tucker yelled.

The two cats shot up the ladder, the three animals leaned against the stone in the wall, and the slate rolled back into place.

Breathlessly they listened as the steps came closer.

"Behind this carton." They crouched behind a tumbled-down carton as Jordan Ivanic walked into the room and threw a switch. He plucked a carton off the top of the neat pile, turned, hit the switch off, and left.

"Let's get out of here before we're trapped," Pewter whispered.

"You know, I think you're right," Mrs. Murphy agreed.

They hurried down the corridor, pushed open the stairwell door, ran back up one flight of stairs, and dashed out onto the loading dock. They jumped off and ran the whole way back to the post office, bursting through the animals' door.

"Where have you been?" Harry noted the time at four-thirty.

"You'll never guess what we found," Pewter breathlessly told her.

"She won't get it." Tucker sat down.

"It's just as well. The last thing we want is Harry back in that hospital." Murphy wondered what to do next.

30

"What is this?" Mim pushed a letter across the counter.

Mrs. Murphy, with quick reflexes, smacked her paw down on the 8" x 11" white sheet of paper before it skidded off onto the floor. *"Got it."*

Pewter, also on the counter, peered down at the typewritten page. She read aloud,

"Meet me. I will be the next victim. I need your help to escape. Why you? You are the only person rich enough not to be corrupted. Put a notice for a lost dog named Bristol on the post office bulletin board if you will help me. I will get back to you with when and where."

Harry slid the paper from underneath the tiger's paw.

"Well?" Miranda walked over to read over her shoulder.

"Well, this is a crackpot of the first water."

Miranda pushed her glasses back up on her head. "I'm calling the sheriff." She flipped up the divider.

"Wait. Let's talk about this for a minute," Harry said.

"This could be the killer playing some kind of weird game." Mim headed for the phone.

"Sit down, Mim. You've had a shock." Miranda propelled her to the table.

"Shock? Seismic." The thin, beautifully dressed woman sank into the wooden kitchen chair at the back table.

"This letter is from someone who knows our community, knows it well." Miranda searched her mind for some explanation but could come up with nothing.

Harry noticed the time, eight-thirty in the morning. She had a habit of checking clocks when she'd walk or drive by, then she'd check her wristwatch, her father's old watch. Ran like a top. Mim usually preceded everyone else into the post office in the morning. Like Harry and Miranda she was an early riser and early risers find each other just as night owls do. She tiptoed around Mim, knowing how hard Larry's death had hit her.

"Trap." Tucker found the letter irritating.

"Possibly." Mrs. Murphy twitched the fur along her spine.

"Flea?" Pewter innocently asked.

268

"In February?" Mrs. Murphy shot her a dirty look.

"We spend much of our time indoors. They could be laying eggs in the carpet, the eggs hatch, and you know the rest of the story."

"You're getting some kind of thrill out of this. Besides, if I had fleas you'd have them, too." The tiger swatted at the gray cat.

"Not me." Pewter smiled, revealing her white fangs. *"I'm allergic to fleas."*

"Doesn't mean you don't get them, Pewter, it means once you do get them you also get scabs all over." Tucker giggled. *"Then Mother has to wash and powder you and it's a big mess."*

"She hides the powder until she's grabbed you." Mrs. Murphy relished Pewter's discomfort at bath time. *"First the sink, a little warm water, baby shampoo, lots of lather. My what a pretty cat you are in soapsuds. Then a rinsing. A second soaping. More rinsing. A dip with medicated junk. Drying with a towel. You look like a rock star with your spiky do. Pewter, the Queen of Hip-Hop."*

"I don't listen to hip-hop." The rotund gray kitty sniffed.

"You hip-hop. You shake one hind leg, then the other. Real disco." Murphy howled with laughter.

"You know." Tucker, on the floor, paced as the humans discussed the letter. *"What if this plea is like Mom with the flea powder? What's hidden?"*

Murphy leapt down to sit next to her friend. *"But we know what's hidden."*

Pewter put her front paws on the wood, then slowly slid down. *"Not exactly, Murphy. We know those machines, those IVAC units are under the basement floor but maybe that was the only place to store them. So we don't really know what's hidden and we don't know what this letter is hiding."*

"Why Mim? Why not Sheriff Shaw?" Tucker frowned, confused.

"Because the writer is tainted somehow. The sheriff would pose a danger. Mim's powerful but not the law." Mrs. Murphy leaned into Tucker. She often sat tight with the dog or slept with her, her head curled up next to Tucker's head.

"Put up the notice. Put one up in the supermarket, too." Harry put her hands together, making a steeple with her forefingers. "Everyone will see it. That we know. Then do like the letter requests: wait for directions."

"Without calling Sheriff Shaw!" Mim was incredulous.

"Well — don't you think he'll want to

keep you under watch? It would be clumsy. The letter writer would notice."

"Are you suggesting I be bait?" Mim slapped her hand on the table.

"No."

"What are you suggesting, Harry?" Miranda folded her arms across her chest.

"That we wait for directions."

"We? You don't know when and where I might receive these directions. I could be hustled into a car and no one would know."

"She's right," Miranda agreed.

"Yeah." Harry sighed. "Instant meeting. Just add danger."

"My point exactly. Harry, let the professionals deal with this." Mim got up and dialed Sheriff Shaw.

"I still think we should try the missing-dog notice by ourselves," Harry said to Miranda, who shook her head no as Mim read the letter over the phone to Rick Shaw.

"Now that Larry Johnson's been killed, Mother won't rest. She wants to find the killer probably worse than Rick Shaw and Coop." Murphy worried. *"I don't know if we can keep her away from the hospital."*

"Well, I know one thing," Tucker solemnly declared. *"We'd better stick with her."*

"And I think what's under the floor is

dangerous. Pewter, those IVAC units aren't down there for lack of space. I predict if someone stumbles onto that room there will be another dead human." Mrs. Murphy put her paw on the postage scale.

31

For Sheriff Rick Shaw and Deputy Cynthia Cooper it was the week from hell. The ballistics report ascertained that Larry Johnson was killed by a shell from a twenty-gauge shotgun.

While Rick spent the week questioning everyone who had been at the hunt meet, the barns, on Larry's patient list, Coop dipped into the state computer file on twenty-gauge shotguns.

There were twenty-six registered firearms of that description in Albemarle County, ranging from a handmade Italian model costing $252,000, owned by Sir H. Vane-Tempest, a very wealthy Englishman who had moved to Crozet five years ago, to the more common $2,789 version, a good working shotgun made by Sturm & Ruger.

Coop patiently called on each shotgun owner. No one reported a firearm stolen. She asked each owner if they would allow the shotgun to be checked to see if it had been fired recently. Everyone agreed. Everyone wrote down the last time they had used their shotgun. Even Vane-Tempest, a pompous man whom she intensely disliked, cooperated.

Of the twenty-six firearms, four had been used recently and each owner readily volunteered when and where they had used their shotgun. All four belonged to the Kettle and Drum Gun Club. None of the four had any connection that Coop could discover to anyone at the hospital.

Being in law enforcement, she expected people to lie to her. She knew in time she might find a connection but she also knew the chances were slim.

The weapon that killed Larry was most likely unregistered. It could have been bought years ago, before registration became the norm in America. It could have been stolen from another state. Could have, should have, would have — it was driving Coop crazy.

Rick and Coop studied patient logs, pored over maintenance records kept by Hank Brevard. They even walked through the delivery of a human kidney right up to the operating room.

The hospital routine was becoming familiar to them. The various doctors, nurses, orderlies, and receptionists were fixed in their minds. The one unit that upset both of them was Tussie Logan's. The sight of those terminally ill children brought them close to tears.

When Rick came back into the office he found Coop bent over the blueprints of the hospital.

"So?" He grunted as he removed his heavy jacket, quick to pluck the cigarette pack from the pocket. He offered her one, which she gratefully took. He lit hers, then he lit his. They both inhaled deeply, then relaxed imperceptibly.

Nicotine's faults were publicized and criticized but the drug's power to soothe temporarily never abated.

She pointed to the center of the blueprint with the glowing tip of the cigarette. "There."

He put his elbows on the table to look closely. "There what? You're back at the boiler room."

"This old part of the building. Eighteen thirty-one, this old square right here. The boiler room and the one hallway off of the boiler room. The rest was added in 1929. And it's been renovated three times since then. Right?"

"Right." He put his weight on his elbows as the pressure eased off his lower back, which felt stiff in the cold.

"The old part was originally built as a granary. Heavy stone flooring, heavy stone walls, whole tree-trunk beams. The original structure will last centuries. I was thinking about that. Now what I've been able to piece together about the history here" — she paused, took another drag — "thanks to Herb Jones's help, he's quite the history buff, well, anyway, he says the rumors always were that the granary was a way station on the Underground Railroad. No one was ever able to prove it but the owners, the Craycrofts, opposed slavery. Peaceably, but opposed, nonetheless. But as Herb says, no one ever proved a thing and the Craycrofts, despite their opposition to slavery, fought for the Confederacy."

"Yeah, well, you tend to do that when people invade your backyard." Rick straightened up.

"The Craycrofts lost everything, like everyone else around here. They sold the granary in 1877 to the Yancys. Herb also said that the granary was used as a makeshift hospital during the war, but then so was every other building in the county."

"Yeah, they shipped in the wounded by rail from Manassas, Richmond, Fredericksburg. God, it must have been awful. Did you know that the War Between the States was the first where the railroad was used?"

"Yes, I did." She pointed again to the boiler room. "If this was a way station on the Underground Railroad then there are probably hidden rooms. I doubt there'd be anything like that in the new part."

"When did the granary cease being a granary?" Rick sat down, realizing he was more tired than he thought.

"Nineteen hundred and eleven. The Krakenbills bought it. Kept it in good repair and used it for hay storage. They were the ones who sold it to Crozet United, Incorporated, the parent company for the hospital. There are Krakenbills in Louisa County. I contacted Roger, the eldest. He said he remembered his great-uncle mentioning the granary. He doesn't remember much else but he, too, had heard stories about the Underground Railroad."

"What you're getting at is that maybe the location of Hank's murder is more important than we thought."

"I don't know. Boss, maybe I'm grasping at straws, but it looked like a hurry-up job."

"Yeah." He exhaled heavily, a spiral of gray-blue smoke swirling upward.

"I keep coming back to how Hank was killed and where he was killed. If this were a revenge killing, the murderer, unless he is stone-stupid, would pick a better place. The risks of killing Hank at work are pretty high — for an outsider. For an insider, knowing the routine and the physical layout of the hospital, killing Hank could be a matter of opportunity as well as planning. The risk diminishes. The way he was killed strongly suggests knowledge of the human body, height, and physical power. Whoever killed him had to hold him long enough to slit his throat from left to right. Hank wasn't a weak man."

"I'll agree with you except on the point about knowledge of the human body. Most of us could slit a throat if we had to. It doesn't take a surgeon."

"But it was so neat, a clean, one-sweep wound."

"I could do that."

"I don't know if I could."

"If your victim were weaker than you or you had him helpless in some way, sure, you could make a neat cut. The trick to slitting a throat is speed and force. If you hesitate or stick the knife straight in instead of starting from the side, you botch it. I've seen the botched jobs."

She tightened her lips. "Yeah, me, too. But boss, the weapon was perfect, sharp."

"A layman could grind a knife to perfection, but I grant you this looks like an inside job, someone picked up a big scalpel or whatever and s-s-s-t. You know, it would be easy to throw away the instrument or return it to where surgical instruments are cleaned. We've been through that."

"Okay. We're on the same wave here." She held out her hands as if on a surfboard, which made him laugh, then cough because he'd inhaled too much. She slapped him on the back, then continued. "Big foxhunt at Harry's farm. Everyone's in a great mood. They view the fox. The fox gets away per usual. People are lined up for the breakfast like a movie premiere. Everyone and her brother is there. You can hardly move it's so packed. The food is great. Larry drinks a little, gets a little loud, and says he'll meet up with me. There couldn't be too many reasons for Larry to meet with me. I'm not a patient. It's not a big stretch to think he had something professional to tell me, my profession, that is. But it's not like it's a big deal. He didn't make it a big deal. Over fifteen or twenty people near the table had to have heard him. But again, it didn't seem like a big deal. He didn't use a dark tone of voice, no hints at evil deeds. However, he knew procedures cold. He knew the people. He probably knew more than even he knew he knew. What I'm saying is that he's known his stuff for so long he forgot how much he did know. An observation from him was worth a hell of a lot more than an observation, say, from Bruce Buxton. See?"

"Kind of."

"I don't think Larry knew what was wrong at Crozet Hospital. Not yet anyway but our killer feared him, feared he'd put two and two together quickly once he sobered up. Whatever Larry did observe, our killer made certain I wouldn't know."

Rick's eyes opened wider. "Our perp was in the room, or if he or she has an accomplice they could have called to warn about Larry spilling the beans." He inhaled. "We know from ballistics and the entry point of the bullet that the killer was flat on the hill about a quarter of a mile from the barn. Larry never knew what hit him. The killer crawls back off the hill in case anyone hears the shots. He was damned lucky those kids keep the radio on full blast but maybe he knew that. Maybe he rides. Or he's a hunt follower. He knew where Larry stabled his horse."

Coop added her thoughts. "He crawls back down the hill, gets in his car or truck, whatever, and pulls away as the sun sets. I checked for tracks. Too many of them. Nothing definitive. I had casts taken just in case."

"Good work." He crossed his arms over his chest, bit his lower lip for a moment.

"There's one last thing."

"What?"

"The attack on Harry."

His face fell. He took a last drag, then stubbed out the cigarette, the odor of smoke and tar wafting up from the ashtray. "Damn."

"In the boiler room."

He looked back at the blueprints. "Damn!"

32

"Box of rocks." Fair touched his forehead with his right forefinger.

"Don't start with me," Harry warned as she walked down the steps to the lower parking lot.

On the tarmac the jet warmed its engine, the whine piercing the still February air. Fair had just returned from his conference.

"You didn't even call to tell me."

"Accident." Harry felt like picking a fight.

"I'm so glad I have a girlfriend with a bald spot." He indicated the small patch on her head with the stitches.

"Yeah, be glad you have a girlfriend. Of course, BoomBoom could always fill in if I'm gone."

"You know, Harry, you find the belt and then hit below it."

"Hey, isn't that where you guys live?"

"Thanks a lot, pardner." He reached her truck, swung his bag over the side.

It dropped into the bed with a thud. He

put his kit bag on the floor of the passenger side.

They said nothing until Harry paid the parking fee, turned right, and drove down to the Y in the road. "I think I'll go the back way. Through Earlysville."

"I should have known when you didn't call me that you'd gotten in trouble. But 'No,' I told myself, 'she knows how intense these conferences are and she's busy, too.' "

"You could have called me." Harry pouted slightly.

"I wish I had. Not that you would have told me."

"Who did?"

"I've known you since grade school, Sheezits." He called her by her childhood nickname. "You don't have farm accidents."

"I broke my collarbone in seventh grade."

"Roller skating."

"Yeah." She scanned her past for a salvaging incident.

"You stuck your nose where it doesn't belong."

"Did not."

"Miranda told me."

"I knew it!" Harry's face reddened. "I'll never tell her anything again."

Naturally, she would.

A few miles west, the panorama of the

Blue Ridge opened before them, deep blue against a grainy, gray sky, a true February sky.

Fair broke the silence. "You could have been killed."

"But I wasn't." She bit her lower lip. "You know, I drove by the hospital and I kind of thought, 'Well, I'll go see where Hank met his maker.' And I walked in the back door. I mean I just didn't think I'd be a threat or whatever I was."

"And now Larry. Oh boy, that's hard to believe. It hasn't really sunk in yet. I think it will when I go by his house or to the next hunt and he's not there."

"Mim's taking it pretty hard. Quietly, obviously."

He stared out at the rolling hills punctuated with barns and houses. "Funny how love persists no matter what."

"Yes."

He looked at her. "Promise me you won't do anything like that again."

"Be specific," she hedged.

"You won't go back into the hospital. You won't snoop around."

"Oh — all right." This was said with no conviction whatsoever.

"Harry."

"Okay, okay, I won't go alone. How's that

for a compromise?"

"Not a very good one. You are the most curious thing."

"Runs in the family."

"And that reminds me, if you don't think about reproducing soon the line stops with you." He spoke like a vet whose specialty was breeding. "You've got that good Hepworth and Minor blood, Harry. Time."

"I see. Who's the stud?"

"I'd thought that would be obvious."

33

"You and I will never see eye to eye." Bruce Buxton slammed the door to Sam Mahanes's office.

Sam, on his feet, hurried to the door, yanking it open. "Because you don't see the whole picture. You only see your part, dammit."

Bruce kept walking but Sam's secretary buried her head in her work.

"Ruth, how do you stand that asshole?" Bruce said as he walked by, ignored the elevator, and opened the door to the stairwell. He needed the steps to cool down.

Sam stopped at Ruth's desk. "He thinks I should open all the books, everything, to Sheriff Shaw. Says forget the lawyers. All they do is make everything worse. This was interspersed with complaints about everything but the weather."

"Perhaps he doesn't hold you responsible for that," Ruth dryly replied.

"Huh? Oh." Sam half smiled, then darkened. "Ruth, you're on the pipeline. What are people saying?"

"About what?"

"For starters, about Hank Brevard. Then Larry."

"Well." She put down her pencil, neatly, parallel to her computer keyboard. "At first no one knew what to make of Hank's murder. He wasn't popular and, well —" She paused, collecting her thoughts. "Larry's killing set them off. Now people think the two are connected."

"Are they criticizing me?"

"Uh — some do, most don't."

"I don't know what more I can do." His voice dropped low. "I'm not hiding anything but I can't just open our books to Rick Shaw. I will allow him to study anything and everything with our lawyers *present*."

"The Board of Directors will find some comfort in that decision, Sam." Her tone of voice betrayed neither agreement nor disagreement. As they were close, Ruth used his first name when it was only the two of them around. Otherwise she called him Mr. Mahanes.

"Bruce also wants me to issue a press statement emphasizing all the good things about Crozet Hospital and also emphasizing that —" He stopped. "What the hell good is a press statement? Larry wasn't killed on hospital grounds. Until it's proven that his murder is connected to Hank's murder, I'd be a damn fool to issue a press statement. All that would do is link the two murders in people's minds — those who haven't made that linkage. You ride out bad publicity. A press statement is just asking for trouble at this time. Now I'm not saying I won't do one —" he paused — "when the time is right."

"How long can we fend off the reporters? We can't stop the television crew from shooting in front of the hospital. We can stop them from coming inside but they've made the connection despite us."

"Six o'clock news." He sat on the edge of her desk. "Well, all Dee" — he used the reporter's name — "said was that a member of the staff was killed. She couldn't say Larry's death was related to Hank's."

"No, but she said Hank was killed two weeks ago. Was it two weeks ago?" Ruth sighed. "It seems like a year."

"Yes, it does." He ran his fingers through his hair, thick wavy hair of which he was quite proud.

"Sam, issue the press statement. A good offense is better than a good defense."

He crossed his arms over his chest. "I hate for that jerk to think he's one ahead of me or that I listened to him."

"Oh, Bruce is Bruce. Ignore him. I do. If he's really obnoxious just imagine what he'd be like as an ob-gyn."

"Huh?"

"He'd think every baby he delivered was his." She tittered.

Sam laughed. "You're right." He slid off her desk, stretching his arms over his head. "Rick or Coop pestering you?"

"Not as much as I thought they would. Mostly they wanted to know hospital routine, my duties, anything unusual. They were to the point. That Coop is an attractive woman. I think I'll tell my nephew about her."

"Ruth, you must have been Cupid in another life."

"I thought I was Cupid in this one." She picked up her pencil, sliding it behind her ear, and turned back to her computer.

"All right. I'll write the damned press release." He trudged back to his office.

34

Coop pulled white cartons of Chinese food out of a brown paper bag, setting them in the middle of Harry's kitchen table. Harry put out the plates, silverware, and napkins.

"Milk, Coke, tea, coffee, beer?"

"Beer." Coop wearily sat down, narrowly avoiding Tucker, who had positioned herself by the chair leg. She appeared glued to it. "I'll have coffee with dessert."

"You got dessert?"

"Yes, but I'm not telling you what it is until we eat this first. Sit down."

"Okay." Harry sat down, reaching for the pork lo mein as Coop dished out cashew chicken.

"I don't do Chinese." Mrs. Murphy sat in the kitchen window.

"Worth a try. You can fish out the pork bits." Pewter extended one talon.

"I had enough to eat," said the tiger cat, who kept her figure.

"I thought you'd be spending the night with Fair after picking him up at the airport."

"Oh, I wasn't in the mood for manly bullshit tonight," Harry airily replied.

"Like what?"

"Like him telling me what to do and how to do it."

"Mother, that's not exactly the way Fair does things. He suggests and you get pissed off." Murphy laughed.

"And what did he tell you to do? Something for your own good." Cynthia mixed soy sauce in her white rice, then dug in with her chopsticks. "Right?"

"Well — well, I know it's for my own good but I don't like hearing it. He told me not to go back to the hospital and not to snoop around anywhere by myself, and then he said I looked like a punk rocker who couldn't quite make it." She pointed to her stitches. "I suppose I could spend the next six weeks wearing a beret."

"Not you, Harry."

"Okay, a baseball cap. Orioles or maybe the Braves. Nah, don't like the logo."

"I was thinking more along the lines of a black cowboy hat — with black chaps and black fringe."

"Coop, is there something about you I should know?" Harry's eyes twinkled.

"Uh — no." She bent her blonde head over the food. "Just a thought. Fair would like it."

"Maybe you ought to play dress-up." Harry giggled.

"For one thing I don't own a pair of chaps and I won't buy the ready-made ones. If you're going to have chaps you've got two choices and only two choices: Chuck Pinnell or Journeyman Saddlery."

"How do you know that?"

"You told me."

"Early Alzheimer's." Harry smacked her head with the butt of her palm.

"Maybe it's not so early."

"Up yours, Coop. I'm a long way from forty."

"Oh — I suppose you were never a whiz at arithmetic. I count three years."

"Thirty-seven is a long way —" Harry smirked slightly. "And you aren't far behind, girlfriend."

"Scary, isn't it? What would I do with those chaps? No one to play dress-up with and I'm not going to wear them in the squad car."

"Oh, why not? It would be such a nice touch. Everyone thinks lady cops are butch anyway."

"You really know how to please a girl." Coop sighed because she knew it was true.

"Yeah, but I didn't say you were butch.

You're not, you know. You're really very feminine. Lots more than I am."

"No, I'm not."

"You're tall and willowy. People think that's feminine until they see the badge and the pressed pleats in your pants. The shoes are winners, too. High heels. You could kick some poor bastard into next week but you'd never get your heel out of his butt. Police brutality."

"Harry." Cynthia laughed.

"See what Fair does to me. Just turns me into an evil wench. I think unclean thoughts."

"You don't need Fair for that. It's just that usually you keep them to yourself."

"Can you imagine me talking like this to Miranda? Smelling salts. And when she came to she'd have to pray for me at the Church of the Holy Light. I love her but there are things you don't say to Mrs. H."

Chopsticks poised in the air, Coop put them down for a moment. "I bet she knows more than she says. That generation didn't talk about stuff."

"Do you really think so?"

"Yeah. I think they did everything we do but they were quiet about it. Not out of shame or anything but because they were raised with guidelines about proper conversation. I bet they didn't even discuss some of this stuff with their doctors."

"The chaps. I wouldn't discuss that either." Harry laughed. "Better chaps than some of those silk things at Victoria's Secret. They look good on the models but if I put something like that on I'd get laughed out of the bedroom."

"I wish they'd stop talking about sex and drop some food," Tucker whined.

"Get on your hind legs. Coop's a sucker for that," Pewter advised. *"I'll rub Mother's legs. It ought to be good for one little piece of cashew chicken."*

The two performed their routine. It worked.

"You guys." Murphy giggled, then glanced back out the window. *"Simon's on a food search."* She saw the possum leave the barn.

"All he has to do is go to the feed room or get under the feed bucket in Tomahawk's stall. That horse throws grain around like there's no tomorrow. He wouldn't be so wasteful if he had to pay the feed bill." Pewter hated food being wasted.

"He's a pig. Wouldn't matter if he paid the bill or not." Murphy liked Tomahawk but was conversant with his faults.

"Any word on Tracy selling his house in Hawaii?"

Harry leaned over to grab another egg roll. "No takers yet but he'll sell it soon. He writes her every day. Isn't that romantic? It's much better than a phone call or e-mail. There's something so personal about a person's handwriting."

"I can't imagine a man sitting down to write me a letter a day."

"Me neither. I suppose Fair would write me a prescription a day — for the horses." She laughed.

"He's a good guy." Coop paused. "You love him?"

"I love him. I always loved him. I don't know about the in-love part, though. Sometimes I look at him and think it's still there. Other times, I don't know. You see, he's all I know. I dated him in high school and married him out of college. I dated a few men after our divorce but nothing clicked. Know what I mean?"

"Does the sun rise in the east?"

"I don't even know if I'm searching for anything or anyone. But he is a good man. And I'm over it."

"What?"

"Over the mess we made."

"At least you have a mess, a past."

"Coop?"

"All I meet are deadbeat dads, drunks,

drug addicts, and the occasional armed burglar. The armed-robbery guys are actually pretty bright. You might even say sexy." The pretty officer smiled.

"Really?" Harry pushed out the last of the lo mein with her chopsticks. "If you want more of this you'd better holler."

"I'll finish off the chicken."

"Deal. So the armed robbers are sexy?"

"Yes. They're usually very masculine, intelligent, risk takers. Unfortunately they don't believe in any form of restraint, hence their profession."

"What about murderers?"

"Funny you ask that. Murderers are usually quite ordinary. Well, set aside the occasional whacked-out serial killer. But the guy who blasts his girlfriend's new lover into kingdom come, ordinary."

"No electricity?"

"No."

"Maybe murder is closer to us than we think. We're all capable of it, but we aren't all capable of armed robbery. Does that make sense?"

"Yes. Given the right set of circumstances or the wrong set, I believe most of us are capable of just about anything."

"Probably true."

"Drop one last little piece of chicken,"

Pewter meowed.

"Pewter, I don't have anything else unless you want fried noodles."

"I'll try them."

Harry laughed and put down a handful of the noodles, which the cat devoured in an instant because Tucker was moving in her direction.

"Your claws click. That always gives you away." Pewter laughed.

"There are more important things in this life than retractable claws."

"Name one," Pewter challenged the dog, although she sounded garbled since her mouth was full.

"The ability to scent a dead body three feet underground."

"Gross!" Pewter grimaced.

"She's trying to get a rise out of you." Mrs. Murphy watched as Simon re-entered the barn. *"Simon's heading for the tack room. I guess he walked around the barn and decided no bears were near. He's a funny fellow."*

"I'd like to know what good possums contribute to the world." Pewter licked her lips with her shockingly pink tongue.

"Think what possums say about cats," Tucker needled the gray cat.

"I catch mice. I dispatch vermin."

"Not lately," came the dry canine reply, which so enraged the fat cat she bopped the corgi right on her sensitive nose.

"Pewter. Hateful." Harry noticed.

"I'm leaving." Pewter turned, sashaying into the living room with the hauteur of a disgruntled cat.

"I think cats and dogs are more expressive than we are." Cynthia laughed as Pewter exaggerated her walk for effect. "They can use their ears, turn them back and forth and out, they can wiggle their whiskers and their tail, they can make the hackles rise on their neck and back. They have lots of facial expressions."

"Pewter's major expression is boredom." Tucker giggled.

"Don't start with me."

"Start? She hasn't stopped," Murphy called from the window.

"Lots of talk. Lots of talk." Harry pointed her finger at each animal in succession, then returned to Coop. "I agree. They are more expressive."

"I'm beat."

"Go in the living room. I'll bring you a cup of coffee and dessert. What is it, by the way?"

"Phish Food. I put it in the freezer."

"Ben and Jerry's. Coop, the best." Harry

raced for the freezer, retrieved the pint of ice cream, pulled two bowls out of the cupboard. "The ice cream can soften while I make coffee. I've got Colombian, hazelnut, chicory, and regular. Oh, I've got decaf, too."

"Colombian." Cynthia sat on the sofa, bent over, and removed her shoes. "Oh, that feels too good. Foot massage. We need someone in Crozet who can give a good foot massage."

"Body massage. It's been years since I had a massage. Oh, they feel so good. I get such knots in my back." She waited for the coffee to run through the coffeemaker, filling the kitchen with rich aroma.

Cynthia got up to retrieve her briefcase, which she had put down by the kitchen door. She reached the sofa and lay down. She couldn't resist. When Harry brought in the coffee and a bowl of ice cream she sat up.

"Work?"

"Yeah. I need just enough energy to go over these bills from the hospital."

"I'll help you."

"It's supposed to be confidential."

"I won't tell anyone. Cross my heart and hope to —"

"Don't finish that," Mrs. Murphy hollered

as she jumped off the kitchen counter. *"Enough has happened around here."*

"Murphy?" Harry wondered if something was wrong with her cat, who hurried over, leaping into her lap.

"Okay, here are the procedure billings, you know, cost of a tonsillectomy. I'll go over the equipment bills."

"What am I looking for?"

"I don't know. Anything that seems off."

Harry's eyes fell onto a bill for a gall-bladder operation. "Jeez, two thousand dollars for the surgeon, a thousand for the anesthesiologist, two hundred a day for a semi-private room. Wow, look at these medication prices. This is outrageous!"

"And this is a nation that doesn't want comprehensive health care. It will kill you — getting sick."

"Sure will at Crozet Hospital." Harry smiled weakly. "Sorry."

Coop flipped her fingers, a dismissive gesture. "You develop gallows humor after a while. Otherwise you lose it."

"Here's a bill for breast removal. When you break down these bills it's like an avalanche. I mean every single physician bills separately. The rent on your room is separate. I can imagine you'd think you'd seen the last bill and here comes another one."

They worked in silence for about an hour, occasionally commenting on the cost of this or the fact that they didn't know so-and-so's sister had a pin put in her leg.

"Hank Brevard kept meticulous records," Harry noted.

"He wrote them out by hand and then I think someone else entered them on the computer. Hank wasn't that computer literate." Coop paused. "Boy, am I dumb. I'd better find out who did that for him."

Harry frowned. "I guess so. After a while everything and everyone seems suspicious. It's weird."

"Salvage Masters."

"Oh, that's a good one. The Dumpster people?"

"No, a company that rehabilitates infusion pumps. You know, the units next to a patient's bed that drip saline solution or morphine or whatever." She studied the bill. "Middleburg postmark. I think I'll drive up there Saturday if Rick says okay."

"He will."

"Want to go with me?"

"Yeah. I'd love to go."

35

"Mug shot." Mrs. Murphy scrutinized the lost-dog photo taped on the wall by the post-boxes.

"Ever notice you hardly ever see photographs of lost cats? We don't get lost." Pewter ran her tongue over her lips.

"Ha. It means people don't care as much about their cats," Tucker said, malice intended.

"Bull!" Pewter snarled and was about to attack the sturdy canine when the first human of the day entered the post office.

Reverend Herb Jones picked up the church's mail, then strode over to the sign. "Now that's a new one."

"What?" Harry called out from behind the divider.

She was dumping out a mail sack, letters cascading over the table, onto the floor.

"Bristol. I thought I knew every dog in this district. Who owns Bristol?" Herb frowned.

"You know, I don't know. The notice was

slipped under the front door. I put it up. I don't recognize the pooch either except that he's awfully cute."

"Yeah. Hope he's found," Herb agreed.

"Where's Miranda?"

"Home. She said she'd be a little late this morning."

"Well, I'd better get a move on. The vestry committee meets this morning and I have to deliver the blow that we must replumb the rectory."

"That will cost a pretty penny."

"Yes, it will." He leaned over the counter for a second. "If money is your objective, Harry, become a plumber."

"I'll remember that."

He waved as he left.

A few minutes later BoomBoom Craycroft, tanned, came in. "I'm back!"

"So I see."

"She really is beautiful," Tucker had to admit.

"A week in Florida in the winter restores my spirits." She stopped. "Except I've come home to such — such sadness."

"No one quite believes it." Harry continued to sort through catalogues.

BoomBoom glanced at the lost-dog notice, said nothing, cleaned out her mailbox, then went over to the counter. "More."

Harry walked over, taking the yellow slip indicating there was more mail than the mailbox could hold. She put the overflow in a white plastic box with handles. She retrieved it, heaving it over the counter.

"Here you go."

"Thanks." BoomBoom picked up the box.

Harry flipped up the divider, trotting to the front door, which she opened. "It's slippery."

"Sometimes I think winter will never end. Thanks."

Harry closed the front door as Miranda entered through the back.

"Yoo-hoo."

"Hi." The animals greeted the older woman.

"Hello, you little furry angels."

"Oh, yes." Tucker flopped over on her back.

"That's more stomach than I care to see," Pewter snipped.

"Look who's talking," Tucker responded.

Tussie hurried through the front door. "Hi, late." She slipped her key in the brass mailbox, scooped out the contents, shut the door with a clang, glancing at the lost-dog notice. "Poor puppy." She dashed out the front door.

Jordan Ivanic followed, read the notice, said nothing.

Later that day Susan dropped by. "We ought to put up posters of marriageable daughters."

"Right next to lost dogs," Harry remarked.

"Or goats."

By the end of the day neither Harry nor Miranda had observed anything unusual regarding the poster. Harry called in to Coop.

"You know, even though Rick must have someone watching Mim, I'd rather she hadn't done that," Miranda worried out loud as Harry spoke to Coop.

"If it's the killer versus Mim, catnip's on Mim," Mrs. Murphy declared.

"It's been a while since I've been up there. I enjoy walking around the shops — after my duty is done, of course." Coop referred to their planned trip to Middleburg.

"You could get measured for chaps."

"Harry."

"Hee hee."

36

"Mother, do you really think you can stay neutral?"

A languid, melancholy Mim replied, "I have no choice."

"You don't think I should run against Dad, do you?"

"No."

A slight red blotch appeared on Little Mim's forehead, a hint of suppressed anger. "Why? He's been mayor long enough."

"I believe in letting sleeping dogs lie." The older woman patted the arm of her overstuffed chair; a fire crackling in the fireplace added to the warm atmosphere of the drawing room.

"Change never happens that way."

"Oh, Marilyn, change happens even when you sleep. I just don't see the point in stirring things up. Your father is a wonderful mayor and this town has flourished under his guidance."

"And your money."

"That, too." Mim glanced out the window. Low gray clouds moved in fast from the west.

"You never support me."

A flicker of irritation crossed Mim's regular, lovely features. "Oh? You live in a handsome house, provided by me. You have a car, clothing, horses, jewelry. You are denied nothing. You had the best education money can buy and when you married, I believe the only wedding more sumptuous was that between Grace Kelly and Prince Rainier. And when you divorced we dealt with that, too. Just exactly what is the problem?"

Pouting, not an attractive trait in a woman in her mid-thirties, Little Mim rose from her chair opposite her mother's and walked to the window. "I want to do something on my own. Is that so hard to understand?"

"No. Get a job."

"Doing what?"

"How should I know, Marilyn? It's your life. You have talents. I think you do a wonderful job with the hunt club newsletter. Really, I do."

"Thanks. Storm's coming in."

"Yes. February never fails to depress."

"Mother." She bit her lower lip, then continued. "I have no purpose in life."

"I'm sorry. No one can provide that for you."

Turning to face her mother, arms crossed over her chest, Little Mim said, "I want to do something."

"Charity work has meaning."

"No. That was for your generation. You married and that was that."

"Marriage might improve your humor." A slight smile played over Mim's lips, mocha lipstick perfectly applied.

"And what's that supposed to mean?"

"Just that we are meant to go in twos. Remember the animals on Noah's Ark?"

The younger woman, lithe and as well dressed as her mother, returned, gracefully lowering herself into the chair. "I'd like to marry again but Blair isn't going to ask me. He's not in love with me."

"I'm glad you realize that. Anyway, he travels too much for his work. Men who travel are never faithful."

"Neither are men who stay at home." Marilyn was fully aware of her father's peccadilloes.

"Touché."

"I'm sorry. That was a low blow."

Mim smoothed her skirt. "The truth isn't tidy, is it?"

"I'm out of sorts. Every time I think of Blair my heart leaps but when I'm with him I don't feel — I don't feel *there*. Does that make sense?"

"Any man that gorgeous will get your blood up. That's the animal in you. When you're with him you don't feel anything because there's nothing coming off his body. When a man likes you, wants you, you feel it. It's electric."

The daughter looked at her mother, a flash of recognition illuminating her features. "Right. Did you feel that for Dad?"

"Eventually. I learned to love your father."

"You were always in love with Larry, weren't you, Mother?"

As they had never discussed this, a surprising silence fell over them for a few moments.

"Yes."

"I'm sorry, Mother." Marilyn meant it.

"Life is strange. Hardly a profound thought but I never know what will happen from one minute to the next even though I live a well-ordered life. The mistake I made, and I share this with you only in the hopes that you won't repeat my mistakes, is that I valued form over substance, appearances over emotion. I was a perfect fool."

"Mother." Little Mim was shocked.

"The money gets in the way, darling. And social expectations are deadening. I ought to know, I've spent a lifetime meeting and enforcing them." She leaned over to turn on the lamp by her chair as the sky darkened. "Going to be a good one."

"First snowflake."

They both stopped to watch the skies open.

Finally, Mim said, "If you're determined to run against your father, go ahead, but consider what you really want to do as mayor. If you win, stick to it. If you lose, support your father."

"I suppose."

"Maybe there's another path. I don't know. I haven't been thinking too clearly these last days."

"It's awful that Larry's dead." Marilyn had loved him as though he were a kindly uncle.

"Quite. Snatched from life. He had so much to give. He'd given so much and someone took aim. I don't think Rick Shaw has one clue."

"They have the ballistics report." Marilyn wanted to sound hopeful.

"Little good it does without the finger that pulled the trigger." Mim's eyes clouded over. "As you age you learn there is such a thing as a good death. His was a good death in that it was swift, and apart from the shock of getting hit with a bullet, I should think the pain didn't last. He died as he lived, no trouble to anyone."

"I don't have any ideas; do you?"

"No, unfortunately. So often you have a premonition, an inkling, a sense of what's wrong or who's wrong. I don't have that. I'd give my eyeteeth to find Larry's murderer. I don't know where to look. The hospital? A lunatic patient? I just have no feel for this."

"I don't think anyone does, but now that you mention the hospital, what do you think of Bruce Buxton?"

"Arrogant."

"That's all?"

"Arrogant and handsome. Does that make you feel better?"

"He's brilliant. Everyone says that."

"I suppose he is."

"But you don't like him, do you?"

"Ah, well, I can't explain it, Marilyn. And it's not important anyway. Are you interested in Bruce? At least he rides reasonably well. You can't possibly be interested in a man who can't ride, you know. Another reason Blair's not for you."

Little Mim laughed because it was true. Horse people shouldn't marry non-horse people. It rarely worked. "That's something."

"Bruce rides like most men. Squeeze, jerk. Squeeze, jerk, but a bit of teaching could improve that. He doesn't intend to be abusive and he's not as abusive as most. Women are better with horses. Always will be." This was stated with ironclad conviction. "Women make up eighty percent of the hunt field but only twenty percent of the accidents."

"Harry's been riding well, hasn't she?"

"You two ought to ride in the hunt pairs when we have our hunter trials."

"Harry and I aren't close."

"You don't have to be close. Your horses are matched."

This was followed by an exhaustive discussion of the merits of relative mounts, carried out with the enthusiasm and total concentration peculiar to horse people. To anyone else the conversation would have been a bloody bore.

"Mother," Little Mim said, changing the subject. "Would you give one of your famous teas and invite Bruce?"

"I can't see the stables." Mim noted the thickness of the falling snow. "A tea?"

"You give the best teas. Things always happen at your parties. I wish I had your gift."

"You could have it if you wanted it, Marilyn. One learns to give parties just as one learns to dress. Oh, what was that I heard Harry and Susan say a few days ago? The 'fashion police.' Yes, the fashion police. They were laughing about Jordan Ivanic's tie and said he needed to be arrested by the fashion police."

"Harry in her white T-shirt, jeans, and paddock boots?"

"Ah, but Marilyn, it works for her. It really does and she has a wonderful body. I wish she and Fair would get back together again but once trust is broken it's hard to mend that fence. Well, a tea? You can learn."

"I can do the physical stuff. I will. I'll help with all that, but you have a gift for putting people together. Like I said, Mother, something always happens at your parties."

"The time Ulrich jumped the fence, cantered across the lawn, and jumped the picnic table was unforgettable." She smiled, remembering a naughty horse.

"What about the time Fair and Blair got into a fistfight and Herb Jones had to break it up? That was pretty exciting."

Mim brightened. "Or the time Aunt Tally cracked her cane over Ned Tucker's head and we had to take Ned to the emergency room."

"Why did Aunt Tally do that?"

"You were eleven at the time, I think. Your brother, Stafford, was thirteen. I'll tell you why. Ned became head of the Republican Party in the county and Aunt Tally took umbrage. She told him Tucker was an old Virginia name and he had no business registering Republican. He could vote Republican but he couldn't register that way. It just wasn't done. And Ned, who is usually an intelligent man, was dumb enough to argue with her. He said Lyndon Johnson handed the South to the Republican Party in 1968 when he signed the Voter Rights Act. That did it. Pow!" Mim clapped her hands. "I suppose Aunt Tally will enliven this tea as well. Let's sic her on Sam Mahanes, who is getting entirely too serious."

"With good reason."

"He's not the only person with troubles. All right. Your tea. How about two weeks from today? March sixth."

"Mother, you're lovely."

"I wouldn't go that far."

37

Bruce dropped by Pediatrics to check on a ten-year-old boy on whom he had operated.

Tussie Logan stood by the sleeping boy, hair dirty blond. She adjusted the drip of the infusion pump, took his pulse, and whispered on his progress to Bruce, who didn't wish to wake him.

They walked back into the hall.

"That pump's old, an IVAC 560 model. I keep pushing Sam for new equipment but I might as well be talking to a wall."

"Forget new pumps. These work perfectly well and the nurses know how to use them." Tussie had no desire to get in the middle of a Bruce versus Sam disagreement. The nurse always loses.

"They can learn."

"Dr. Buxton, they are overworked now. Keep it simple. The old pumps are really simple."

"You sound like Sam."

Her face tightened. "I hope not."

"Cheap."

"We do have budget restraints."

"We're falling way behind the technology curve, Nurse Logan. He's got to spend money to catch up. Go in debt, if necessary. He's too cheap, I tell you."

"Dr. Buxton, I can't really criticize the director of this hospital. It's not a wise policy." A flicker of fear danced in her hazel eyes. "And if you're going to fight for new equipment, fight for another MRI unit or something. Leave the nurses out of it."

"Afraid to lose your job?" He snorted. "Cover your ass. Ah, yes, the great American answer to the future, cover your ass."

"If you'll excuse me." She turned, walking down the hall to disappear into another patient's room.

"Chickenshit. Everyone around here is just chickenshit." Disgusted, he headed back toward his office in the newest wing of the hospital.

38

Chain store after chain store lined Route 29; fast-food restaurants, large signs blazing, further added to the dolorous destruction of what had once been beautiful and usable farmland. The strip, as it was known, could have been anywhere in the United States: same stores, same merchandise, same food. Whatever comfort value there was in consistency was lost aesthetically.

Back in the late sixties the Barracks Road shopping center at the intersection of Garth Road and Emmet Street, Route 29, broadcast the first hint of things to come. It seemed so far out then, three miles north of the University of Virginia.

By the year 2000 the shopping centers had marched north almost to the Greene County line. Even Greene County had a shopping center, at the intersection of Routes 29 and 33.

The city of Warrenton wisely submitted to a beltway around its old town. Charlottesville eschewed this solution to traffic congestion, with the result that anyone wishing to travel through that fair city could expect to lose a half hour to forty-five minutes, depending on the time of day.

As Harry and Coop headed north on Route 29 they wondered how long before gridlock would become a fact of life.

They chatted through Culpeper, the Blue Ridge standing sentinel to their left, the west. At Warrenton they latched onto Route 17 North which ran them straight up to Route 50 where they turned right and within six miles, they were at the door of Salvage Masters, a new four-story building nestled in the wealthy hills of Upperville, ten miles west of Middleburg proper.

Harry's chaps, needing repair, were tossed in the back of the Jeep, Coop's personal vehicle. She didn't want to draw attention to herself by driving a squad car, although she could have flown up Route 29 without fear of reprisal from another policeman lurking in the hollows, radar at the ready. The small towns relied on that income although they were loath to admit it, ever declaring public safety as their primary concern for ticketing speeders.

"Think my chaps will be okay?" Harry asked automatically, then grinned.

"There must be millions of people here

just waiting to steal a pair of chaps needing repair — because you wore them." The blonde woman laughed as she picked up a leather envelope containing papers.

When they knocked on the door, a pleasant assistant ushered them in.

Joe Cramer, a tall muscular man at six four walked out of his office. "Hello. Come on in. Would either of you like coffee, or a Coke?"

"No thanks. I'm Deputy Cynthia Cooper and this is Mary Minor Haristeen, Harry, who has been involved in the case." Cynthia shook his hand, as did Harry.

"Come on." He guided them into his office, a comfortable space.

"This is quite an operation." Coop looked around at the employees seated at benches, working on IVAC units.

"Infusion pumps are sent to us from all over the world. These machines are built to last and for the most part, they do."

"You aren't from Virginia, are you, Mr. Cramer?" The lean deputy smiled. "Do you mind giving me a little background about how you developed this business?"

"No. I'm originally from Long Island. Went to college in the Northeast and started working in the medical industry. I was fascinated by the technology of medicine. I worked for years for a huge corporation in New Jersey, Medtronic. That's when I came up with the idea of rehabilitating infusion pumps and other equipment. The smaller hospitals can afford to repair their equipment and they can often afford to buy used equipment, but they often can't afford to buy new equipment. As I said, most of these machines are well built and will last for decades if properly maintained."

"Do you visit your accounts?"

"Yes. I haven't visited our accounts in India," he answered in his warm light baritone. "But I've visited many of the accounts here."

"What about Crozet Hospital?"

"Oh, I think I was there four years ago. I haven't had much business from them in the last few years."

"You haven't?" Cynthia's voice rose.

"No. And the machines need to be serviced every six months."

"Let me show you something." She pulled invoices out of the leather envelope, placing them before him.

Joe studied the invoices, then hit a button on his telephone. "Honey, can you come over to the shop for a minute?"

A voice answered. "Sure. Be a minute."

"My wife," he said. "We put everything on

the computer but I trust her memory more than the computer." He punched another button. "Michael, pull up the Crozet Hospital file, will you?"

"Okay."

A tall, elegant woman swept into Joe's office. "Hello."

"Honey, this is Deputy Cynthia Cooper from the Albemarle Sheriff's Department and Mary Haristeen. Uh, Harry."

"Laura Cramer." She shook their hands.

"Do you remember the last time we got an order from Crozet Hospital?"

"Oh — at least four years."

Just then Michael walked into the office. "Here."

Joe reached up for the papers as Michael left. He and Laura read over the figures. "Here, Deputy, look at this."

She reached for the papers. The bills stopped four years ago. "They've given us no notice of moving their business," Laura said.

"Well, Mr. and Mrs. Cramer, the last billing date on the last invoice I have is December second of last year."

"It's our letterhead," Joe said, as Coop handed him an invoice.

"It's our paper, too." Laura studied the invoices, tapping them with her forefinger.

"But Joe, these aren't our numbers." She looked up at Coop and Harry. "We have our own numbering system. These fake invoices copied the numbers from four years ago, running them up sequentially. But each year I alter the numbers. It's our internal code for keeping track of business, repair cycles, and it's all in those numbers."

"It'd be a pretty easy matter to print up invoices with your logo," Harry volunteered. "Someone with a good laser printer could do it and it would be cheaper than going to a printer. Also, no records of the printing job."

"Some of those laser systems are very sophisticated," Laura said, obviously upset.

"Has there been a problem with the equipment? Is that why you're here?" Joe asked because the reputation of his business was vitally important to him.

"No. Not that we know of." Coop walked around and sat back down, as did Harry.

"Can you tell me just what it is that you check on the infusion pumps, if check is the correct term?"

"We check for electrical safety, something like good current leakage. Or a power cord might be damaged. Sometimes orderlies will drop a unit. Stuff happens. We take the unit apart and check the circuits. Here, let me show you." He stood up and ushered them into the spanking-clean shop area.

"Here." Laura pointed to the digital screen on the face of the unit, above a keyboard of numbers like telephone push buttons. "The nurse punches in the flow, the time frame, the amount of fluid, and the rate, which is displayed here." She pointed to the screen. "The nurse on duty or doctor has only to look on the screen to know how much is left in the unit, whether to increase flow or whatever."

Harry remembered Larry punching in information on a unit.

"And you can put any fluid in the bag?" Coop pointed to boxes filled with sterile bags.

Joe nodded. "Sure. Blood. Morphine. Saline solution. Anesthesia. OBs use IVAC units to drop Pitocin, which stimulates the uterus to go into labor. The infusion pump is very versatile."

"And simple," Laura added.

"Here." Joe picked up a unit from the table. "You can even medicate yourself." He placed a round button attached to a black cord into Coop's hand. "You hit the button and you get more drip."

"Are these units well made?" Harry was curious.

"Oh sure. They're built to last and it's like everything else, newer models are more expensive, more bells and whistles, but I service units that are twenty years old — they usually come in from Third World countries."

"May I ask you something?" Laura smiled.

"Of course."

"Is someone stealing IVACs and selling them to poor countries?"

"What we have are two murders which we believe are connected, and I think we just found the connection. We don't know if the units are sold on the black market or not. What we have to go on right now are these false bills."

"Murders?" Laura's eyes widened.

"Yes, the plant manager of the hospital was killed three weeks ago and a doctor was killed just a week ago." She paused. "Both of those men must have stumbled onto something relating to these billings."

"Have you added up the amount of the billings? You've got three years' worth." Laura checked the figures and the dates.

"Yes, we have. It comes to seven hundred fifty thousand dollars for that time period."

"Someone's rolling in dough," Laura flatly stated.

"We've looked for that, too, Mr. and Mrs. Cramer. We didn't know this was the problem but we knew something had to be going on. We had no reports of suspicious patient deaths. We thought there might be a black market in human organs."

"There is." Joe leaned forward. "A huge black market."

"We found that out, too, but we also discovered that wasn't our problem. You two have shown me what's at stake here, a lot of money and more to come, I should guess."

"Joe, I think we'd better contact our lawyers. Officer, do you mind if I make copies of these?"

"No, but I ask you both to keep quiet about this. You can't sue anyone until we catch them and we won't catch them if they have warning."

"I understand," Laura agreed.

"This just knocks me out." Joe shook his head.

"The only reason the sheriff and I noticed these particular invoices, and it took time, I might add, was we crawled over the hospital, over billings, maintenance bills, you name it, but what finally caught our eye was that these bills were so neat."

"What do you mean?" Laura was curious.

"Well, they have a receipt date, as you can

326

see." Coop pointed to the round red circle in the middle of each bill. "They have a pay date." She pointed to another circle, this one in blue with a date running across it diagonally. "But the invoices are so white and crisp."

"What do you mean?" Laura picked up an invoice.

"The other bills and invoices had gone through a couple of hands, a couple of shufflings. Fingerprints were on the paper, corners were a little dog-eared. These are pristine. It was a long shot but it was just peculiar enough for me to come up here."

"I'm glad you did." Joe, upset, looked into the young officer's eyes.

"Is there anyone who stands out in your mind at Crozet Hospital?" Coop had been making notes in her notebook.

"No. Well, I met the director and the assistant director, that sort of thing. I talked to a few of the nurses. The nurses are the ones who use the infusion pumps. That's why the simpler the model, the better it is. You can make these devices too complicated. Nurses have to use them, they're overburdened, tired — keep it simple." His voice boomed.

"How serious would a malfunctioning unit be?" Coop asked.

"Life and death." Laura folded her long

fingers together as if in prayer. "An improper dosage could kill a patient."

After they left Salvage Masters they drove east on Route 50, ten miles into Middleburg. Harry took her chaps to Journeyman Saddlery to have them repaired, since Chuck Pinnell in Charlottesville was off to another Olympics. As he was one of the best leatherworkers in the nation, with a deep understanding of riders' needs, he had been invited to the Olympics to repair tack for all the competitors, not just Americans.

"Coop, look at these neat colors and the trims you can get, too."

Cynthia felt the samples, played with putting colors together. "It really is beautiful."

"They can put your initials on the back or on the side. They can make leather rosebuds on the belt or whatever. It's just incredible."

"I can see that."

"Mine's a plain pair of pigskin chaps with cream trim and my initials on the back, see?" Harry showed her the back of the chaps belt.

"Uh-huh." Cynthia was gravitating toward black calfskin.

"You know, if you had a pair of chaps made to your body, you might even learn to jump. I'd let you ride Gin Fizz. He's a sweetie. Then, too, chaps have other uses." She had a devilish glitter in her eye.

Coop weakened, allowing herself to be measured. She chose black calfskin, smooth side out, no fringe, and a thin green contrasting strip down the leg and on the belt, also calfskin. She had her initials centered on the back of the belt in a small diamond configuration. The waiting period would be three months.

All the way back to Crozet the two women discussed uses for the chaps as well as the pressing matter at hand: how to trap the killer or killers into making a mistake.

It only takes one mistake.

39

The two cats and the dog had heard about the trip to Upperville and Middleburg. They huddled in the back of the post office by the animal door. Outside a hard frost was melting as the temperature at ten in the morning was forty-five degrees and rising quickly. February could run you crazy with the wild weather fluctuations.

"That's what those machines are we found. The pumps that should have gone to Salvage Masters." Pewter held her tail in her paw. She'd meant to clean it but in the excitement of the news she'd forgotten.

Mrs. Murphy, already one step ahead of her, replied, *"Yes, of course, but that's not the real problem. You see —"* As the two animals drew closer to her she lowered her voice. *"Those machines have to be rehabbed. That's why they're down there. Whoever is stashing them can't put them back into use without cleaning them, right?"*

"Why not?" Tucker asked.

"Either they won't work or they'll work improperly. Which means complaints to Salvage Masters and the game is up. Whoever is doing this has to crawl down in that space and clean the pumps. I should think that part wouldn't be too hard. Well, the person has to get in and out undetected. What's difficult is if a machine needs more work than just cleaning. See?" Mrs. Murphy swept her pointed, refined ears forward.

"No, I don't see," Pewter confessed.

"I do." Tucker licked the gray cat's face. *"Someone has to understand these machines."*

"Oh." Pewter's face brightened. *"I get it."*

"Think it through," Murphy counseled patiently. *"The infusion pumps are small. One person, a small person, a child even, can pick them up, roll them, move them around. The hospital routine isn't ruffled. For years these pumps have been removed for cleaning. Right?"* The dog and other cat nodded in agreement. *"Whoever picks them up is in on it."*

"Not necessarily," Tucker contradicted her. *"An orderly or janitor could pick them up and take them to the basement for*

331

shipping out. Then they could be removed to where we found them."

"*True.*" The pretty tiger was getting excited because she felt she was getting close to figuring this out. "*That's a good point, Tucker. The fewer people who know, the better. And someone has to run off the fake invoices. H-m-m.*"

"*Okay, let's review.*" Tucker caught Murphy's excitement. "*We have a person or persons good at using a computer. It sounds easy, copying a bill, but it isn't and the paper matches, too. So they're pretty good. We have a person or persons with mechanical skill. Right?*"

"*Right,*" the two kitties echoed.

"*And there has to be someone higher up. Someone who can cover for them. Someone very, very smart because the chances are, that's the mastermind behind this. That person recruited the others. How often does an employee woo the boss into crime?*" Tucker stood up, panting from her mental efforts.

"*Well done, Tucker.*" Mrs. Murphy rubbed along the dog's body.

"*How can we get a human to the hidden room?*" Pewter cocked her head, her long whiskers twitching.

"*We can't,*" Mrs. Murphy flatly replied.

"First off, anyone we might lure there in the hospital could be in on it. We'd wait down-stairs and who is downstairs but the plant crew, as Sam Mahanes calls them. You know one of them has to be in on it. Has to be. We'd be toast."

"Hank Brevard." Pewter's green eyes grew large. "He was the one. And he had his throat slit."

"Maybe he got greedy. If he'd kept at his task why kill him? Think about it. Whoever is on top of this sordid little pyramid is creaming the bulk of the profits. Hank fig-ured out somewhere along the line that he was an important person in the profit chain and he wanted more. He asks for more or threatens. Sayonara." Murphy glanced at Miranda and Harry sorting out the parcels, tossing them in various bins or putting them on the shelves, numbers like the postboxes.

"Which means if the money is to keep rolling in, our Number One Guy will soon need to recruit someone else." Tucker was getting an uneasy feeling.

"He might be able to do the work him-self," Pewter said.

"That's possible but if he's high up on the totem pole he isn't going to have the time, number one, and number two, he isn't going to be seen heading to the basement a lot. Eventually that would be a tip-off, especially after Hank's death." Mrs. Murphy's mind raced along.

"When Mom got clunked on the head — it must have been him." Tucker hoped Harry wouldn't go back to the hospital but she knew her mother's burning curiosity, which was why she'd been feeling uneasy.

"Everyone knows that Harry is both smart and curious. Smart for a human. I hope as long as she stays away from the hospital, she's okay, but she's friends with Coop. If I were the killer that would be worrisome. Look how fast he struck when Larry was finding discrepancies, and they probably weren't critical yet because if they were Larry would have gone straight to Sheriff Shaw. He wouldn't have waited." The tiger began to pace.

"If it were just one person . . ." Pewter's voice trailed off; then she spoke louder. "We've got at least two. Mom might be able to handle one but two — well, I don't know."

"And no bites yet on Bristol, the missing dog? We've got to find out who that is," Mrs. Murphy fretted.

"Mim would tell Rick if anything had

happened," Tucker said.

"Well, nothing's happened on that front yet." Murphy sighed. They were wrong about that.

48

Fair stood at the divider counter sorting out his mail. "You know Dr. Flynn's got two gorgeous stallions standing at Barracks Stud."

"Yeah. I thought I'd breed Poptart in a few years. She's still pretty young and I need her. If she's bred . . ." Harry's voice trailed off as there was no need to say she'd be out of work for at least the last three months of her pregnancy and then out of work until the foal was weaned.

"I like Fred Astaire, too." Fair mentioned a beautifully bred Thoroughbred stallion at Albemarle Stud.

"Doesn't everyone?" Harry smiled as she threw metered mail in one pile, since it needed a second hand-cancellation for the date.

"Now what's the difference between one stallion and another?" Mrs. Hogendobber, not a horse person, asked.

"Kind of the difference between one man and another." Fair laughed.

"Don't get racy. I'll blush." Miranda's

cheeks did turn rosier.

"It depends on what you're looking for, Miranda. Let's say you have a good Thoroughbred mare, she's well bred and she has good conformation. She didn't win a lot of races but she's pretty good. You'll search around — and you can do this on the Net, by the way — for a stallion whose bloodlines are compatible and who also has good conformation. You might want more speed or more bone or more staying power. That's in the blood. Breeding is as much an art as a science."

"Don't forget luck." Harry pressed the heavy rubber stamp in the maroon postal ink.

"There sure is that," the tall blond man agreed. "Miranda, if breeding were just a matter of study, we'd all be winning the Triple Crown. So much can happen. If you get a live foal —"

"What do you mean, a live foal?" The older woman assumed they'd all be live.

"A mare can slip or not catch in the first place." Noticing the puzzled look he explained, "A mare can not get pregnant even though you've done everything by the book. Or she can get pregnant yet abort early in the pregnancy. Strange as it may sound, it isn't that easy to get mares pregnant. A conception rate of sixty percent by a vet specializing in breeding is respectable. There's a vet in Pennsylvania who averages in the ninety percent range, but he's extraordinary. Let's say your mare gives birth. A mare can have a breech delivery the same as a woman but it's much worse for a mare. If those long legs with hooves get twisted up or tear her womb you can imagine the crisis. Foals can strangle on the umbilical cord or be starved for oxygen and never be quite right. They can be born dead."

"It sounds awful."

"Most times it isn't but sometimes it really is and your heart sinks to your toes. You know how much the owner has put into the breeding both financially and emotionally. Around here people are attached to their mares. We don't have huge breeding establishments so just about everything I see is a homebred. Lots of emotion."

"Yes, I can see that. Why, if Mrs. Murphy had kittens I think I'd be so concerned for her."

"Thank you." Murphy, half asleep in the mail cart, yawned.

Pewter, curled up next to her, giggled. *"Some mother you'd be."*

"Look who's talking. You selfish thing, you'd starve your own children if there

338

weren't enough food. I can see the head-
lines now. 'Cat starves kittens. Is fat as a
tick.' "

"Shut up."

"You started it."

"Did not," Pewter hissed.

"Did too."

"Not."

"Too." Murphy swatted Pewter right on
the head.

"Bully!" Pewter rolled over to grapple with
the thinner cat.

A great hissing, growling, and flailing was
heard from the mail cart. Harry and
Miranda tiptoed over to view the excitement. Fair watched from the other side of
the counter.

Tucker, on her side, lifted her head, then
dropped it. "Cats."

"Fatty, fatty, two by four," Murphy sang
out.

"Mean. Hateful and mean!" Pewter was
holding her own.

The mail cart rolled a bit. Harry, devilish,
gave it a shove.

"Hey!" Murphy clambered over the side,
dropped to the ground, put her ears back,
and stomped right by her mother.

"Whee!" Pewter crouched down for the
ride.

Harry trotted over, grabbed the end of the mail cart. "Okey dokey, smoky. Here we go." She pushed the mail cart all around the back of the post office as Pewter rose up to put her paws on the front. The cat loved it. Murphy sulked, finally going over to Tucker to sit next to the dog, who wanted no part of a cat fight.

"It's a three-ring circus around here." Miranda laughed.

"You look good in hunter green. I meant to tell you that when I walked in." Fair complimented her dress.

"Why, thank you, Fair. Now where were we before Mrs. Murphy and Pewter interrupted us?"

"Mares. Actually once you deliver a healthy foal life begins to shine a little. There are always worries. The mare's milk could be lacking in proper nutrition. The foal's legs could be crooked although usually they straighten out and if not then I go to work. Nothing intrusive. I believe less is more and let nature do her work. But short of a foal running through a board fence in a thunderstorm, once you've got a healthy baby on the ground, you're doing great."

"What about diseases?"

"Usually protection comes in the mother's milk. In that sense it's like kittens or puppies. They receive immunity from the mother. In time that immunity wears off and then you need to be vigilant. But nature truly is amazing and a foal arrives much more prepared to negotiate the world than a human baby. With both babies, the more they're handled the better they become. I think, anyway."

"You're the doctor." Mrs. H. smiled.

"Here, why don't you take these back?" He shoved bills across the counter.

"Happy to." She playfully grabbed them.

"Want mine, too?" Harry usually got to her own mail last.

"We could burn them," Fair suggested.

"They'd just come back," Harry ruefully observed.

"Somewhere in this vast nation exists a person with an incredible mind, a person who can crack computer codes. I pray that person will wipe out everyone's IRS files and save our country. I dream about it at night. I believe in a national sales tax. Then everyone knows what they're paying. No hidden taxes. If the government can't run itself on those monies then the government can cut back. If I have to cut back as a private citizen I can expect my government to do the same. That's exactly what I think."

"Bravo." Harry finished canceling the metered mail. "Run for office."

"Little Mim has beat me to it." He shuffled his mail, organizing it into a pile according to letter size.

"That rebellion has taken second place to the mess around here. Maybe that's a good thing. Little Mim doesn't seem to know what she's searching for but young people worry more these days than we did."

"I don't know," said Harry. "Maybe after a long time you forget. You know, you forget the pain but hold on to the good part of the memory."

"Could be. Could be." Miranda smiled at Fair, who smiled back, as both were hoping Harry had done this with memories of her marriage.

"Tucker, why don't we sneak out tonight and go to the hospital? I bet those pumps get brought in as well as cleaned at night." Pewter called out from the mail cart. *"That's a seven-mile hike and it's cold at night, real cold."* Her voice lowered.

"I don't mean from the farm, dimwit. I mean just before Harry leaves work we run off."

"Oh, I don't know. She'll catch us." Pewter wanted to go home after work. Supper beckoned.

"Not if we run under Mrs. Hogendob-ber's porch."

"Murphy, we could head straight to the hospital. All we have to do is go through yards. One road crossing but we can handle that." Tucker was thinking out loud.

"If we do that, she'll follow us. If we get close enough to the hospital I know she'll go in. She'll forget her promises and just go right in. Can't have that." Mrs. Murphy knew her human to the bone.

"It will be cold," came the mournful whine from the mail cart.

"That's why you have fur," Murphy tartly replied.

"Fine."

Murphy and Tucker looked at one another and shrugged.

At closing the tiger and corgi blasted out the back animal door. Pewter stuck close to Harry as she chased her bad pets. Although curious, the gray cat wanted to snuggle up on the sofa in front of the fire after her tuna supper. She wasn't that curious.

Harry and Miranda tried to cut off the cat and dog but the animals easily eluded them.

"Every now and then." Harry shook her head.

"I'll keep my eyes open for them."

"Thanks, Miranda. I'll leave the animal

door unlocked, too. I don't know what it is. They get a notion." She glanced up at the sky. "At least it looks like it will be a clear night. No storms rolling in."

Defeated, Harry bundled Pewter into the cab of the old truck to head home.

"They're very naughty." Pewter sat right next to Harry.

"You're a good kitty." Harry rubbed her head.

"I'd like fresh tuna, please," Pewter purred, half closing her eyes, which gave her a sweet countenance.

Murphy and Tucker reached the hospital just as the loading dock was shutting down. They scooted in, hearing the big rolling doors lock behind them.

"Going to be a long night," Murphy observed.

"Yeah but someone might open the back door later. We'll get out."

"No matter what, we know we can escape in the morning. I bet if we scrounge around we'll find something to eat."

They could hear the elevator doors open and close. The shift was changing. Day workers were going home and the night crew, much smaller in number, was coming to work. Then silence. Not even a footfall.

Just to make sure they remembered the

layout they walked down the halls, checked the boiler room in the center, poked their heads into those closet doors that were open.

Finally they walked into the carton room.

"Clever, leaving this door open, filling it with cartons. As though there is nothing to hide," Murphy noted.

"You can hide better than I can." Tucker searched the room. *"What if I lie flat over here in the darkest corner and you push a carton over me. I think that will work. After all, no one is expecting a corgi here."*

"Right."

As Murphy covered up Tucker they both heard a footfall, a light footfall.

Wordlessly, the cat climbed to the top of the cartons, wedging herself between two of them. She could see everything. Tucker's face, ears covered, poked out from the carton in the dark corner. Both held their breath.

Tussie Logan softly walked inside carrying a pump. She pressed the stone in the wall. The floor door slid aside. She climbed down the ladder, pressed a button down there, and the floor quietly closed up.

Neither animal moved. Three hours later the floor yawned open. Tussie climbed up the ladder, then pressed the stone. She watched the flagstone roll back, tested it with her foot, brushed off her hands, put her nurse's cap back on, and left, yawning as she walked.

They could hear her move down the hall but she didn't go to the elevator bank. Instead she opened the back door and left.

Tucker grunted as she shook off the carton. *"That floor is cold."*

"Let's see if we can get out of here."

The two hurried to the lone door at the end of the hall.

Tucker stood on her hind legs. *"You maybe can do this."*

Murphy reached up but it was a little high. *"Nope."*

"Get on my back."

The cat hopped onto the corgi's strong back. She easily reached the doorknob and her clever paws did the rest. They opened the door and scooted out without bothering to close it.

Within twenty minutes they were scratching at Miranda's back door.

She opened it. "Nine-thirty at night and cold. Now just what were you two bad critters doing out there?"

"If only we could tell you," Mrs. Murphy sighed.

"Come on. Bet you're hungry," said the

kindly woman, who would feed the world if she could figure out how.

When the phone rang at ten that same cold night Mim, early to bed, grudgingly picked it up.

A muffled voice said, "Your barn, tomorrow morning at nine." Then hung up.

Mim had caller ID and quickly called Sheriff Shaw at home.

"823–9497." He repeated the number as she read it to him.

"She must have had fabric or something over the mouthpiece but it was a woman," Mim stated, "and she sounded familiar."

"Thanks. You've done good work. I'll have someone in the hayloft tomorrow and another officer flat in the backseat of your car. Park your car at the barn."

"I will."

When Rick checked the phone number it turned out to be the pay phone in the supermarket parking lot.

Harry chastised Mrs. Murphy and Tucker, neither of whom appeared remorseful, which only infuriated her more. She thanked Miranda for keeping them overnight. That was at seven in the morning.

By seven-thirty Rob Collier had dropped

off two canvas sacks of mail, a light day. As Harry sorted mail and Miranda tackled the packages and manila envelopes, the two bold creatures told Pewter everything.

"Nurse Logan. Tussie Logan?" Pewter couldn't believe it. *"It's hard to imagine her as a killer."*

"We didn't say she was the killer. Only that she went down into the room and came back out three hours later. We assume she's cleaning the infusion pumps." Mrs. Murphy allowed herself a lordly tone.

"Remember the first three letters of assume." Pewter smarted off.

41

A spiral of blue smoke lazed upward for a few feet, then flattened out. Whenever smoke descended hunters felt that scent would be good. Rick, not being a foxhunter, would have gladly picked up a good scent, figuratively speaking. He felt he was on the cusp of knowledge yet it eluded him like a receding wave.

The temperature hovered in the low forties but the air carried the hint of snow. He looked west at the gunmetal-blue clouds peeping over the tops of the Blue Ridge Mountains. Turning up the collar of his jacket, he stood on a knoll a half mile from Mim's barn. Coop, next to him, held a cell phone in her hand. They waited for the call from the barn.

"You know I've always felt that killers, like painters, eventually leave a body of work behind so distinctive that you can identify them — by looking at the canvas. Some people kill out of self-defense. Understandable. Admirable even, and hard to fault." A plume of air escaped his lips.

"As long as those killers are men. If a wife kills in self-defense against an abusive husband people find reasons why she shouldn't have done so. In fact, boss, killing seems to still be male turf."

"Yep, for the most part it is. We jealously guard our propensity for violence. That's the real reason the services have trouble with women in combat. Scares the men." He half laughed. "If she's got an Uzi, she's as powerful as I am."

She hunched up. The wind picked up. She checked her watch. Nine-fifteen. No call.

They waited until ten-thirty, then walked back to the barn. Mim and the two officers at the barn were bitterly disappointed.

Mim returned to her house accompanied by one of the officers.

"Stay in the barn office until noon unless you hear from me," Rick ordered the other man. Then he and Cooper trudged through the woods to their squad car parked in the hay shed on a farm road. The ground was frozen. They'd drive out without getting stuck.

Once inside the car they sat for a moment while the heater warmed the vehicle and Rick squashed his cigarette in the ashtray.

"Boss." Coop unzipped her coat. "Harry had an idea."

"Sweet Jesus." He whistled.

"The Cramers foxhunt with Middleburg Hunt and Orange, too."

"What's that supposed to mean?" He turned toward her, his heavy beard shadow giving his jaw a bluish tinge.

"According to Harry it means they hunt with fast packs, they're good riders."

"So what?"

"So, she said invite them down to hunt. It might rattle our killer."

"Harry thought of that, did she?" He leaned back, putting both hands behind his head. "Remind me to take that girl to lunch."

"The sight of them might provoke our guy to do something stupid."

"We still have to keep somebody with them. No chances. Can you ride good enough to stay with them?"

"No, but Graham Pitsenberger can and so can Lieutenant-Colonel Dennis Foster. They're both tough guys. They'll be armed, .38s tucked away in arm holsters or the small of the back. We can trust them."

"You've asked them?"

"Yes. Graham will come over from Staunton. Dennis will drive down from Leesburg. Harry said she'll mount them."

"That sounds exciting," he wryly noted.

"I'll go with the Hilltoppers."

"God, Cooper, I can't keep track of all this horse lingo."

"Hilltoppers don't jump. It will take me a while before I can negotiate those jumps. I will though." A determined set to her jaw made her look the way she must have looked as a child when told no by her mother.

"I'll stick to fishing. Not that I have the time. I've been promising Herb we'd go over to Highland County to fish for the last four years." He sighed, cracking his knuckles behind his head.

"You haven't spit on dogs or cussed Christians so I guess it's all right?"

"Where do you get these expressions?" He smiled at her. "I'm a Virginia boy and I haven't heard some of them."

"I get around." She winked.

"When are the Cramers coming?"

"This Saturday."

"I'll try to get there for part of it, anyway."

"Roger."

"Let's cruise." He put the car in gear. "Maybe if we're lucky we'll catch this perp before there's more harm done."

What neither of them knew was that they were already too late.

42

"Ran down over everything, part of my ceiling fell in." Randy Sands, bone white, coughed, composed himself, and continued, "so I banged on the door and shouted and then I opened the door. I guess that's when I knew something was — was not right." He coughed again.

Rick sympathetically put his arm around Randy's thin shoulders. "Quite a shock, Randy."

"Well, I yelled for her but she didn't answer so I went straight to the bathroom." His lower lip trembled. "The rest you know."

In the background the rescue squad removed the body of Tussie Logan. The fingerprint team had come and gone.

Coop figured from the body that Tussie had been in the tub perhaps four or five hours. Whoever shot her had come up behind her and shot down through the heart, one shot.

"Randy, how long have you owned this

house?" Rick asked as Coop joined him.

"Since Momma died." Randy thought this information was sufficient.

"When was that?"

"Nineteen ninety-two." He fidgeted when the body was rolled out on the gurney even though it was in a body bag. "She was a good-looking woman. I hated to see her like that."

"Yes." Rick guided him to the sofa. "Sit down, Randy. Your first impressions are valuable to us and I know you're shaken but I have to ask questions."

Shaken though he was, it wasn't often that Randy Sands was the center of attention. He sat on the wicker sofa, brightly colored cushions behind him. Rick sat in a chair opposite the sofa. Coop quietly examined each room in the airy upstairs apartment.

"Did Tussie lock her doors?"

The clapboard house with the wraparound porch built in 1904 was halfway between Charlottesville and Crozet, situated back off Garth Road. The location was convenient to the hospital yet afforded privacy and a touch of the country. Randy couldn't always keep up with the forty-two acres. Tussie enjoyed mowing the lawn on the riding mower, edging the flower beds, and hanging plants on the porch.

"Where were you today?"

"At work. I came home around five-thirty. Finished a little early today. That's when I found Tussie."

"Where do you work, Randy?"

"Chromatech. Off the downtown mall. My bosses Lucia and Chuck Morse can verify my hours." A slightly belligerent tone infected his voice.

"I'm sure they can. Now do you have any idea who would kill Tussie?"

"No." He shook his head.

"Drugs?"

"No. Never."

"Drinking?"

"No. Well, socially but I never saw her drunk. I can't imagine who would do this."

"Is anything obvious missing? Jewelry? Money? Paintings?"

"I didn't check her jewelry box. I stayed right here in the living room. I —" He didn't want to say he was afraid to walk from room to room.

"Boss." Cynthia Cooper called from the glassed-in back porch, which had been a sleeping loft in the old days.

"Excuse me, Randy. You wait here." Rick walked down the hallway to the back.

The porch overlooked the meadows, the mountains beyond. Filled with light, it was a wonderful place to work. A bookshelf rested against the back wall. Her desk, a door over two file cabinets, was in the middle of the narrow room, coldish except for a space heater on the floor.

"Here." Coop pointed to a very expensive computer and laser printer.

"Huh. Must have cost close to six thousand dollars."

"This computer and printer can do anything. The quality is very high."

"Invoices?" Rick wanted another cigarette but stopped himself from reaching for the pack in his inside coat pocket. "Maybe."

"Is everything all right?" Randy's querulous voice wafted back to them.

"Yes, fine," Rick called back. "Coop, can you get into the computer?"

"Yes, I think so."

"I'll keep Randy busy. Maybe I'll walk him outside. He can show me if there's a back way in." Rick winked and returned to the slender man in the corduroy pants.

Coop sat down, flicked on the computer. Tussie had lots of e-mail. She had been plugged into a nurses' chat room. She'd taped a list of passwords on the side of her computer, a defense against forgetfulness perhaps. Coop went through the passwords finally hitting pay dirt with "Nightingale."

Coop perused the messages. She then pulled up the graphics package, which was extensive.

"I could sit here all day and play with this," Coop said to herself, wishing she could afford the same system.

Tussie had a code. Coop couldn't crack it.

After checking out what she could, she shut off the computer and walked to the bedroom. With gloved hands she lifted the lid on the leather jewelry box. Earrings, bracelets, and necklaces were thrown in together. She opened the top drawer of the dresser. Silk underwear was jumbled. A green savings bankbook rested under the eggplant-colored underwear.

She pulled it out, flipped the white pages to the last balance. "Wow." She whistled.

Tussie's savings account balance as of February 25 was $139,990.36.

"I'm beginning to get the picture," Coop said to herself.

Once she and Rick were together in the squad car she informed him of her finds. They wondered where and how Hank Brevard had hidden his profits. To date they'd found nothing in that department.

Rick picked up the phone, calling in to headquarters. He ordered the department computer whiz to see if he could crack

Tussie's code.

"Screwy, isn't it?" Coop wiggled down in her seat, hunching her shoulders. "What's the plan, boss?"

"First we'll go to Sam Mahanes, which means he'll call for his lawyers."

"Right. Then he'll express grief."

"Then we'll go to Bruce Buxton."

"More shock and dismay but in a different way."

"We'll go to her Pediatric unit. And then you and I are going to walk through this hospital one more time. As many times as it takes over the next few days, weeks, or whatever. We know there are false billings. We know those infusion pumps have to be cleaned and rehabbed. They have to be in that hospital somewhere. Damn, it's right under our noses!"

Coop, having heard that before, sat up straight and said nothing. She was wondering why a woman like Tussie Logan got involved in the scam in the first place. Tussie seemed like a nice enough person. She knew right from wrong. She knew what she was doing was wrong — even before the murders. Maybe Tussie was one of the murderers. How does a woman like that get into something like this? She knew what Tussie Logan had done was wrong and she knew

Tussie knew it was wrong.

Coop expected more of women than men. It surprised her. She'd never thought of herself as a sexist but her response to Tussie's criminal behavior gave her a gleam of insight into her own self. She wasn't sure she liked it.

43

The Church of the Holy Light, in order to raise money for Herb's God's Love group, was holding a bake sale at the small old train station. Given that the ladies of the church had earned fame for their skills, the place was mobbed.

Miranda Hogendobber baked orange-glazed cinnamon buns as well as luscious breads.

Harry held down the fort at the post office. She and Miranda spelled one another. Sometimes it was nice to scoot out of work early or take a long lunch.

Everyone noticed when the Rescue Squad ambulance pulled out of the brick garage and they also noticed when it drove by, heading out of town.

Big Mim, as Crozet's leading citizen, felt she should be informed of every single event the moment it occurred. She flipped out her tiny cell phone, dialing the sheriff's office.

"Mother." Little Mim thought her mother could have at least walked outside to call, but then again it was cold.

"Don't tell me what to do." She tapped her foot, clad in exquisite crocodile loafers. "Ah, hello. Is the sheriff in? Well, have him call me then, Natalie." She dropped her voice as she worked over the daytime dispatcher. "You don't know who just rolled by in the ambulance, do you? Well, have him call me on my cell phone. Thanks. Bye." She pressed the Off button, folded her phone, slipping it in her purse.

"People do have heart attacks without consulting you." The daughter smiled sweetly as she drove home a light barb.

"They shouldn't. They shouldn't do anything without consulting me." Mim smiled sweetly right back. "I suppose I ought to buy some brownies."

"The orange cinnamons are all gone."

"Really, Miranda should open her own bakery. She's got a gift." Mim noticed the squad car with Rick and Coop stopping at the post office. "Here." She handed her daughter fifty dollars. "I'm going across the street."

"Without me?"

"Oh, Marilyn. Just buy the stuff and join me." Mim was out the door before she finished her sentence.

Rick and Cooper set foot in the post office

but before they could open their mouths, Mim charged in. "Did Natalie call you?"

"About one minute ago." He exhaled from his nostrils. "I was going to call you as soon as I finished here."

Big Mim's eyebrows raised up. What could be so important that Harry had to be consulted first?

"Bad news." Pewter trotted over from the small table in the rear.

"Why don't you all come back here?" Harry flipped up the divider as Mrs. Murphy stretched herself on the narrow shelf behind the postboxes. Tucker, awake, watched.

Rick realized he was going to have to tell Mim something, so he thought he'd get that over with first. "Randy Sands found Tussie Logan in her bathtub shot to death."

"What?" Mim clapped her hands together, a gesture of surprise.

"How did he know?" Harry asked the pointed question.

"The water was running and it came through his ceiling below. He came home from work, noticed it, and ran upstairs. He's in a bad way. I called Reverend Jones to go on out there."

"Shot." Mim sat down hard in one of the wooden chairs at the table.

"Well, that's no surprise to us," Mrs. Murphy said.

"Being in on it and being dead are two different things," Tucker sagely noted.

"Ugh." Pewter hated the thought of dead big bodies. She didn't mind mice, mole, or bird bodies but anything larger than that turned her stomach.

"Good Lord. I wonder if it was Tussie who called me?" Mim was incredulous.

"Her death ought to tell you that." Murphy paced on the narrow ledge.

"If they knew what we knew, it would." Tucker had more patience with human frailty than the cat.

"How long had she been dead?" Harry was figuring in her mind whether the killer crept up by night or by day.

Rick added, "It's hard to tell. Tom Yancy will know."

"Struggle?" Harry was still reeling from the news of the murder and that Tussie was the chain-letter writer.

"No," Coop simply stated.

"Whoever it was may have been known to her but having anyone walk into your bath ought to provoke some sort of response from a lady." Mim saw her daughter, laden with food, leave the train station to put the booty in her car.

"I don't know but it wouldn't be terribly difficult to walk into a bathroom and pull the trigger. She wouldn't have time to struggle. This was fast and effective." Rick slipped a cigarette out of the pack. "Ladies?"

"No. I thought you quit." Mim didn't care if anyone smoked or not.

"I quit frequently." He lit up.

"Why do humans do that?" Pewter hated the smell.

"To soothe their nerves," Murphy said.

"It ruins their lungs." Tucker also hated the smell.

"You don't see cats smoking," Pewter smugly said, secure that this proved yet again the superiority of cats.

Murphy kept pacing. *"Rick's not just here to deliver the news. Mom wouldn't be first for that."*

"Yeah, that's true," Tucker agreed.

"Harry, I think we'd better cancel having the Cramers hunt tomorrow. It's too dangerous. And I'm going to have Coop stay with you at night until —" He noticed Little Mim walking toward the post office.

"The Cramers?" Mim's voice rose. "Do I know the Cramers?"

"No." Harry quickly spoke for she, too, saw Little Mim. "They hunt with Orange and Middleburg."

365

"Must be good." Mim wanted to know what was going on.

"Mrs. Sanburne." Rick leaned over. "We're close to our killer here. I know you like to be in on everything but right now I would expose you to danger, serious danger. The reason I'm here with Harry is that she was struck over the head at the hospital."

Mim raised an eyebrow, saying nothing, since Miranda had sworn her to secrecy when she told her, but Mim had figured it out anyway. Rick continued. "I can't take a chance. The killer or killers may think she knows more than she does."

"And I don't know anything." Harry shrugged. "Wish I did."

"What do the Cramers have to do with Harry?"

"Well, uh, we were going to hunt together tomorrow. They're in the hospital business and —"

"Mrs. Sanburne, I promise you I'll fill you in as soon as we're —" He paused, searching for the right words. "Over the hump. Now could I ask you to intercept your daughter before she gets in here? Just give me two minutes with Harry."

Mollified slightly, Mim stood up, walked over, flipping up the divider, and caught Marilyn just as her hand was on the doorknob. She ushered her back toward the car across the street.

"Rick. Let the Cramers hunt. It will be the straw that breaks the camel's back. We've got Graham, we've got Dennis. They're military men. They're horsemen. They know what they're doing. They can protect the Cramers. Dennis is riding down with them in their rig and he'll ride back. I really believe we can shake our gorilla out of the tree tomorrow."

"It's a hell of a chance." Rick ran his fingers through his thinning hair. He knew Harry had a point but he hated to risk civilians, as he thought of them.

"Coop, I know we can do this. I wouldn't use the Cramers as bait if I didn't think it would flush him out," Harry pleaded.

"Yeah, Harry, I know, but I just saw Tussie Logan."

Rick and Coop stared at one another.

Rick puffed, then put down his cigarette. "Okay."

44

The Hunt Club hounds met at Tally Urquhart's farm at ten in the morning. Rose Hill, one of the oldest and most beautiful farms in Albemarle County, was a plum fixture, fixture being what meeting places are called.

The home itself, built of bricks baked onsite in the mid-eighteenth century, glowed with the patina of age. Tally herself glowed with the patina of age at ninety-two. She said ninety-two. Mim, her niece, swore that Tally was a hair older but at least everyone agreed she was triumphantly in her nineties.

Tally would stride into a room, still walking mostly upright, shake her silver-headed cane, a hound's head, at the congregation and declare, "I am two years older than God so do what I say and get out of my way."

And people did. Even Mim.

Years ago, back in the 1960s, Tally had been Master of the Jefferson Hunt. Her imperiousness wore thin but her ample contributions to the treasury ensured a long mastership. She finally retired on her eightieth birthday, amid much fanfare.

Everyone thought Mim would vie to be Master but she declined, saying she had enough to do, which was true. But truthfully, Mim wanted to keep her hunting pure fun and if she were Master it would be pure politics. She practiced that in other arenas.

Jane Arnold found herself elected Master and had remained at her post ever since.

A chill from the mountains settled into the meadows. Harry's hands were so cold she stiffly fastened Poptart's girth. She had introduced Laura and Joe Cramer to Jane per custom. There was no need to introduce Graham Pitsenberger, Joint-Master of Glenmore Hunt, nor Lt. Col. Dennis Foster, the Director of the Master of Foxhounds of America Association.

Master and staff didn't know the true reason for their company. Jane graciously invited these guests to ride up front with her.

Harry breathed a sigh of relief. If Joe and Laura were up front, nothing much could happen that she could foresee. If they fell behind, well, anything was possible.

Aunt Tally waved everyone off, then hurried back to the house before the chill could get her. Also, she was hosting the breakfast and it had to be perfect.

Dennis and Graham had conferred by phone before the hunt. Each man wore a .38 under his coat, low near the belt so the gun could be easily retrieved if needed.

Susan, Little Mim, and Harry rode behind Big Mim, who rode immediately behind the Cramers and the two men. It would never do to pass Big Mim in the hunt field, but since her Thoroughbreds were fast and she was a consummate rider, there was little chance that would happen.

The hounds hit right behind the cattle barns and within minutes everyone was flying up the hill behind the barns, down into the narrow ravine, across the creek, and then they boomed over open meadows which would soon be sown with oats.

Sam Mahanes rode in the middle of the pack, as did the bulk of the field. A few stragglers, struggling at the creek, brought up the rear.

Dr. Bruce Buxton rode back with the Hilltoppers since he was trying a new horse. Being a cautious rider, he wasn't ready to ride a new horse in the first flight.

They flew along for fifteen minutes, then stopped. The hounds, noses to the ground, tried to figure out just where Reynard lost them. A lovely tricolored female ran up a large tree, blown over in a windstorm, its top branches caught in the branches of another large tree. The angle of the fallen tree must have been thirty degrees. The top of the tree hung over a large, swift-moving creek.

Finally a brave hound plunged into the creek and started working on the other side.

"He's on this side," the hound called out to his companions.

"I knew it!" the tricolor female, still on the tree, shouted. *"He ran up this tree and dropped into the creek. Swam to the other side. Oh, he's a smart one, he is."*

Within a minute the whole pack had crossed the creek. The humans and horses, however, slipped and slid, trying to find a negotiable crossing. Jane, leading the humans, rode about one hundred yards downstream to find a better place. She motioned for the others to follow her quickly for the hounds were streaking across the meadow.

Laura Cramer, sitting her horse beautifully, jumped down the bank, trotted across the creek, and then jumped out. Her husband followed. Mim, of course, rode this as though she were at Madison Square Garden. Everybody made it except for a little girl on a pony. The water swirled up over the saddle. She let out a yell. Her mom retrieved her, and both walked back home, the kid crying her eyes out, not because she was cold and wet but because her mother made her stop hunting. She didn't care if she caught a cold. It would mean she might miss some school. Mothers could be mean.

Harry and Poptart observed a movement out of the corner of their eyes. The fox had turned, heading back toward the creek.

Harry stopped, turned her half-bred in the direction of the fox, took off her hunt cap, counted to twenty to give the fox a sporting chance, and then said, "Tally Ho."

Jane raised her whip hand, stopping the field. Everyone got a splendid view of a medium-sized red fox rolling along at a trot. He reached the creek, jumped in, but didn't emerge on the other side. He swam downstream, finally jumping out, and he then walked across a log, stopped, checked where the hounds were. Then he decided to put some distance between himself and these canine cousins.

Graham stood up in his stirrups and laughed. He was a man who enjoyed being outsmarted by this varmint. Dennis noticed the First Whipper-In flying along the top of the ridge ahead of the hounds but to the right of the fox. No hunting person, staff or field, ever wants to turn the fox.

The Huntsman watched proudly as his hounds curved back, soared off the bank into the creek, coming out on the other side. Now they had to find the scent, which was along the bank but a good football field or more downstream. The Huntsman jumped straight down the bank.

Laura whispered to Joe, "Think we'll have to do that?"

"You go first." He laughed.

Jane wheeled back, deciding that discretion was the better part of valor. She'd recross at their original crossing site and then gallop along the stream to try and catch up, for she knew the Huntsman would push his hounds up to the line of scent as fast as he could.

Within minutes the hounds sang out. Harry's blood raced. Susan giggled. She always giggled when the pedal pushed to the metal.

They slopped across the creek, jumped up the bank, and thundered alongside it, jumping fallen logs, dodging debris. The path opened up; an abandoned meadow beckoned ahead, a few scraggly opportunistic cedars marring it.

They shot across that meadow, hounds now flying. They crossed a narrow creek, much easier, and headed up the side of a steep hill, the tree line silhouetted against a gray, threatening sky.

Once they reached the crest of the hill, the hounds turned toward the mountains. The field began to stretch out. Some whose horses were not in condition pooped out. Others bought some real estate, mud stains advertising the fact. About half the field was still riding hard when the crest of the ridge thinned out, finally dipping into a wide ravine with yet another swift-running creek in it.

They reached the bottom to watch all the hounds furiously digging at an old tree trunk. The fox had ducked into his den. There was no way the hounds, much too big for the den, could flush him out, plus he had lots of hidden exits if things grew too hot. But the Huntsman dismounted to blow, "Gone to ground." The hounds leapt up, dug, bayed, full of themselves.

The fox moved farther back into the den, utterly disgusted with the noise. Why a member of the canine family would want to live with humans baffled the fox. Humans smelled bad, plus they were so dumb. No amount of regular food could overcome those flaws.

After a fulsome celebration, the Huntsman mounted back up.

"Shall I hunt them back, Master?"

"Oh, why not?" She smiled.

On the way back they picked up a bit of scent but by the time Tally's farm came into view, fingers and toes craved warmth.

Everyone untacked their horses, threw sweat sheets and then blankets over them, tied them to the trailers, and hurried into Tally's beautiful house.

Harry thought to herself, "So far, so good."

45

"Why, the fences were four feet then. We rode Thoroughbreds of course and flew like the wind." Tally leaned on her cane. It wasn't her back that had given out on her but her left knee and she refused to have arthroscopic surgery. She said she was too damned old to have some doctor punching holes in her knee.

Dennis listened, a twinkle in his eyes. The fences were always bigger when recalled at a distance of decades but in truth, they were.

A crowd filled the house: Miranda, Ned Tucker, Jordan Ivanic, Herb Jones, plus stablehands, more lawyers and doctors, and the neighbors for miles around. When Miss Tally threw a hunt breakfast, best to be there.

"Sam," Joe Cramer greeted him warmly. "I didn't have time to talk to you during the hunt. Say, it was a good one, wasn't it?"

"Those creek crossings —" Sam noticed Bruce out of the corner of his eye. "Well, I haven't seen you for some time, Joe. I'm glad you could come on down and hunt with us."

"Yes, Harry invited us," Joe almost said but caught himself.

Cynthia Cooper brushed by, a plate loaded with food, including biscuits drenched in redeye gravy, her favorite.

Bruce joined Joe and Sam. He spoke to Joe. "Forgive me. I know I've met you but I can't recall where."

"Salvage Masters. Joe Cramer." Joe held out his hand. "We rehab infusion pumps, every brand."

"Why, yes, of course." Bruce warily shook his hand. "What brings you to Crozet?"

"Harry Haristeen invited my wife and I to hunt today. You know, February is usually a good month."

Laura glided up next to her husband. "The dog foxes are courting."

"My wife, Laura. Laura, this is Dr. Bruce Buxton and Sam Mahanes, director of Crozet Hospital."

"Glad to meet you." She shook their hands.

"You ride quite well," Sam said admiringly.

"Good horse," she said.

"Good hands." Graham Pitsenberger, smiling, squeezed into the group, the fireplace immediately behind them providing much needed warmth. "Time to thaw out."

"My butt's cold, too." Bruce smiled.

"Sam." Joe held his hands behind his back to the fire. "You know, your infusion pumps are way overdue on a cleaning." Joe just blurted this out in the excitement of it all. He was supposed to say nothing.

Sam paused a moment. "They are?"

"Years."

"I'll look into that. I can't imagine it because our plant manager, Hank Brevard, was meticulous in his duties. I'll check the records."

Troubled, Bruce cleared his throat. "We've had a shake-up at the hospital, Mr. and Mrs. Cramer. You may have heard."

Joe and Laura played dumb, as did Graham.

Sam, jovially, touched Joe's elbow as he spoke to Bruce. "No need to go over that, Bruce. Foxhunting shouldn't be plagued with work troubles. Joe, I'll get out the files Monday and give you a call."

"Here's my card." Joe slipped his hand into his inside hacking jacket, producing a business card printed on expensive paper, really printed, not thermographed.

He'd changed from his hunting coat to a hacking jacket for the breakfast, which was proper. Not that Tally would have pitched a fit. She didn't care if anyone came into her house in a muddy or torn frock or melton so long as they regaled her with stories. She did draw the line at lots of makeup in the hunt field though. Tally felt that hunting favored the naturally beautiful woman while exposing the artificial one.

Sam took the card, excusing himself. As he headed for the bar, Bruce tagged after him.

"Sam, what's going on? The equipment is overdue for cleaning." He gulped down his drink. "Why the hell won't you listen to me about this — our reputation is taking a beating."

"Let's have this discussion at another time."

"It's a damned sorry mess if we're using pumps that need work. It's beyond sorry."

"Bruce." Sam's voice was firm but low. "As far as I know those infusion pumps are working beautifully. The nurses would report it to the head nurse in a heartbeat. You know that. But I will definitely check the records. Hank would never let anything get out of hand or worn down. He just wouldn't and I don't think Bobby Minifee will either, once he feels comfortable in his position."

Rick Shaw and Big Mim whispered to one

another in the corner for a moment.

"When will Tussie's death be written up in the paper?"

"Tomorrow." Rick sighed. "I used every chit I had to hold the story. The only people who know are you, Marilyn, Harry, and Randy."

"Rescue Squad."

"They understand perfectly well. Diana Robb can shut up the two people who came out with her for another twenty-four hours."

"I hope so." Mim's eyes darted around the room.

"Randy called the hospital and told her boss that Tussie had a family emergency. She wouldn't be in to work until Sunday."

"If this ruse works, Rick, our fox should bolt the den."

Rick smiled. "You hunters crack me up."

She smiled and they parted to mix with the others.

Little Mim cleverly maneuvered toward Bruce Buxton who, face flushed, was now talking with Harry, Susan, and Miranda.

"You all will be receiving invitations to one of Mother's teas," Little Mim said, her luxurious chestnut hair falling straight to her shoulders.

"More mail to sort." Harry winked.

Miranda's stomach growled. She put her

hand on it, saying, "News from the interior."

"Time to eat," Susan added. "Harry, you've only eaten once. You must be ready for another plate."

"Cold makes me hungry."

The three women made a beeline for the table, leaving Marilyn to flirt with Bruce, who didn't seem to mind.

Fair strode through the door.

Tally called out to him. "Why didn't you hunt today?"

"Breeding season, Miss Urquhart. But I had to drop by to see you."

"Liar. You dropped by for the food!" He kissed her cheek.

"I came to see you." He kissed the other cheek. "Prettiest girl in the county."

"You go." She blushed a little. "Go on, your girlfriend's back at the table. She can eat, Fair, my, how she can eat. In my day a lady hid her appetite. Of course, she never puts on a pound. Me neither."

"Your figure is the envy of women half your age."

"Fifty!" Tally triumphantly said.

"Actually, I was thinking more like thirty-five."

"Mercy. You get out of here before I forget myself." She pushed him toward the dining room.

Fair cut into the line to be with Harry.

"Cheater," Susan humorously complained.

"Tally called me a liar. You're calling me a cheater. Anyone else want to unburden themselves?" He stared down at his ex-wife's pretty head. "I retract that offer."

Harry reached for and squeezed his hand. Laura Cramer was on the other side of the table.

"This is a lively group." Laura laughed.

"Wait until the drinks hit." Susan giggled.

Harry introduced Fair to Laura as they moved around the table.

He gallantly carried her plate, put both plates down on the long coffee table, and headed to the bar for Cokes for each of them. Fair never drank during the day, although he did drink socially.

Cooper walked over. "Some party."

"Have you had anything to eat?"

"Yes. Too much. I'm going back for dessert."

"Come sit with us." Harry indicated they'd sit on the floor.

The Cramers also sat on the floor, using the coffee table as their table. Graham, Dennis, Cooper, Susan, and Miranda squeezed in. Fair and Joe talked medical talk, since veterinary medicine used many of the same procedures and machines as human medical science. In fact, some procedures successful on humans were pioneered by veterinarians.

Graham regaled Cynthia Cooper with tales of training green racehorses to use the starting gate. Dennis Foster and Laura compared packs of hounds in northern Virginia, always a subject of passionate interest to foxhunters. Susan listened intently and Laura invited her, the whole table, to join them at Middleburg Hunt for a ripsnorter.

At one point Joe leaned over, whispering to Harry what he'd said to Sam and Bruce. Just then Jordan Ivanic bent over to say his hellos and Joe repeated what he'd told Sam and Bruce to Jordan, who blanched.

"I'll look into it. We've had some unfortunate occurrences." Jordan smiled tightly.

"I think murder qualifies as an unfortunate occurrence." Graham picked up a piece of corn bread.

"Now, Mr. Pitsenberger, we only know that Hank Brevard was killed in the basement of the hospital. We have no information that would connect other irregularities to that incident," Jordan smoothly replied.

"That's not what the newspaper says," Graham needled him.

"Newspapers sell issues for the benefit of

advertisers. Now if you all will excuse me. It's nice to see you again." Jordan nodded to the Cramers.

"That's a cool cucumber," Graham remarked as Jordan was out of earshot.

"He wasn't so cool when Hank was murdered," Susan filled him in. "At least that's what I heard."

The visiting hunters had been well briefed about Hank's demise and Larry Johnson's murder. They knew nothing about Tussie Logan.

"For a small community you don't lack for excitement," Laura dryly said.

A shout at the front door attracted everyone's attention.

"George Moore, what are you doing here?" Tally laughed as a tall man breezed through her front door.

"I'm here to sweep you off your feet." He picked her up.

"Brute!" She threw up her hands in mock despair.

He carefully placed her down. "Have you eaten any of your own food?"

"No. I've been the hostess with the mostest."

"Well, come on. I'll be your breakfast date." He slipped her arm through his, walking her to the table.

Everyone knew George so there was lots of catcalling and waving.

Little Mim teased Bruce Buxton. "With a name like George, you have a lot to live up to in Virginia."

The breakfast rolled on for hours. Tally had hired a pianist, which augmented the already high spirits. After everyone had eaten they crowded around the piano to sing, a habit common to Tally's generation and all but lost by the time Harry's generation was raised.

As the guests finally left one by one, Dennis accompanied the Cramers.

Rick quietly watched everyone from the front windows of the house. Coop used the excuse of helping Harry load her horses to go back to the trailers.

"I'll ride home with you." Cynthia's voice indicated this was an order not a request.

"Great."

"Rick's going to push Sam and Jordan about the records and he wants me to stick with you."

"I'd say there's someone at this breakfast today who is sweating bullets."

"You know, here's where the human ego baffles me. Why not take the money and run? If you're the kingpin of this scam, you know the noose is being tightened — just run," Coop said.

"Maybe the money is not easily retrieved."

"All the more reason to run." Coop shrugged.

"I think it's ego. He thinks he can outsmart all of us."

"Could be. He's done a good job so far." Coop waved as the Cramers and Dennis pulled out.

By the time Harry and Coop reached the farm, unloaded the horses, fed them, cleaned up, they were tired.

As they discussed the events of the day, the animals listened.

"I hate to admit this but I'm hungry again." Harry laughed.

"I can always eat."

They raided the refrigerator.

"You know, Mom has that chirpy quality," Tucker noticed.

"That means she's going to do something really dumb." Murphy said what Tucker and Pewter were thinking.

46

Rick walked into his office just as the dispatcher told him to pick up line one.

"Sheriff Shaw."

"Hi, Sam Mahanes. I dropped back by the hospital after Tally's breakfast and we do have records for cleaning out the infusion pumps. Joe Cramer must have been confused."

"Where are you now?"

"Home."

"Can anyone working a computer terminal at the hospital pull up a maintenance file?"

"No. If people could do that they could also get into medical records, which are strictly confidential. The only people accessing the maintenance file would be myself. Well, Ruth, of course, Hank Brevard, and now Bobby Minifee."

"What about the men working with Bobby? Someone like Booty Weyman. Wouldn't Bobby teach him to use the computer? Anybody responsible for equipment, for shipping, would have to access the records."

"I'll double-check with Bobby on Monday. I'm not sure. I always assumed Hank gave marching orders and that was that."

"Maybe he did but it would have made his life a lot easier if someone could work the computer, otherwise he'd have been bugged on his days off, on vacation." Rick paused. "And Jordan Ivanic. As your second-in-command he would have the maintenance records or know how to get them."

Sam airily dismissed Jordan. "He could, I suppose, if he felt it germane but Jordan shows little interest in those matters. He likes to focus on 'above the line' as he calls it. He feels that maintenance, orderlies, janitorial, and even nurses are 'below the line.'"

"Speaking of nurses, are you on good terms with Tussie Logan?"

"Yes. She's one of our best." A questioning note filtered through Sam's even voice.

"H-m-m, why don't you meet me in your office in about an hour? Jordan will be on duty this weekend. We can all go over this together."

"Sheriff, an oversight about infusion pumps seems small beer compared to the murders."

"On the contrary, Sam, this may be the key." He paused. "Anything not quite on the tracks at Crozet Hospital interests me right now. And one other little thing. Joe and Laura Cramer have examined the invoices. The billing numbers aren't their billing numbers. These invoices are bogus, Sam." Rick could hear a sharp intake of breath.

"In an hour. Eight-fifteen."

47

"Coop, are you going to spend the night?" Harry innocently asked.

"Yes." Cynthia checked her watch. It had been losing time.

"Seven." Harry answered without being asked.

"I'd much rather the damn thing gained time than lost it. Well, it only cost me forty dollars so I suppose I could afford another one. There's no sense wearing good watches on my job." She reset her watch, to synchronize with Harry's: seven o'clock.

"Those Navy Seals watches are pretty neat. They glow in the dark."

"So do people who live near nuclear reactors," Coop joked.

"Ha ha." Harry stuck out her tongue. "Wouldn't it be helpful if you could read the dial in the dark? What if you're creeping up on a suspect or you have to coordinate times, synchronize in the dark?"

"Your fervid imagination just runs riot."

"You should live here." Pewter yawned.

"Coop, there's two of us. I've got a .38 pistol. You've got your service revolver."

"Harry, where is this leading?"

"To Crozet Hospital."

"What?!"

"Now hear me out. Three people are dead. My stitches still itch. Joe baited Sam, Bruce, and Jordan. Right?"

"Right."

"What we're looking for has to be in that basement. Has to be."

"Rick Shaw and I crawled over that basement with a fine-tooth comb. We studied the blueprints. We tapped the walls to see if any are hollow. I don't see how we could have missed anything."

"The floor," Murphy practically screeched in frustration.

"Pussycat, do you have a tummy ache?" Harry swung her legs off the sofa but Murphy jumped on her lap to save her the trip to the chair.

"I am fine. I am better than fine. What you want is underneath your feet."

"Yeah!" Pewter joined the chorus.

"It's so obvious once you know," Tucker barked.

"Pipe down." Harry covered her ears and they shut up.

"Something provoked them."

"Human stupidity," Murphy growled.

"Maybe you need a tiny shot of Pepto-Bismol."

"Never." Mrs. Murphy shot off Harry's lap so fast she left tiny claw marks in Harry's thigh.

"Ouch. Murphy, behave yourself."

"You ought to listen to us." Tucker stared at her mother, her liquid brown eyes soulful.

"Here's my idea. We take our guns. We take a good flashlight and we go back down there together. I even think we should take Mrs. Murphy, Pewter, and Tucker. They can sense and smell things we can't. Coop, you know Rick won't let me or the kids down there and what we need is there. Has to be."

"You're repeating yourself."

"This is our only chance. It's nighttime. There won't be as many people around. The loading dock will be closed. We'll have to contend with whoever is on night duty, assuming we can find him. Come on. You're a trained officer of the law. You can handle any situation."

It was the appeal to Cooper's vanity that wore down her defenses. "It's one thing if I gamble with my life, it's another if I gamble with yours."

"What about mine?" an insulted Pewter yowled.

"God, Pewter, you can't be hungry again." Harry returned her attention to Cynthia Cooper. "You gamble every day you put your foot out of bed. Life is a gamble. I really want to get whoever killed Larry Johnson. I can't say I'm motivated by Hank's death or Tussie's, not that I wished them dead, but Larry was my doctor, my friend, and a good man. I'm doing this for him."

Cooper thought a long time. "If I take you, will you shut up? As in never mention this to Rick?"

"Scout's honor."

Another long pause. "All right."

"Oh brother." Tucker hid her eyes behind her paws.

48

Harry drove her old blue truck around to the back of the hospital. Everyone in town knew that truck but it was less obvious than Coop's squad car. She parked next to the back door. Had Harry parked out in the open parking lot even though she was at the rear of the hospital, the truck would have been more noticeable.

Cynthia checked her watch. It was seven-fifteen.

Harry double-checked hers. "Seven-fifteen."

The young officer checked her .357, which she wore in a shoulder holster. It was a heavy, long-barreled revolver. She favored long barrels since she felt they gave her more accuracy, not that she looked forward to shooting anyone.

Harry shoved her .38 into the top of her jeans.

"Mom, you ought to get a holster," Tucker advised.

"She ought to get a new brain. She has

no business being here." Pewter, a grumbler by nature, was nonetheless correct.

"We'd better be on red alert. We can't turn her back." Murphy's tail puffed up, then relaxed. She had a bad feeling about this.

Coop opened the back door as the animals scampered in. Harry noiselessly stepped through and Coop shut the door without clicking the latch. They walked down toward the boiler room, stopped, and listened. Far away they could hear the rattle of the elevator cables; the doors would open and close but they heard no one step out. Then the cables rattled more.

The animals listened intently. They, too, heard no one.

The two women stepped inside the boiler room, the large boiler gurgling and spewing for the night was cold. Coop checked the pressure gauge. She had respect for these old units. The trick was keeping the pressure in the middle of the gauge, which looked like a fat thermometer.

"This place was supposed to be on the Underground Railroad. The first thing we checked when Hank was killed was whether the wall was hollow behind what had been the old fireplace. Nothing," Cynthia whispered.

"You checked all the walls?"

"In every single room."

"Follow me," Mrs. Murphy commanded.

"Yeah, come on," Tucker seconded her best friend.

As the animals pushed and prodded the two humans, Sam Mahanes pulled into his reserved parking space right next to Jordan Ivanic's car. It was seven twenty-five. If the two of them were to meet with Rick Shaw at eight-fifteen then he'd better prepare Jordan, who, he felt, was a ninny. While Rick asked them about the invoices, Ivanic was capable of babbling about an anesthesiologist who nearly lost a patient. Those things happened in hospitals and Sam was determined that everyone stay on track.

Down in the basement, after a combination of nips, yowls, and pleading, Harry and Coop at last followed Mrs. Murphy and Tucker. Pewter walked along, too, but in a foul mood. Mrs. Murphy and Tucker were showing off too much for her and the only reason she accompanied everyone tonight was that her curiosity got the best of her.

In the distance the animals and humans heard a siren. Someone was being rushed to the emergency room. In the country that usually meant a heart attack, a car accident, or a farm accident.

"In here!" The tiger's tail stood straight up.

Harry reached for the light but Coop put her hand over Harry's. "No." She clicked on the flashlight, half closing the door behind her.

The cartons, neatly stacked, offered no clue to the treasure below.

Tucker ran to the wall, stood on her hind legs, and pressed the stone. Although low to the ground and short, the corgi was powerfully built with heavy bones. The flagstone opened with a sliding sound and thump.

"I'll be damned," Cooper swore under her breath as she flashed the light into the entrance.

In the distance the elevator chains rattled, the doors opened and closed.

The humans didn't hear but the animals did.

"Human. Human off the elevator." Pewter's fur stood straight up.

"Quick. Down the hatch!" Mrs. Murphy hopped onto the ladder, her paws making a soft sound on the wood as she hurried down into the hiding room.

"Murphy!" Harry whispered loudly.

Pewter, no fool, followed suit. Tucker, never one for ladders, turned around and backed down with encouragement from the cats.

By now the humans could hear a distant footfall heading their way.

"Come on." Harry grabbed the top of the ladder, swung herself around, and slid down, her feet on the outside.

Cooper reached down, giving Harry the flashlight, but as she turned around to climb down she knocked over a carton. It tumbled down. She grabbed it, putting it back up, then dropped down the ladder.

"How do we close this damn thing?" Harry realized she might have trapped everyone.

Mrs. Murphy pressed a round red button on the side of the ladder. The top slowly closed.

"Murphy," Harry whispered.

"Hide. Get in the back here and hide behind the machines," the tiger advised.

As the animals ran to the back, the humans heard the heavy footsteps overhead. Whoever was up there was bigger than they were. They moved to the back, crouching down behind pumps stacked on a table.

Cynthia put her finger to her lips, pulled out her gun. Harry did the same. Then Coop cut the flashlight.

The flagstone slid open.

"Can you smell him?" Mrs. Murphy asked Tucker.

"Too far away. All I can smell is this dank cellar."

The light was turned on. The humans crouched lower. One foot touched the top rung of the ladder, then stopped.

"Hey." Bobby Minifee's voice sounded loud and clear. "What are you doing?"

They heard a crack and a thud and then Bobby was tossed down the ladder. He landed heavily, blood pouring from his head. The flagstone closed overhead.

Pewter and Murphy ran to Bobby. Coop crept forward. Overhead they heard something heavy being pulled over the sliding trapdoor.

Harry, too, quietly moved forward. The two women bent over the crumpled young man. Harry took his pulse. Coop opened his eye.

"His pulse is strong," Harry whispered.

Coop looked around for towels, an old shirt, anything. "We've got to wrap his head up. See if you can find anything."

"Here." She handed Coop a smock, unaware that it had been Tussie Logan's.

Coop tore it into strips, wrapping Bobby's head as best she could. "Let's get him off this cold floor."

Harry cleared off a table and with effort they put him on top of it.

As the humans tended to Bobby, Mrs. Murphy considered their options. *"Coop and Mom are armed. That's cold comfort."*

"I'd rather have them armed than un-armed," Pewter sensibly replied.

"We'd better find a way out of here. For all we know, he's sitting up there trying to figure out how to kill us all."

"There's something over the trapdoor but since it's a sliding door, we could try." Pewter didn't like the cold, damp hole.

"Try what? To open the door?" Tucker asked.

"Yeah, press the button and see what happens." Pewter reached out with her paw.

"Pewter, no," Murphy ordered. *"You don't know what's sitting on the trapdoor. You don't know what will fall down. Hospitals have all kinds of stuff like sulfuric acid. Whatever he put up there he figured would either hold us or hurt us. He's a quick thinker. Remember Larry Johnson."*

"And he's merciless. Remember Hank Brevard and Tussie Logan," Tucker thoughtfully added.

"My hunch is, he'll come back. He doesn't know who's down here but he sus-pects something. And he has to come back to kill Bobby. He heard the carton drop. I know he did. He was moving up faster

than the humans could hear." Mrs. Murphy's tail twitched back and forth. She was agitated.

"I don't fancy being a duck in a shooting gallery," Pewter wailed.

"Get a grip," Tucker growled.

"I'm as tough as you are. I'm expressing my feelings, that's all."

"Express them once we're out of this mess." Mrs. Murphy prowled along the walls. "Pewter, take that wall. Tucker, the back. Listen for anything. If this was part of the Underground Railroad then there has to be a tunnel off this room. They had to get the slaves out of here somehow."

"Why couldn't they take them out in the middle of the night? Out the back door?" Pewter did, however, go to the wall to listen.

"If everyone is still telling stories about the Underground Railroad, this place was closely watched. Since no one was ever caught, I believe they had tunnels or at least one tunnel." Murphy strained to hear anything in the walls.

"Hey." Pewter's green eyes glittered. "Rats."

Mrs. Murphy and Tucker trotted over, putting their ears to the wall. They could hear the claws click as the rats moved about;

occasionally they'd catch a snippet of conversation.

"*Now, how do we get in?*" Tucker sniffed the floor, moving along the wall. "*Nothing but mildew.*"

"*Pewter, you check the ceiling, I'll study the wall.*" Mrs. Murphy slowly walked along the wall.

"*Why am I checking the ceiling?*" Pewter rankled at taking orders and she'd been taking too many, in her mind.

"*Maybe the way they got out was to crawl between the ceiling and the floorboards upstairs.*"

"*Murphy,*" Tucker said, "*the rats sound lower than that.*"

"*We've got to try everything.*" Murphy walked the length of the wall, then returned, stopping at a large stone at the base. "*Tucker, Pewter, let's push. This might be it.*"

They grunted and groaned, feeling the stone budge.

"*Harry!*" Tucker barked.

Harry turned from Bobby to see her three friends pushing the stone. She walked over, knelt down, putting her own shoulder to the large stone. Sure enough it rolled in. "Coop!"

Cooper turned her flashlight into the

small dark cavern and a narrow tunnel appeared, rats scurrying in all directions. One would have to walk hunched over but it could be done. "It *was* part of the Underground Railroad!"

"He's back!" Tucker barked as she heard the heavy burden being slowly slid off the trapdoor.

"He knows we're here now," Murphy warned after Tucker barked.

Harry heard it, too. She ran back and cut the lights. "Let's go." She ducked down and squeezed into the tunnel, crawling on all fours. Cooper followed as the animals ran past them. The two women rolled the stone back in place, then stood up, bending over to keep from bumping their heads.

"Bobby, we left Bobby." Harry's face bled white.

"Harry, we'll have to leave him to God. Let's hope whoever this is comes after us first. He had to have heard Tucker."

"Sorry," Tucker whimpered.

"No time for that," Mrs. Murphy crisply meowed. *"We've got to go wherever this leads and hope we make it."* She shot ahead followed by Pewter, who was feeling claustrophobic.

The humans ran along as fast as they could, flashlight bobbing. Harry noticed scratchings along the wall. She reached for Cooper's hand, halting her for a moment. She took the flashlight, turning it on the wall. It read: *Bappy Crewes, age 26m 1853.* They ran along knowing that Bappy, buried in the wall, never found freedom. Right now they hoped that they would.

"He's rolling the stone." Tucker could hear behind them.

"Nip at their heels, Tucker. Make them go faster. We don't know what's at the end of this and it might take us a little time to figure it out."

"Oh, great," Pewter moaned when Murphy said that.

"Your eyes are the best. Run ahead. Maybe you can figure it out," Tucker told the cats.

The two cats sped away as the light dimmed. The tunnel turned hard right. The rats cursed them. They skidded, turned right, then finally reached the end of the tunnel. They waited a moment while their eyes adjusted. They could see the flashlight shining on the wall where the tunnel turned right.

"We have to go up. There's no other way," Pewter observed.

"Oh, thank the Great Cat in the Sky." Murphy breathed a prayer. A ladder made

from six-inch tree trunks lay on its side. *"Maybe we can make it."*

Harry and Cooper now turned right; they were running harder now because whoever was behind them was firing into the dark.

Harry saw the ladder since Murphy was helpfully sitting on it. The two women hoisted it up. Cooper turned to train her gun on the turn in the tunnel.

"Get up and push with all your might!" the deputy said between gritted teeth.

Harry's foot went through one rotted rung but the rest were okay. She pushed and the top opened with surprising ease. She reached down, picking up Murphy, whom she tossed up. Then she did the same for Pewter and finally she carried Tucker, much heavier, under her arm.

She turned back for Coop, who extinguished the flashlight so as not to give their pursuer, who was approaching the right-hand turn, a target. Cooper, in great shape, leapt up, grabbing the top rung. She was out of the tunnel in moments.

"Where are we?" Pewter asked.

Harry quickly flopped down the heavy lid. "Let's get out of here."

"We're in the old switching station." Cooper was amazed. "My God, they literally put them on the trains."

"Smart people, our ancestors." Harry opened the door to the old switching station and they plunged into the darkness, running for all they were worth.

"Down here." Cynthia scrambled down a ditch by the side of the railroad tracks, the typical drainage ditch. "Lie flat. If he comes out I might be able to drop him."

They waited for fifteen minutes in the bitter cold but the door to the switching station never opened.

The railroad, begun by Claudius Crozet in 1849, had been in continuous use since then, with upgrades. The small switching station had been replaced by computers housed in large stations in the major cities. A nerve network fanned out from there, so the individual stations had fallen into disuse.

"Let's go back." Coop, shivering, stood up, brushing herself off.

"Mrs. Murphy, Pewter, and Tucker, I think we owe you big time."

"We're not out of the woods yet." Murphy's senses stayed razor sharp as Tucker's hackles rose.

"I vote for warmth." Pewter moved ahead toward the hospital parking lot.

Cynthia checked her wristwatch. "Eight-ten." As they drew closer to the front door she noticed Rick's squad car. "Well, we might get our asses chewed out but let's find him."

They walked into the main reception area just as Sam Mahanes, disheveled, was greeting Rick. Cooper's hands were torn up and the sleeves of Harry's jacket were shredded where her arms had slid against the stone wall when her foot went through the rotted rung of the ladder to the switching house.

"You look like the dogs got at you under the porch." Rick frowned. "And just what are you doing here?"

It took a second but both Harry and Coop looked down at Sam's shoes, scuffed with dirt on the soles.

"Harry, you've got to take those animals out of here. This is a hospital," Sam reprimanded her as he moved toward the front door.

"He smells like the tunnel!" Tucker hit him from behind. If they'd been playing football the corgi would have been penalized for clipping.

Harry may have been a human but she trusted her dog. "Coop, it's him!"

Sam lurched to his feet, kicked at the dog, and ran for all he was worth.

"Stop!" Cooper dropped to one knee.

He didn't stop, reaching the revolving door. Coop fired one shot and blew out his kneecap. He dropped like a stone.

The few people in the hospital at that hour screamed. The receptionist ducked behind the desk. Rick ran up and hand-cuffed Sam's hands behind him.

"Call a doctor," he shouted at the receptionist.

"Call two," Cooper also shouted. "There's a man badly injured in the basement. I'll take the doctor to him."

Sam was cussing and spitting, blood flowing from his shattered kneecap.

"How'd you know?" Rick admiringly asked his deputy.

"It's a long story." She smiled.

49

"That's so awful about Tussie Logan." Miranda wrung her hands.

The group of dear friends gathered at Miranda's house that Sunday morning. The article about Tussie's murder was front-page news. Harry and Cooper filled them in on all that happened.

"He made enough money. He didn't have to steal any." Big Mim was horrified by the whole episode.

" 'And he said to them, Take heed, and beware of all covetousness; for a man's life does not consist in the abundance of his possessions.' Luke, chapter twelve, verse fifteen." Miranda recalled the Scriptures.

"Well, that's what's wrong with this country. It's money. All anyone ever thinks about is money." Mim tapped her foot on the rug.

"Mimsy, that's easy for you to say. You inherited a boatload of it." Miranda was the only one in the room who could say that to Mim.

Fair sat so close to his ex-wife he was glued to her. "I'll never forgive myself for not keeping a closer watch over you."

"Fair, honey, it's breeding season. You can't. You have to earn a living. We all do. Well, most of us do."

"All right. I was born with a silver spoon in my mouth but that doesn't mean I don't understand this nation's malaise. I do. I can't help being born who and what I am any more than the rest of you," Mim said.

"Of course, dear, but I simply wanted to point out that it's rather easy to declare money the root of all evil when one is secure." Miranda's voice was soothing.

Susan, rather disappointed to have missed the action, asked, "I thought Sam Mahanes had an alibi for Hank Brevard's death?"

"He was in his work space, as he calls it." Cooper nodded. "Rick questioned Sally Mahanes in a relaxed way. The night of Hank's murder she didn't see him come in. He used the private entrance to his shop. It was easy for him to slip in. He left the radio on. Easy. Hank got greedy, threatened him, and Sam took him out. Quick. Efficient."

"And Larry?" Mim's lower lip trembled a moment.

"We'll never know what Larry knew." Cooper shook her head. "But he was such an intelligent man. Sam took no prisoners. Poor Tussie, after Hank's murder she must have lived in terror."

"Caught in a web and couldn't get out." Miranda felt the nurse's life had been squandered.

"And how much money are we talking about?" Mim got down to brass tacks.

"Close to a million over the years. Just out of Crozet Hospital. He confessed that they billed for more than infusion pumps. They worked this scam on anything they could fix, including air conditioners. But the IVAC units — easy to fix, Tussie knew them inside and out — were the cash cow."

"Well, I thank you for apprehending Larry's killer. I feel I owe you a reward, Cynthia, Harry." Mim's voice was low but steady as she fought with her own emotions.

"I was doing my duty, Mrs. Sanburne. You don't owe me a thing."

"And I don't deserve anything either. The real detectives were Mrs. Murphy, Pewter, and Tucker. How they figured out where the hiding room was, I'll never know, and then they discovered the tunnel. They're the ones."

Mim eyed the three animals eagerly looking at her. "Then I shall make a large contribution to the local SPCA."

"No! Food!" Pewter wailed.

"Good God." Murphy grimaced. *"At least, ask for catnip."*

"Perhaps my largesse is unappreciated." Mim laughed.

"No." Harry smiled. "They want treats."

"And they shall have them!" Mim smiled. "Liver and kidneys and chicken. I'll cook them myself."

"This is wonderful." Tucker turned a circle. She was that excited.

A knock on the door drew their attention.

"Come in," Miranda called out.

Little Mim, face flushed, let herself in, hurriedly taking off her gorgeous sheepskin coat dyed hunter green; even the baby lamb's wool was dyed hunter green. "I'm sorry I'm late but Daddy and I just had a meeting. I'm going to run for vice-mayor and he's going to create the position. So now, Mother, will you support me?"

"With enthusiasm." Big Mim smiled.

"Why does it take people so long to find the obvious solution?" Pewter tilted her head as she spoke to Murphy.

"Too much time on their hands." Tucker turned another circle just thinking about kidneys.

"She's probably right. When they had to fight lions and tigers and bears, when they

had to till the soil and run from thunder-bolts, they didn't have time to think about themselves so much," Pewter thoughtfully added.

"Who was it said, 'The unexamined life is not worth living'? That contradicts your point," Tucker said.

"Yeah, who said that?" Pewter asked.

"Not a cat so who cares?" Mrs. Murphy burst into uproarious laughter.

Dear Reader,

You'll never guess what just happened. My Aunt Betty makes catnip sockies. She brought in two huge bags full, two hundred little toys just loaded, jammed, stuffed, reeking of potent, powerful, intoxicating home-grown Virginia catnip. She placed the bags on two kitchen chairs and then left the room. I expect something diverted her attention because Pewter and I shredded the bags, wallowed in all those toys.

Mother walked in to find us sound asleep, burrowed in those sockies. Now Aunt Betty has to make a bunch more since we've "tested" these. Mother says she can't send them out. I argued that they'd be even more valuable but she said I really ought to shut up.

A few other things. No, Mother still hasn't gotten up the money to totally repair her bridge. Many of you write and ask. More dogs seem interested in our bridge than cats. This doesn't mean I think dogs are reading. No. I bet their humans read to them.

Another question you ask is are there

other cats on the farm. Mother says I have to name them, that I'm selfish and hogging all the limelight. Oh? Do my friends write mysteries? No. They chase mice, moles, birds, skinks, lizards, and even the chickens (who chase right back). I'm the one who works around here! But to keep the peace allow me to introduce my friends. First my daughter, Ibid. She looks just like me except she has green eyes. Pewter you know, of course. Every time someone knocks on the door, Pewter rushes out to greet them since she believes they've come to see her. Oh, the ego. She has a double, Gracie Louise, and together they play tricks on people. One jumps out from the left then runs away and a few seconds later the other one jumps out from the right. Personally, I think they've read too many plays, from Plautus to Shakespeare, about twins. Then there's Mr. Murphy, a large tiger cat named for Mrs. Murphy, obviously. He's hunting quite a bit, but a nice fellow. There's another tiger cat, Nenee. The calicos are Pippin and Peaches. All very pretty, young, slim. Loretta is about four months old. She follows me around when she isn't shadowing Mother. Usually I can put up with her questions but some days she plucks my last nerve. Maybelline guards the lower barn and Zydeco commands the upper.

As you can see there are many of us. Everyone has all their shots and everyone gets spayed. If a stray has kittens, she gets spayed after her babies are weaned.

Mother gives speeches for various animal shelters and SPCAs. She loves animals, sometimes to the despair of her friends because she's always taking in some stray. She's even fed and gotten shots for fox cubs.

We also have ten dogs. With the exception of Liška, an ancient Shiba Inu, and Godzilla, the Jack Russell, they, too, are strays or hounds rescued from the pound.

Together, over the years, Mother and I have placed many abandoned animals in homes. We're proud of our efforts.

We don't understand how humans can bear children or have animals and then mistreat them. Cats don't do that. Nor dogs.

I was talking to Pewter the other day and I said, concerning humans, "They left Eden. We didn't."

Nuff said.

Oh, one lovely thing happened to Mom. As you've probably gathered, all her money goes toward animals and she doesn't have very much left for herself. She doesn't mind but when her best clothes were stolen a few years ago on a book tour she hadn't the money to replace them, especially at today's prices. One day the postman dropped off a large box. She signed for it. I helped her open it. Four beautiful Turnbull & Asser shirts were inside, made to Mom's pattern, registered at that British company. I wanted to wear them but she wouldn't let me touch them. The colors: lavender, silky blue, and a black patterned one, and a pink — ain't life grand!

We called Turnbull & Asser in New York (the home company is on Jermyn Street, London). Yes, they had taken the order but they wouldn't tell us who sent the shirts.

Now, that's a mystery.

I love everyone.

Affectionately Yours,
Sneaky Pie

www.ritamaebrown.com
or
Sneaky Pie Brown
P.O. Box 696
Crowzet, VA 22932

The employees of Thorndike Press hope you have enjoyed this Large Print book. All our Large Print titles are designed for easy reading, and all our books are made to last. Other Thorndike Press Large Print books are available at your library, through selected bookstores, or directly from us.

For information about titles, please call:

(800) 223-1244
(800) 223-????
To share your comments, please write:

Publisher
Thorndike Press
295 Kennedy Memorial Drive
Waterville, ME 04901